The Pilgrim Glass

The Pilgrim Glass

JULIE K. ROSE

Copyright © 2010 by Julie K. Rose

All rights reserved. Except as permitted by the U.S. Copyright Act of 1976, no part of this publication may be reproduced, distributed, or transmitted in any form or by any means, or stored in a database retrieval system, without the prior written permission of the author.

First edition: December 2010

The characters and events in this book are fictitious. Any similarity to real persons, living or dead, is coincidental and not intended by the author.

ISBN 978-0-557-81074-1

Photo Credit: Mother Mary Window by The Brainstorm Lab
iStockphoto.com

Printed in the United States of America

For Craig.

Chapter One

THE GLASS SWIRLED and shifted in the uncertain light, its edges sharp and unpredictable, beautiful and strange in its imperfections. He turned it over gently in his hand, caressed its smooth surface, then held it close to his eye, watching the room through its shadowy waves, falling into its blue depths. He hummed tunelessly under his breath, swinging back and forth in his broken desk chair, following the tracery of indigo light across the room.

"I'll never get it done in time," he muttered, holding the glass between his fingertips like an offering. "Damn."

Jonas pocketed the glass and opened the door to his studio, stepping out into the surprising and silent darkness. He flicked his lighter and the end of his cigarette glowed crimson, the smoke swirling lazily around his head as he watched the last lilacked clouds turn to grey and then to black and then disappear into the night. Holding the cigarette precariously between his lips, he rubbed his itching eyes with his knuckles and took a long drag.

Leaning against the stucco wall, in the dim glow of the studio's light, Jonas examined his fingers. Ragged nails. Thin white scars – more than he could count. Traces of blue and red paint on his knuckles and cuticles. *Jesus, I'm a mess*. He shook his head and took another long drag, eyes closed and head resting against the wall.

Half an hour later, the evening wind had risen and was rustling the leaves of the massive eucalyptus at the edge of his property. He glanced at the dark sky, dotted with stars, then peered into his now-empty Marlboro pack. With a sigh, he stubbed out the last cigarette and flicked the butt into the gloom of his backyard.

The studio seemed unnaturally bright and harsh, though lit only by a single low lamp in the corner, and the work table cluttered, littered with fragments of glass, and tools, and cut lead came. After a moment's hesitation, he tossed the piece back onto the work table; it splintered into a sapphire arabesque.

Jonas picked up his diary and made a note of the next day's appointments. St. Joseph's in San Jose; that was a big one. Well, maybe not as big as others he'd done, but the best job he'd had lately.

The quiet of the studio was broken by the shrill ring of the phone. Jonas stumbled over a lead spool holder next to the desk and grabbed the phone before it went to the machine. "Ow! Yeah?"

"Mr. Flycatcher?"

"Yes."

"I am glad I caught you. This is Geneviève Chevrey. From UNESCO –" she finished expectantly.

"Yes…" he said, dropping into his chair.

The line was silent for a long moment. "We are the agency that looks after the world's cultural treasures," she said.

Jonas imagined the pinched look on her face and the tapping of her perfectly manicured nails and smiled. "Yes, I know what UNESCO is. What can I do for you, Madame Chevrey?"

The line was silent for a moment. "Vézelay," she intoned.

"Yes?"

"We need some assistance with the glass there."

Vézelay: typical of the Burgundian Romanesque church– high, perfect vaulted spaces and beautiful clear light. No selenium red or cadmium blue in sight. "What kind of assistance?" he asked, now only half-interested.

"They have found a stained window."

"You're shitting me!"

Madame Chevrey laughed. "No, Mr. Flycatcher, I am most certainly not shitting you."

"So…wow…OK, so where? How?" Jonas scanned the room – the soldering iron and the came bender and the safety glasses, and the glass jewel-like in the faint light – as if he'd find the answer there.

"Our workmen were doing some routine maintenance on the

crypt and found a small piece. About half a metre high and a quarter wide."

"Date?"

"It is hard to tell…it is certainly quite early. The leadwork is primitive, and the color range is rather limited…"

"The subject?"

"The Magdalene."

Jonas leaned forward, elbows on knees, the phone cradled precariously on his shoulder. He stared at his fingers, but did not see them. The line was silent for ten, fifteen, twenty seconds as he examined the implements of his craft, his work.

"Mr. Flycatcher?"

"Are you sure?" he breathed.

"Oh, of course," Madame Chevrey laughed. "It is most certainly the Magdalene."

He shook his head but did not correct her. *No. About me.* "Its condition?" he asked.

"There is considerable damage to the outer leading, of course…"

"Of course."

"…and broken fragments on her gown…"

"And the grisalle?"

"Primitive."

"Hmm…"

"There is a most amazing rendering of the unguent jar which is intact," Madame Chevrey said, warming to the subject. "The leadwork of the hair is quite incredible, very delicate and extremely complex."

"Hmmm…" Jonas muttered, mostly to himself, as he made a mental checklist of his tricks and tools and alchemy. He examined his latest restoration, the story of Job, rendering pain and suffering untold in luminous blues and luxurious purples.

"And there is the most unusual border -"

"So when do you need me?" Jonas cut in.

"Are you still available?"

"Madame?"

"I had heard that you were no longer taking assignments in Europe."

Jonas furrowed his eyebrows. "I haven't done any in a while, if that's what you mean. But I am definitely available."

"Well, the restoration needs to be complete in time for the Feast of the Magdalene this summer. As part of our millennial celebrations."

"When is that?"

"22nd July."

"No way," Jonas snorted, standing up and running his rough fingers over the glass on the work table.

"I beg your pardon?" Madame Chevrey asked, her accent more pronounced and clipped.

"There is no way I can complete a restoration of this magnitude in under a month."

"That is unfortunate, Mr. Flycatcher. Because that is all the time we have."

"Why didn't you call me earlier?" he asked, his voice rising in anger, and panic. "I would need four times that time to restore something of such significance and detail. There's research, and I need to gather materials…and then of course there's the shipping time back and forth from Burgundy. These things take time."

"I am aware of that," she replied flatly.

"I can't do quality work in such a ridiculously short amount of time," he said, pacing.

"Well, that ridiculously short amount of time is all you get – should you deign to take this assignment," she replied, irritation coloring each syllable.

Jonas stopped pacing, shook his head, and ran a hand over his short-cropped wavy hair, gold curled with red. He took a deep breath…Vézelay. Unbidden, a vision of flaming red and deepest orange filled his mind. He was transfixed, staring out the dark, blank window, for a moment. Just as quickly, he returned to himself. Then he laughed out loud, a shimmering sound that filled the small workroom and surprised even him. "Yeah, I'll do it."

"D'accord," she responded. "Luckily, the glass is not in the wall of course so we save time."

"How quickly can you get it crated and shipped?"

Silence.

"Mr. Flycatcher, surely you realize that given the rarity of this piece, and its condition, there is no way we will be able to ship it to California. You will need to work onsite."

His smile faded. "Oh. Right. Of course," he replied, turning to look out the window into the dark yard. He could still make out the towering eucalyptus and the stand of coast redwoods, shadowy and still in the darkened distance.

"We will pay for your travel and per diem expenses," she continued.

"Right, right..." he muttered, searching through the drawers in his desk for a new pack of smokes.

"There is a direct flight to de Gaulle on Air France from San Francisco every evening. How quickly can you make arrangements to be here?"

Jonas found a crumpled pack, half-empty, and headed for the porch. "Mmmm...," he started, cradling the phone on his shoulder and lighting his cigarette. "I can be there in three days?" he suggested, blowing out smoke in a great sigh.

"Excellent. I will let them know you are coming. When you arrive, ask for Abbott Dubay at the cathedral. He will help you find a place to stay. I will email you with the proposed terms of the contract tomorrow, and you can fax me your signed copy, and we shall go from there."

"Mmm," Jonas nodded.

"Mr. Flycatcher?" Madame Chevrey prompted.

"Yes?" he asked, coming out of his daze.

"God speed on your journey."

"Thank you for the opportunity," he recovered.

"Au revoir."

"Au revoir." He clicked off the phone and set it on the deck railing and watched the moon crawl toward the hill's ridge. He blew smoke across it like a cloud.

Shit.

Two days later, after a sleepless night, Jonas awoke early and wandered out the back door. The towering redwoods were there, watching over the property and the first rays of sunshine finally cresting the mountains and flooding the San Lorenzo valley. The pale jade-green eucalyptus waved at him in the bright blue breeze, and he inhaled the light and the color, gulping it like a steadying drink. He lit a cigarette with a shaking hand and tossed the match into the green lawn, still wet with fog.

Jonas shook his head again, blowing the smoke lazily through his nose. "I'm just nervous," he muttered aloud to his reflection in the kitchen window.

He stubbed out the half-smoked cigarette under his heel and walked down the path to his locked workshop. He opened the door on the dark studio; the light was cool and violet, spilling through the unfinished replica of the window of the *Résurrection des morts* from his beloved Ste. Chapelle onto the scattered papers and the smooth sheets of colored glass which rested, untouched, waiting for his hands and the light to bring them back to life. His life, for ten years.

On his makeshift desk, a brown leather book peeked out from under a pile of papers. Jonas picked it up and brushed dust from its rich cover, supple and earthy. He flipped through pages and pages of drawings – doodles and form studies but mostly designs, colored for intricate and exquisite stained glass. He pulled up the office chair with the broken wheel and immersed himself in the past.

Some of the designs were dated; others lost in the years, a pleasant surprise. He could remember each design, what he was thinking, the feeling of each color and line. But the drawings slowly dwindled. In their place, and all over the desk, scribbled notes about repairs and clients: Small churches and synagogues. Large regional churches and public buildings.

This could make my career. "If I don't fuck it up," Jonas muttered. He shook his head and left the workshop, slamming the door behind him; the notebook was pressed under his arm.

He wandered through the rooms of his small house. He watched a little TV. He realphabetized his already impeccable CD collection. He tried to eat some lunch, but failed. He succeeded in smoking a lot of cigarettes. Finally, a car horn sounded in the driveway at 1:05.

He stuck his head out his front door. "Hey – I'll be right out," he hollered at the van driver.

He flung his backpack over his shoulder and picked up his suitcase. He threw a long, dark coat over his shoulders and backpack, not bothering to shrug into the sleeves. A wooden-handled umbrella stood next to the door and he grabbed it along with his suitcase. With a deep breath, he pulled the door closed behind him. *I can do this. Right?*

Chapter Two

"GOD DAMN, MOVE IT!" Jonas shouted, waving the dinosaur of a delivery truck out of his way. He returned the driver's gesture with gusto and laid on the horn, swerving and cutting off a taxi.

The *route péripherique* around Paris was, as always, packed and dangerous, a single-minded mass of humanity making a pilgrimage to Paris and back again. But it was the only way to get from Charles de Gaulle to the A6, and Jonas gritted his teeth as he tried again to merge onto the roadway. He slid The Clash into the CD player and rolled down the windows, yelling at motorists swerving around him.

After one hour and 10 maddening kilometers, he reached the A6–*l'autoroute du soleil*, Paris to Lyon, finally unclenching his jaw. Half an hour later, escaping the depressingly large shantytowns and mind-numbing sameness of the suburbs, he reached the first fingers of the countryside and pulled off into a tree-lined rest area. He turned off the CD player, shut off the engine, and got out to stretch his legs.

Leaning against the door of his rented Renault, he lit a cigarette and closed his burning eyes. He hadn't slept at all on the flight from San Francisco. He'd watched, mesmerized, the slow progress of his plane, hour by hour, on his seat's video monitor.

The hangover aftermath of a bottle of Burgundy wasn't helping his concentration on the road, and he looked gratefully around at the quiet, quintessentially French rest-stop, rows of slender trees lining the narrow lane, symmetrical and pleasingly logical, graceful and soft in the hazy overcast. He studied the tracery of intertwining leaves and branches and boles, the play of jade and silver green, and the tension in his shoulders dissolved. He leaned back and squinted, blurring the waving forms and lines, inhaling the wet greenness.

A car pulled in beside him long minutes later and his eyes fluttered open. With a great yawn, Jonas stubbed out his cigarette and spread a roadmap on the hood of his car. At least two hours of driving to go on the A6 to Avallon, then winding local roads to Vézelay were ahead. With a last glance around at the waving trees, he got back into his car.

As he eased back onto the autoroute, the sun broke through the low cloudbank and suddenly the grey and hazy world was brilliant and green and blue. Jonas smiled and rolled down the window. The road was a shimmering thread of silver in the broken sunlight, the gently rolling hills damasked in emerald. Thick forests of hardwoods edged the road, then gave way suddenly to broad swaths of quilted pastureland. Every tree, every lonely delicate wildflower, every blade of grass luminous, as if the very life ready to burst caused the world to illuminate from within.

Two hours later, exhilarated and exhausted, he paid the toll at the *péage* in Avallon and pulled onto the two-lane N151. The Renault panted, catching its breath and thankful for the 50km per hour speed limit. Jonas eventually pulled to the side of the road and shut off the engine. He sat on the hood of the grateful car and pulled the pack of cigarettes out of his pocket. Empty. "Shit," he grumbled, crumpling the packet and tossing it in a ball into the back seat of the car where his lost luggage should have been.

He urged the car back into life, crossed the bridge over the Cousin River, and headed down the road to Vézelay. The landscape had changed, grown even more beautiful. Wide swaths of rolling pastureland had given way to close valleys and hills clothed in pine forests. The sun faded behind a veil of grey clouds, and the hilly Morvan parkland away to the southeast looked dark and forbidding and seductive.

He pulled into the tiny town of St Père sous Vézelay, hugging the winding banks of the Cure River. The houses and shops were tattered and careworn, with a shabby grace and quiet reserve born of many long centuries along the pilgrim's road. Spying a *tabac*, he pulled off as best he could and crossed the narrow, empty road. *Bonjour. Bonjour, uh – what's the word for cigarettes? Bonjour. Bonjour.* He pushed open the door and found the *tabac* was empty, save for an old man behind the counter.

"Bonjour," Jonas said to the top of the man's head.

"Bonjour," the old man nodded, lifting his eyes from his newspaper.

Jonas stood silent. *Where the hell is my French when I need it?* He cleared his throat. "Uh – les – uh – cigarettes, s'il vous plait."

The old man put his newspaper down and regarded Jonas with a quirked eyebrow. "Américain?" he asked.

"Oui," he nodded with a small shrug of the shoulders.

The old man smiled and pulled out a pack of Gitanes. He pushed them with scarred and gnarled fingers across the counter.

"Uh, pas des Marlboros?" Jonas asked.

The old man shook his head.

"D'accord, d'accord. Deux, s'il vous plait," Jonas replied, pulling out a wad of Euros from his pocket. "Combien?"

"Dix Euros."

"Dix?!"

The old man shrugged and returned to his newspaper. Jonas rolled his eyes; yet he liked this old man with the stained ancient hands and the green cardigan sweater. "D'accord," he said, pushing a ten-Euro note across the counter. The old man pulled out another pack and looked Jonas over. "Est-tu un pélerin?"

"Uh, oui?" Jonas replied, shrugging his shoulders. He grabbed the cigarettes and walked to the door. "Merci bien," he called back. The old man did not answer. *Maybe that means vagrant?* Jonas sniffed his t-shirt as he walked back across the road to his car. *Well shit, no wonder. I haven't had a shower in two days.*

He leaned against the car and lit a Gitane. He inhaled deeply and spluttered. He shrugged his shoulders and took a slower drag, letting the harsh smoke warm his lungs. *What the hell is a pélerin?*

Jonas started the car and watched clouds chase each other across the sun again as it sunk behind the hill. The narrow road wound languid around the base of the verdant hill, climbing slowly as if enjoying the journey, or hesitating.

The sun dipped in and out of the gathering clouds, inconstant and beautiful. Bright sunflowers lined the roadway, chattering and gossiping in groups, their color a shock against the shadowed hillside. Beautiful and dignified beech and oak, clothed in summer greens swayed in the evening breeze and pointed their long-fingered branches, urging Jonas ever upward around the next bend.

He slowed the car and pulled to a stop at the side of the road next to an ancient vineyard, its guyots of lush Aligoté neat and ordered and clinging to the side of the hill. Lighting a Gitane and inhaling – slow, slow – he reached into the back seat of the car, unsure of what he was searching for. Rifling through his backpack, he pulled out his brown leather notebook.

Sitting on the hood of the car, he held the harsh cigarette between his lips and turned to a blank page, just beyond a to-do list and directions to a prospective customer's offices. He looked up and, squinting, picked out the patterns in the vines and the tall trees beyond. His pencil hovered over the page for five minutes. He finally snapped the book shut and squeezed his eyes closed.

He pointed the car back up the meandering road, and soon found the town entrance in the honey-colored limestone of the medieval wall. The city came upon him all at once, rising over one hundred meters, sandy-grey and ancient, stark and overpowering after the gentle river valley. Jonas pulled into the first parking area he could find and turned off the engine. He sat with arms and forehead resting on the steering wheel. *This is going to suck. Damn it.*

Jonas shook his head and took a deep breath. He stepped out of the car and onto the precarious cobblestones of the Place du

Champ-de-Foire. He stared up the hill at the ancient town. The late evening sun had given up, retiring behind the hill; the darkness covered the town like a veil.

With a shaking hand he lit a cigarette and watched a tourist bus retreat from the height to the welcoming valley below. The town emptied around him and the cigarette burned down to his fingers. "Ow! Shit!" he grumbled. He dropped it and with a sigh, ground it under his heel, turning to grab his backpack from the back seat. He shrugged the backpack onto his shoulders, threw his coat over the backpack, and grabbed his long wooden-handled umbrella. He turned back to the steep street and squared his shoulders. *Come on.*

The rue St. Etienne snaked up the steep hill under dark clouds. The two- and three-storeyed houses and shops lining the narrow street were ancient and beautiful, lush red flowers peeking over the top of wooden window boxes; but they hid their true faces behind shuttered doors and windows of forest green. The street was quiet, save for a small knot of tourists hurrying down the hill, anxious to leave the town before nightfall, as if the ancient town gates would close and bolt them in.

Jonas was breathing hard by the time he passed the Hotel de Ville and reached the rue St. Pierre at the Maison de Colombs. "I have to stop smoking," he muttered, leaning on his umbrella. He spied a blue sign, barely visible in the gathering gloom: *l'eglise, 50m.* He stood for a moment, catching his breath and calculating how far 50 meters uphill really is, when a flame flickered into life just outside his range of vision.

He snapped his head around and saw only a single bulb glowing in the window of a small shop. He crossed the street and pressed his forehead against the cool glass. Black and white photos lined the walls, of the church and townsfolk and Vézelay's narrow winding streets and traceries of ancient leafless trees, beautiful and melancholy.

A figure moved in the back of the shop, graceful and ghostly, flickering in and out of sight. He spread his fingers against the glass and a sigh of longing and regret escaped his lips. He shook his head. *What the hell?*

Almost without thinking, he tried the door but it would not give. A hand-written sign gave some explanation: *Ouvert 10h à 16h.* "Damn," he grunted, and turned to make the final push up the hill.

The confines of the rue St. Pierre opened suddenly into a modest plaza and parking lot groveling in the gloom at the feet of a hulking colossus. He tugged the backpack off his shoulders and dropped it at his feet. Panting, he craned his neck and slowly took in the massive outlines of the ancient cathedral of Sainte-Marie-Madeleine de Vézelay against the darkling sky.

Suddenly, light trembled beneath the massive doors and moments later a figure emerged, tall and spectral and dark against the sudden burst of radiance.

Jonas shivered.

Chapter Three

Pons must never know. I must fly, quickly, a shadow in the wood. The offering is mine; it is of my hand, it is of my soul. Cluny is many miles away. If I leave by the octave... The messenger assures me the Abbot will be feasting with his monks and nobles for days to come. When he is yet crossing the Cure, lazy on a fat mare, I will abase myself at the shrine of the Magdalene. She, who sprinkled her very tears on the feet of the Saviour. She, apostle to the apostles. The offering is mine alone to give; he will not take it from me.

The sun now calls me to the garden. Like the light of the blessed Magdalene's hair, and my hair, is the golden sun, and the sky as blue as her eyes, and my eyes, that looked upon the Saviour and was made holy. All has been made ready. But for one detail.

The offering is wrapped in white linen, like a shroud, in the corner of the garden. The last piece is in my hand, but I am afraid to place it. It is too poor, too base. I pull out the bundle and unwrap it, carefully, reverently, and it shimmers in the sun. The last piece.

It shimmers too, but crimson, as if fired from within by the very fervor of the Baptist. His feast day draws nigh.

I place the final piece and the offering is complete. I am ready.

I turn back to the small cottage and take my place at the table. The sun illuminates the page and makes my close work more bearable. I pull my hair into a plait and dip my nib into the lazuli.

The day has arrived for my departure. Praise holy St. John, and may his blessings find me on my road. The early morning is fine and warm, and my offering is secure deep in my satchel, with dark bread and new cheese, and cherries from Auxerre. The road is long – a day's journey to Beaune. If I encounter no difficulties along the way, I shall climb the holy hill at Vézelay on the eve of the Feast of the Magdalene.

My feet touch the dirt path outside the garden walls for the first time in months. The road draws west and the sun warms my back, yet I am chilled. The journey has at last begun.

"Huh? Ungh." *Where am I?* Meredith's head snapped up and she squinted in the dimness. The day had slipped away outside her window, though she could still make out clouds like thieves stealing just beyond her vision. She pushed dark curls from her face and groaned as she rolled her shoulders back and stretched her neck.

The table where she'd fallen asleep was littered with negatives and still-tacky black and white photos, redolent with a pleasing warm acidic smell from the chemicals in her darkroom. She felt her face and found a negative stuck to her cheek. *Coffee. Definitely.* She shook her head and shuffled to the stairway.

As she started down the steps, the dream came back to her

with a force that threatened to send her headfirst down the stairs.

She grabbed the railing with a gasp, then leaned against the shadowed wall. She shivered, and a vision of the – medieval? – woman, serene and determined, appeared in her mind. "What was *that* about?" she muttered.

She gathered her wits and made her way downstairs. As she flicked on the light at the bottom of the stairs, another disconcerting thought came to her. *Who the hell is Pons?* Meredith stood with her hand on the light switch, replaying the dream word by word. *Word by word?* The dream, still fresh, was not realized as a series of images, but as a story. She shivered and contemplated her small shop, walls covered in ethereal black and white photos, as if the strange woman might be hovering just outside her range of vision, on the other side of the black windows on the rue St Pierre.

She hurried across the shop to what passed for her kitchen in the back and fumbled in the darkness for the kettle and a canister of coffee. She was bending over the small stove when a shiver stole up from behind and pricked the back of her neck. She straightened sharply and dropped the kettle with a clatter.

A few moments later, she heard the door to the shop rattling. A thrill of fear passed through her, leaving her woozy. She edged back into the shop, and peeked around the corner. She snapped off the light, and as her eyes adjusted to the sudden darkness, thought she saw a figure floating away, up the street.

It was just a dream.

She shivered.

Chapter Four

*T*HIS WILL MAKE MY CAREER. *If I don't fuck it up. I can't screw this up. How am I going to –*

Jonas' musing was cut short with a shiver as a figure emerged from the shadowed cathedral and glided down the stairs, nearly tripping over Jonas at the base. He was an older man, perhaps in his late 50s, in priest's garb, his thin face scored with wrinkles and his large mouth pursed in concern – or annoyance. "Merde," he muttered under his breath, and pushed silver hair from his eyes. He leaned down and put a long elegant hand on Jonas' shoulder. "Pardon, monsieur. D'accord?" he asked, looking Jonas intently in the face.

Jonas struggled out of his fog. "Huh?"

"Vous êtes un pélerin?"

"Huh?" he replied. Then, under his breath, "Ugh, fucking French…"

The man stood up straight and looked down at Jonas, hands on his hips. Then he laughed, a deep rumbling guffaw that echoed around the empty plaza like thunder. Jonas snapped his head up to look at the man, who suddenly smiled down at him, showing a great number of very white teeth.

"Monsieur Flycatcher, yes?" he said, offering his hand. Jonas accepted it and was pulled to his feet.

"Yes. How did you –"

"Madame Chevrey."

"She must have warned you about me," Jonas said, standing up. "And you are?"

"Abbot Dubay."

"Of course."

Jonas folded his arms.

"Is this your first time in France?" Dubay asked.

"Does it matter?"

"Of course."

Jonas scowled. "No. I was a graduate student about ten years ago. In Paris."

"Eh, oui? It is a remarkable place."

"Sure."

The plaza was silent. Dubay too folded his arms.

"What else did Madame Chevrey say?" Jonas asked.

"I think she described you as 'unbearably rude,'" Dubay said, smoothing his vestments. Jonas chuckled under his breath. "And that you are extremely talented. She refused to consider anyone else for this assignment."

Are you kidding?

Jonas patted his pocket for cigarettes. He did not take them out. "Of course," he said, standing straight. "Who recommended me?"

"I do not know. Genevieve was very close about this project," Dubay said, looking Jonas over. "You must be very tired. You probably haven't slept or – ah – showered for a day or two."

Jonas snorted. "At least," he said, relaxing.

"Then let us find Soeur Fabienne," Dubay said, taking Jonas by the elbow and attempting to lead him towards the cathedral. "She has arranged for your lodging tonight; I will introduce you to your workshop tomorrow. And where is your luggage? Is this all you have?" he asked, pointing at the backpack.

"No, they lost my bag."

"We shall inquire after it in the morning. For now, let us find Soeur Fabienne."

Dubay pushed open the heavy oak door and stepped through the central portal of the cathedral; Jonas followed him into the wide narthex. The far right door to the nave was open, spilling candlelight and throwing the massive tympanum into deep contrast. Dubay walked through to the basilica, its massive space glowing beyond the door, but Jonas slowed to a standstill.

The tympanum, the original portal to the church, rose majestic and disquieting. Faceless apostles carrying the law of God in books opened and closed, ornamented and plain, shared the space with demonic possession and hunchbacks and mutes cured. Siamese twins and dog-headed men and pig-snouted lovers. Persian archers and African pygmies. Signs of the zodiac and storm clouds and in the midst Christ in his mandorla, whorls and spirals and holy light shooting from his outstretched hands. The shadowy light served to make the twisting figures more menacing, the riot of movement and imagery crowded together more overwhelming.

"Monsieur Flycatcher?"

Jonas tore his gaze from the sculpture to look at the Abbot. "Yes?"

"Soeur Fabienne?"

"What about her?"

"We need to arrange for your sleeping quarters. But if you would prefer to sleep in here tonight, I can certainly arrange that," he said, folding his arms. "It is a bit draughty, but quiet enough. You would not have any company."

Jonas shivered. "I think I'd have too much company in here," he murmured.

Dubay nodded and gazed up at the tympanum. "Yes, they are very much alive," he mused. "I remember the first time I came to Vézelay. It was just over five years ago. I was at the cathedral in Autun, which at the time I believed to be the most spectacular expression of Romanesque art and faith in the world. Of course, that was pure arrogance, as it was 'my' church," he laughed. "Certainly, the spaces there are awe-inspiring, and the Autun tympanum is awesome and frightening."

"More frightening than this?" Jonas asked.

"Ah, but this is not frightening. The Autun work is the Last Judgment, wicked bodies writhing in their final and everlasting torment. Even in broad daylight it makes me shiver."

Jonas nodded.

"But this–" he said, gesturing to the figure of Christ enthroned "—this is the spreading of the Word, and the ending of sickness. The deaf shall hear and the mute shall speak and the lame shall walk again…"

Dubay and Jonas stared at the figures.

"Two years ago, I arrived for good. It was in the afternoon and I jostled with tourists for my first look at the cathedral. I was so beguiled with the soaring light inside the nave that I walked past the tympanum with only a moment's glance. And that was a mistake. Because every detail on this building, every joint and doorframe and capital tell a story."

Jonas looked around the narthex.

"So it is a good thing that you did not arrive in the daylight, to become tempted by the light of the nave."

"I think I remember studying this in grad school. But you sure don't get what it *feels* like, what it *does* to you…" Jonas muttered, shrugging his shoulders.

At that moment, the door on the far right opened, and a small woman in a plain gray dress and headscarf walked into the narthex.

"Aah! Soeur Fabienne! Pardon me, Monsieur Flycatcher," Dubay said, taking leave of Jonas and walking to meet the woman. They had an extended conversation in quiet tones, leaving Jonas to gather his belongings.

Dubay nodded to the woman and returned to Jonas. "D'accord. Soeur Fabienne will take you to your room, and I will take leave of you here for the evening. Please come see me in the morning – at 10? – to look into your luggage and discuss the glass."

"Sure, sure thing," Jonas replied, a hitch in his breathing. *The glass.*

"Bon nuit. A dèmain," Dubay said, shaking Jonas' hand warmly. Jonas watched him walk through the doors into the fiery orange of the candlelit nave.

"Monsieur?" Soeur Fabienne prompted.

Jonas turned back to the nun and nodded. He followed her out into the night. He pulled the pack of Gitanes from his pocket and offered one to the nun. She refused with the shake of her head and pursed lips, and he laughed.

After only a block, they reached the lodging house and he ground the cigarette out under his heel. She led him through a small parlor and up a flight of narrow wooden steps to his room, looking not out over the rue St Pierre, but onto a side street, lined with mature beech and oak.

"Merci," he nodded as she pulled the door closed. He looked around his small room in the light from the streetlamp: a twin bed, a dresser, and a chair. He sat on the bed – *Hard, of course* – and slowly took off his high tops. He kicked them into a corner and lay down, fully clothed, too tired to get undressed. *Can I do this?*

Chapter Five

THE SOFT KNOCK on his bedroom door told him it was well past the hour he needed to get up. He rolled over with a grunt and cocooned in the covers against the cool darkness. Blessed silence surrounded him for two minutes. Then another gentle but insistent knock.

"Monseigneur?"

Dubay sighed. "Oui, oui, un moment," he croaked. He threw the covers off and stood quickly, before the urge to lie back down again overtook him. In his years of service to the church, and all his years as a Catholic, he had never quite understood why prayers had to start before dawn. Who do you impress with prayers at 5 a.m.? God? Time doesn't exist for God. But there was no sense in arguing with thousands of years of tradition.

He shuffled to his small bathroom and flicked the single bulb on, squinting against its harshness. He reached in and turned on the shower, then turned to face the small round mirror above the chipped white sink. Ooooof," he muttered, shaking his head. His short-cropped grey hair spiked in odd angles all over his head. He passed a long, thin hand, marked with deep and jagged scars, over his stubbly chin and cursed for the thousandth time the prohibition against beards.

After a short and painful interlude with the razor, he stepped into the frigid shower. The cold water wasn't a sign of piety or self-abasement; Dubay simply knew that if he didn't take a cold shower, he'd stand in there all morning, letting the hot water and steam envelop him. Better to get in and out quick and not be tempted. He stepped out, shivering, and pulled the towel around his waist, rushing into his bedroom, which was somewhat warmer.

"Monseigneur!" A surprised and clearly very frightened novice of his order stood on the threshold of his room, coffee tray in hand. Dubay choked back a laugh at the look of confusion and embarrassment on his face, but smiled, "Thank you. Right there on the desk is fine."

The novice scurried to the well-ordered desk and dropped the coffee tray, spilling cream and rattling silverware. He refused to look the Abbot in the face as he backed toward the door. "I apologize, I had not realized –"

Dubay couldn't quite remember the name of this thin dark-haired young man, who looked as if he had joined them at Vézelay straight out of his nursery. He smiled. "There is nothing to apologize for. You were simply following the instructions of the good Soeur Marie, and have not yet learned that she has a –

how shall we say – unique sense of humor." The novice smiled but his eyes darted to the open door to the hallway.

Dubay folded his hands with as much dignity as he could muster standing half-naked in the cold pre-dawn. "Thank you. That will be all," he said gravely.

The novice tried all at once to bow and run out the door. He tripped on his robes, knocked his elbow against the doorframe, and stumbled down the hall, cheeks flaming. Dubay shook his head, snickering, and closed the door.

He crossed the room to the worn and ancient armoire in the corner. Rows of neatly pressed designer shirts and carefully tailored slacks hung side-by-side with his vestments in the musty closet. He selected a pair of tan linen pants and a crisp white shirt and laid them carefully on the unmade bed, then returned to the drawer, filled with silk polka-dot boxers of every shade. He hummed a passage from Dvorak's New World Symphony as he dressed and poured himself a cup of black coffee, his humming buzzing on the rim of the delicate china.

Dubay set the cup down and pushed the coffee tray and largely undrunk coffee to the side. He pulled his diary toward him and chewed thoughtfully on the cap of his fountain pen. *Mmmm... Jean at 1300. Flycatcher this morning. What an odd name.*

He flipped through the rest of the week's appointments, then set the diary down and scanned the massive cherrywood bookshelf, which took up an entire wall, and selected a slim burgundy-leather volume. He turned to the first chapter and returned to his chair. As he sat, a small photo slipped from the pages of the book and fluttered to the floor.

Dubay stooped to retrieve the photo and gasped. "Oh. Oh," he whispered, dropping into his chair. A young woman, in her early thirties, perhaps, with long, curling black hair grinned at him, the murky Seine flowing lazily in the distance. He turned the photo over with shaking hands.

Michel – je t'aime!

May, 1982.

There was no signature.

Dubay sat staring at the photo, tracing its edges with his thumb, Augustine's *Confessions* forgotten on the desk. Fifteen minutes later, his alarm clock rang five o'clock. He placed the photo back into the book, downed the rest of his coffee, and bolted out the door.

Chapter Six

SHE REACHED OUT to him, long hair whipping around her face, obscuring her eyes but not the movement of her lips. She stood near the window, her arms wide and pleading, a writhing smoke stalking her every swaying movement, curling around her head and darkening the folds of her scarlet dress. Her lips rounded and grimaced, muttering words he felt he could see if only he could hold them in his hand. He reached out for her and she shattered into a thousand jeweled pieces.

Jonas caught his breath and awoke, shivering. He sat up and looked around the room, searching for a flash of scarlet. "Just a dream, Jonas, just a dream," he whispered to the dark. He took a deep breath and turned his head to look out the open window.

The graceful oak outside his window had been joined by the sailing moon, a silvered boat in the vast sky-sea. He watched the argent vessel rise and fall in the swells of the wide swaying branches, but could not return to sleep.

Sighing, he sat up and swung his legs over the side of the small bed. *Crap, didn't I even get undressed?* He stood and stretched, pulling his t-shirt off as he did. He folded it and laid it neatly on the small wooden chair in the corner of the room; he caught a side view of himself in the small mirror, and scowled at the short red scars along his arm and upper torso. He turned and pushed open the tall, narrow window and squeezed past the worn wooden frame where he half-sat, half-leaned on the stone casing.

The night was deeply blue and quiet. In the distance, a door suddenly creaked open and slammed shut, and he could hear hurrying feet on a nearby street, the *clip-clop* of their heels echoing lonely in the darkness. Jonas pulled out a Gitane and added his silvery smoke to the night. He watched the swaying branches and empty street, guessing at the time in California and wondering where the hell his luggage was and wondering for the thousandth time what he was doing there, and let the cigarette burn down to his fingers. With an impatient grunt he took a last drag, and flicking the butt out the window, turned back to his bed.

He pulled off his jeans and, folding them, placed them neatly on top of his t-shirt. He shuffled over to the small bed and crawled in, rolling onto his side and pulling his knees tight to his chest. He yawned and drifted back to sleep.

"Monsieur Flycatcher?"

"Huh – wha?"

Jonas sat up and looked in confusion around the small room. Warm light swirled through the open window. The sound of people chattering under his window wafted in, along with the rumble of diesel engines at the base of the hill. He'd half expected the swaying woman, but instead, the door creaked open and Dubay stepped in, smiling. "Jetlag?"

"Mmm," Jonas nodded. "What time is it?" He rubbed his eyes with the heels of his hands.

"Nearly nine-fifteen."

Jonas stopped rubbing his eyes and looked at Dubay in surprise. "Wow. Really?"

"Indeed."

"Crap," Jonas said, throwing the covers off. "Did my luggage show up?" he asked, standing and walking to the folded jeans on the chair for his pack of cigarettes. Empty. "Damn," he muttered. He turned and looked at Dubay, who he found was watching him, with narrowed eyes, move around the room in his plaid boxers. Jonas stood with his back to the attenuated window, the morning sun streaming behind him, throwing his face into shadow. An areole shone about his head, touching his short reddish curls with fire. "Abbot Dubay?" Jonas prompted.

"Those scars. On your side and your arm. How did you get them?"

"That's none of your goddamned business."

Jonas and Dubay stared at each other for a long minute. Jonas folded his freckled white arms but did not move.

"They are in such an unusual pattern, I thought perhaps they were intentional," Dubay said.

Jonas turned his back to Dubay and pulled on his jeans and t-shirt. He turned back and folded his arms again. Dubay leaned against the doorframe and too folded his arms. "I should like to hear the story someday."

"Yeah, listen, it's none of your fucking business, OK?" Jonas said, sitting on the bed and pulling on his shoes.

Dubay nodded, an eyebrow quirked.

"So, let's just drop it and go find out about my luggage."

"We can certainly inquire after your luggage."

"Good."

"Excellent."

"Fine."

"Fine."

Silence.

"Can we go now?"

"Most certainly," Dubay smiled, but did not move.

"God damn, I need some cigarettes," Jonas said, pushing an impatient hand through his hair and without a word or a glance back, walked out the door and down the narrow steps.

Jonas passed through the dark and quiet front parlor to the street, nodding a greeting to Soeur Fabienne. He turned and waited, arms folded, for Dubay to follow. A small group of tourists across the street, puffing and wide-eyed, hiked to the cathedral's plaza. He watched them cross the last few meters and stop in the middle of the parking lot, necks craned and mouths slack. Dubay joined him and watched the procession. "Cameras. Any second now," he said.

On cue, all five tourists pulled out their cameras and looked at the massive and imposing cathedral only through their viewfinders. After a minute or two of furious clicking, the flurry ended. Three of the tourists proceeded to the portal and narthex; two others simply turned around and walked back down the hill.

"They're not going in," Jonas said flatly.

Dubay took Jonas by the elbow and turned him downhill, toward the town. "Hmm? Oh, no, of course not. They can now put a tick next to Vézelay and be done."

"Does it make you crazy?"

"It is disappointing, certainly, but there are so many other things in this world that can make me crazy. I cannot dwell on it."

"But it's *your* cathedral – don't you want them to come in and – and, I don't know, be converted or something?"

Dubay stopped and turned to face Jonas. "There are many reasons people are drawn to the cathedral," he said. "If they step through the doors and are moved or touched by the glory of the work of man in the name of God, then that is enough. And even if they come this far, to only see the doors and the towers, it is something at least. It is not my job to convert; it is my job to live the word of God and conserve his works in stone."

Jonas shrugged and they continued down the hill. "Well, it would drive me insane. All the work and artistry that went into that structure...all the pain. It's just wrong that people aren't more moved by it."

Dubay smiled. "Here we are." He opened the door to a small *tabac* and followed Jonas in. "Bonjour, madame," he said to the ancient old woman behind the counter. She nodded but did not reply. An old man stood at the counter as well, but did not seem to be buying anything. He put his cigarette into his mouth and offered his hand to Dubay, who shook it and smiled. The old man said nothing, only grunted, and returned to *Le Figaro*.

Jonas raised his eyebrows. "Gitanes, s'il vous plâit," he said to the old woman.

"Combien?"

"Uh, deux."

She looked at him and took a long drag on her cigarette. "Hmmph," she grunted, then disappeared behind the counter in a puff of smoke.

Jonas looked around while the woman fished out the cigarettes. The small store, not much larger than Jonas' bedroom, smelled of stale cigarette smoke and sickly sweet old lady perfume. Dubay flipped idly through a magazine, immune to the behavior of the denizens of the tabac.

The old woman reappeared with two packs of Gitanes. "Vingt Euros," she said, blowing smoke out her nose.

"Dix?! Est-tu fou?" Dubay looked up from his magazine and laughed in surprise. "You are not going to pay ten Euros per pack, are you?"

"I guess. It's what I paid down in St Père."

"Oh, that is ridiculous." Dubay leaned over the counter and had a low conversation that Jonas could not follow. At the end, the old woman folded her arms and shook her head. Dubay smiled, and Jonas noticed for the first time how young the Abbot seemed – grey, but prematurely. He had plenty of wrinkles, but his blue eyes were bright. Beautiful, even. Dubay raised his eyebrows, at once pleading with and teasing the old woman.

"D'accord, d'accord," she said, waving a dismissive hand at Dubay. "Cinq Euros," she said shortly to Jonas. He pulled out his crumpled wad of bills and handed her a five-Euro note. "Merci beaucoup," he said, taking the cigarettes.

Dubay took Jonas by the elbow and steered him out the door. "Merci bien," Dubay called over his shoulder, and shut the door behind him.

"How did you do that?" Jonas asked as Dubay led him across the street.

"Hmmm?"

"How did you get her to lower her price?"

"I explained a few things to her."

"Like what?"

"I told her that you are a novitiate at the cathedral and these were your last cigarettes before committing yourself to the life of God."

"You what?" Jonas stopped in the middle of the street and looked at Dubay.

"She felt as if she was doing her duty to God."

"You're kidding me."

"Plus, she thinks I am attractive," Dubay smiled and led the way to a small café up the street from the *tabac*.

"You are insane."

"That is entirely possible," Dubay nodded, and pushed open the door of the café, following Jonas through. The scent of strong coffee fought unsuccessfully with the smell of cigarette smoke. "Bonjour," he called to the owner, who was leaning against the bar and reading the paper. The owner nodded and put his paper down as Dubay and Jonas sat at a table near the tall front window. He sauntered over and looked expectantly at Dubay.

"Un croissant, une tatine, et deux café au lait, s'il vous plâit," Dubay said. "Anything else?" he asked Jonas.

"Orange juice. And scrambled eggs and bacon, and maybe some toast."

"Et jus d'orange."

The owner nodded and shuffled away. "Uh – monsieur?" Jonas called after him. "Et deux oeufs, aussi," he said, scowling at Dubay. Dubay did not reply, but instead looked out the window.

Jonas pulled out his Gitanes and lit one, throwing the spent match on the table. He inhaled deeply and leaned forward, resting his head in his hands, running his finger back and forth along the scar from his eye to his temple. It was delicate in a way – much more fine than the scars on his chest and arms. No jagged edges, no crazy change of direction and roadmap spiderweb. Neat and clean and very red. He sometimes thought it might be on fire; he was often surprised to touch it and find it smooth and cool.

He blew the last lungful of smoke out his nose and leaned back in his chair to grab a plastic ashtray from the small table behind. He stubbed out his cigarette and realized Dubay was still looking out the café's window. He followed Dubay's gaze.

"That's a photography studio, right?" he asked.

"Yes," Dubay replied to the window.

"Some pretty interesting stuff in there. I tried to get in last night, but they close too damn early."

"Peculiar."

"What's peculiar?"

"Hmmm?"

"What's peculiar?"

"It is nothing."

Jonas watched as a dark-haired woman emerged and stood at the door of the shop, staring up the street at the cathedral and crossing herself over and over. She shook her head violently, then crossed herself again and repeated the pattern precisely, over and over, a chaotic swirl of sepia curls and long fair arms. Jonas and Dubay watched, transfixed.

"She's so beautiful," Jonas muttered, shaking his head. "I wonder what she's saying."

Dubay did not reply.

"What's wrong with her?" Jonas asked after many minutes had passed.

Dubay turned and looked at Jonas, eyes glassy and unfocused; he shivered.

"Pardon, monsieur," the café owner said, placing a plate of oily eggs and a cup of café au lait in front of Jonas. "Merci," he mumbled, looking at Dubay through narrowed eyes. Dubay busied himself with his croissant and Jonas noticed for the first time how long and thin his hands were – and how scarred.

"So, Jonas – may I call you Jonas?" he asked, his tone bright.

"Sure."

"We have quite a lot to accomplish today. We need to inquire after your luggage of course, and see about the workshop space I have found for you. It might also serve for a flat, if you find the Centre Sainte-Madeleine too confining. Let's finish here quickly, so we can make it to my office before the hordes descend."

"When can I see the glass?"

"Today possibly; tomorrow certainly. I want you to be in the right frame of mind when you see it first." He began humming.

"You realize that's one day less I have to finish the job."

"Yes."

"You realize it's making a fucking impossible job even more fucking impossible?" Jonas took a swift gulp of his café au lait and scalded his tongue. "Ow, shit."

Dubay sipped his coffee and nodded. "We all have our crosses to bear, Jonas," he smiled.

"I just want to make sure I do the best job possible within your timeframe," Jonas said, struggling to keep an even tone. "But I can't very well do that without my tools or the goddamned glass."

"Patience, Jonas. It does not appear to be one of your stronger points. You ought to try to learn it sometime. It is a virtue, they say."

Jonas shoveled a forkful of oily over-salted eggs into his mouth in reply. Dubay sat back and folded his arms, watching Jonas eat. Five silent minutes later, Dubay paid the check and they exited to the rue St Pierre.

"Where are we going?" Jonas asked.

"To my office. I thought you were anxious to have your luggage sorted out?"

"I thought you told me patience was a virtue."

Dubay laughed. "So I did, so I did."

They passed through the square at the feet of the cathedral, then turned the corner and saw the chapter house, a long building jutting from the south side of the great cathedral, grand and imposing of its own accord, but dwarfed by the storeys-high basilica.

Dubay gave a genial nod to the clutch of tourists peeking over the fence to the courtyard between the cathedral and chapter house; he opened the gate and ushered Jonas through. The mid-morning sun was rising to its full above the monastery, bringing the small, dark building into sharp contrast with the soaring, bright cathedral.

As they walked, Jonas looked around the walled courtyard, a paved parking lot but for a long, narrow patch of green, covered in rows of neatly organized and pruned rose bushes. "Gorgeous rose bushes. Who tends them?"

Dubay stopped and smiled broadly. "I do. I find it very soothing."

Jonas sauntered over to the bushes and cupped a bloom in his hand. "Beautiful. The colors are so delicate. It looks like, I don't know, that hazy background that Fragonard used. Or, maybe," he continued, brushing his hands along the row of flowers, "a Gainsborough. You know? Subtle, off to the side. Don't want to distract from the sitter. You know?" he asked, looking over his shoulder.

Dubay stood with his head cocked slightly and a strange expression on his face – a mix of surprise and something that Jonas couldn't place. "Do you paint?"

Jonas turned to face Dubay. "Me? Oh, hell no."

Dubay nodded. "I see," he said, walking again towards the monastery's door. Jonas fell in beside him and they walked in silence. Dubay guided Jonas through the door and down a cool shadowy corridor, not yet touched by the morning's sun. A nun, dressed in a plain grey skirt and a simple dark headscarf, knelt next to a long, low bench, dark and shiny with age and use. She dipped a brush into the bucket next to her, and continued to scrub the floor.

"Soeur Marie," Dubay said, approaching her with a smirk.

She leaned back on her heels and smiled. "Monseigneur," she replied.

Dubay leaned down and whispered something into her ear. She giggled and shook her head. Dubay folded his arms, shook his head, and walked on, indicating to Jonas to follow him.

"What was that about?" Jonas asked.

"Soeur Marie and I have a score to settle. She has a— challenging sense of humor."

They began to climb a narrow stone staircase. "A score to settle? That doesn't sound very priestly, you know," Jonas said.

"You obviously don't know the history of the Catholic church."

Dubay opened the door to his office and Jonas followed him through. The room was small and cramped; every available inch of wall space was covered with bookshelves. "Have a seat, Jonas," Dubay said, sitting at his desk and motioning to the matching dark leather chair opposite. Jonas ignored him, lingering instead at the small window. He heard Dubay rummaging on his desk, picking up the phone, and then speaking briskly to someone in French; he focused his attention on the view.

Dubay's office faced east, and looked down not on the town clutching at the legs of the cathedral, but over a small grassy park covered with spreading shade trees, deeply green and cool, even in the bright morning light. He turned and looked at Dubay. "Do you mind if I open the window?" he asked. Dubay nodded and waved his hand dismissively. "Oui, oui, je suis ici," he said into the phone, turning away from Jonas.

Jonas unlatched the window and pushed it wide. The abbey's hilltop view beyond the park was spectacular. Jonas inhaled, feeling the green fields wash over him, the tree-topped hillsides lifting him into the fresco blue sky, the wild forest land beyond prickling his skin. The varieties of green in just one eyeful was staggering: rich and green and full of bursting life and tempting shadows. Jonas folded his arms and smiled.

A few minutes later, Dubay touched Jonas on the shoulder. "I have tracked down your luggage," he said, offering Jonas the leather chair once again. Jonas sat obediently as Dubay returned to his chair. "Your clothes are in Portugal," he said. Then putting a hand up, "I do not know how, and neither does the airline. However, the good news is that your box – I presume of tools? – is on its way, and should be here by tomorrow morning."

"Thank God," Jonas breathed.

"Indeed."

"So," Jonas said, standing and pulling out his cigarettes, "mind if I smoke in here?"

"I do," Dubay replied. Jonas took the cigarette out of his mouth, and Dubay ushered him through the door to the corridor and stone staircase. "Let us see about your workshop next; I believe you will be able to move in today. That will give you a chance to start tomorrow morning when your tools arrive."

They hastened down the long corridor, past Soeur Marie and her scrubbing, and out into the courtyard. "I apologize for hurrying you like this; I have quite a bit of paperwork to complete this morning before my meeting with Monsieur Merimée – the mayor," he explained to Jonas' quizzical look. "He likes to meet with me once per week to discuss the running of his church," he said with a quirk of his eyebrow. "He kindly offers suggestions for improvement and I buy him wine and ignore his advice. He is fortunate that he is my friend."

Jonas raised his eyebrows.

"The abbots who preceded me, since the monastery was founded here –in the ninth century – have not been particularly amenable to the opinions of the townspeople," Dubay said, steering Jonas north across the plaza toward the narrow rue de l'Argenterie.

"You see," Dubay continued, "the abbey and church had become a center for pilgrimage in the middle ages, thanks to the holy relics of the Magdalene – and that meant money, and a good deal of it. When it became a real industry, oh, around 1080 or so, the Pope took notice and put the monks, abbey, and cathedral under the purview of the monks of Cluny, here in Burgundy. And since the cathedral was under the dual control of the Holy See and the monks of Cluny, the abbot and the monks here were untouchable. The good burghers of the town were none too pleased with this turn of events," Dubay said, warming to the subject, his eyes flashing. "They of course wanted more of the cut, as it were – exclusive rights to housing the pilgrims, more access to sell to them in the marketplace and along the pilgrimage road in the valley. This was the start of the Burgundian pilgrimage road to Compostela in Spain, so quite lucrative. The church would have none of it – and open warfare erupted in the streets."

"No shit," Jonas said, staring down the ancient lane with eyes narrowed.

"Oh, yes, it is a colorful history – quite different than our sleepy town now. This was a center of political intrigue, a stage for the power struggles between the Dukes of Nevers, the Burgundian elite, even the King of France and the Pope. And it has not been pretty. Oh no. In fact, the townspeople actually murdered one of the abbots…" Dubay stopped and turned around to look back at the massive cathedral. After a few moments, he shook his head and continued. "It is certainly not the money-making proposition it was in the twelfth and thirteenth centuries, but Vézelay still depends on the pilgrim-tourist industry," he said. "There is a good deal of money at stake. So, I meet with monsieur the mayor and listen to his suggestions."

"And ignore them," Jonas smiled.

"Absolutely. Ah! Here we are," Dubay said. Number 23 rue de l'Argenterie stood in the middle of a long row of houses, stepped and staggered along the hill, all built of the same honey-colored stone, all faced with green shutters and covered by timbered roofs, dark with age. Dubay pushed the heavy door open and followed Jonas through.

"It is quite small and narrow, but wait until you see the view from the first storey. In the back there –" he motioned past a wooden staircase to a small room "—there is a small kitchen area, and a small garden beyond. But come with me," he said, waving Jonas toward the staircase. "I think you will like the workshop."

They climbed the narrow staircase; Jonas gasped when he reached the top.

"Nice, yes?" Dubay asked.

Jonas nodded. The workspace was small – not more than twenty feet square, and most of it taken by a sturdy wooden worktable. But the windows, and their view, was outstanding. The room faced north, looking out beyond the ancient ramparts to the rolling and wooded countryside beyond. Fields of sunflowers turned to face him and Jonas pushed open the heavy windows, catching the scant breeze.

"The view is especially nice, but I thought the steady northern light would allow you to really *see* the colors of the glass," Dubay said, smiling and somewhat tentative.

Jonas turned reluctantly from the windows. "It really is perfect," he said. "Thank you."

"My pleasure," Dubay said, inclining his head. "There is only one drawback: there is no telephone."

"That's OK, I have my –" Jonas patted his jeans pockets and groaned. "Mobile. Which is sitting on my dresser at home. Of course."

"We will have to communicate the old fashioned way, face to face."

Jonas nodded and paced around the room, peering under the table, shaking it and testing its sturdiness, noting the quality of the light and the dimensions of the room.

Dubay folded his arms and watched Jonas, smiling. "I will meet you at the cathedral tomorrow morning at 10 to give you the glass. I want to make sure you are settled in before you bring it here."

Jonas stopped his investigation and nodded. "Yeah, that's fine. Oh, and do you have the fifty-percent deposit? Madame Chevrey didn't mention in the contract if she was bringing it down, or if she was going to send it to you ahead of time."

"Yes, yes, of course. I shall turn it over to you tomorrow morning. She is also having the countersigned contract sent over – I expect it tomorrow. I believe there is an amendment to the agreement that states if you do not complete the work on time – by the eve of the Magdalene's feast – you forfeit the second fifty percent."

"Are you kidding me?" Jonas said. "I would never have come if I'd known those terms – and why are they changing terms on me after I already signed an agreement? That's insane. I can't do business like that." Jonas stood with his back to the windows and folded his arms, breathing heavily.

"Soyez gentil, Jonas. Mon Dieu, I am not trying to cheat you," Dubay said, his blue eyes glittering. "When you come to retrieve the glass tomorrow, we will review the contract together and call Madame Chevrey if there are any further negotiations to be made. D'accord?" Dubay ran his hands through his hair and took a deep breath. "D'accord?"

Jonas stared out the window. "This is bullshit. You know that, right? Fucking bullshit. You don't change a contract after it's been signed. After I've flown all the way over here."

Dubay squeezed his eyes shut and rubbed his temples. "Yes, Jonas. I am aware. You may discuss it with Madame Chevrey."

"Sorry. Sorry. It's not you. It's just –" Jonas said, shaking his head. "Nothing. No big deal. Ten o'clock tomorrow. I'll be there."

"Fine. Enjoy your view," Dubay said and, with a curt nod, turned and descended the narrow staircase. Jonas heard the front door close and felt in his pocket for his cigarettes. *How am I going to do this? I have to do this. It's my last chance.* He looked around the room, shadowed and untouched by the morning, an image teasing just beyond his eyes of swirling red.

Chapter Seven

THE ALARM CLOCK bleated at her from the crowded nightstand. Meredith lay sprawled across the bed, one arm flung above her head, the covers rumpled in a heap at her feet. She reached down and pulled the covers up against the cold dawn, and turning onto her side, jammed a pillow over her head.

Another five minutes passed, and the alarm clock showed no signs of relenting. With more speed and dexterity than was natural for her so early in the morning, in one movement she yanked off the covers and pillow, slapped the alarm clock into submission, and threw herself back into a fetal position. She reveled silently in her victory. *Just a few more minutes...*

The alarm clock resumed its wailing cry. Knocking over piles of books and papers in her half-finished dream, she groped for the clock. She groaned and sat up, resting her chin in her hands, her dark brown curls making a curtain against the pink dawn outside her bare window. And then the image knocked her into wakefulness, as it had each morning for the last eighteen years, guilt a gnawing beast scrabbling in the pit of her stomach: a whir of burning color, red and orange, scorching heat and searing glass, and then their faces, pale and slack.

And suddenly, a new image.

The night has been cold but I am fortunate. St. Christopher has been my blessed protector and my journey to the walls of Beaune have been solitary and the roads soft and flat. When I reach the main pilgrim road to Vézelay the dangers and temptations will be greater. But that will be as the saints decree. I shake out my cloak, my bedding for the night, and wrap it about my shoulders. I approach the northern gate and request entry to venerate St. Catherine at the cathedral.

Not that goddamned dream again. Meredith shuddered. *I've got to get out of here.* She pulled on a pair of old jeans and a sweatshirt to cover her t-shirt, and not bothering to lace up her hiking boots, grabbed her Hasselblad and photo bag and hurtled down the narrow staircase, taking the steps two at a time. She hesitated at the bottom of the stairs and, pulling her hair into an untidy ponytail, looked with longing at the tiny kitchen beyond her dark shop. She peered out at the gathering pink dawn and shook her head. *Coffee later.*

She stepped out onto the cold rue St Pierre and hugged her sides against the chill. The serpentine line of the ancient walls echoed the melody of the rolling hills beautifully, a harmony and counterpoint in light and dark at that hour of the morning. She walked down the winding street, past closed and quiet homes and shops that made up her neighborhood for the past year, and headed for the junction of the rue St Pierre and the rue Etienne.

The chill air and shadowy streets helped push the strange dream to the back of her mind. Meredith pulled out her camera and framed the street and the lamps, still shining in the early dawn, but did not take the shot.

She shook her head and hurried toward the corner – she'd reach the ramparts from the west end, working her way up from the porte Neuve to the tour Rouge, and perhaps up to the tour des Ursulines. *You're going to lose the light*. She shook her head in disgust and broke into a jog around the corner.

"Meredith! Mon Dieu, where are you going in such a hurry this morning?" A tiny old woman with unnaturally dark hair and cobwebs of wrinkles grasped Meredith by the elbow to keep from falling.

"Oh, Marie-Laure, I am so sorry!" Meredith said, abashed, brushing imagined dirt from Marie-Laure's navy cotton dress. "Are you alright?"

"Fine, fine, ma chère," Marie-Laure replied, smiling and patting Meredith on the arm.

"What are you doing up so early?"

"Sniffing the wind. And where are you running to so early? I thought you have already shot this side of town."

"Mmm, I have. I'm doing the ramparts this morning. I need to do the north towers," Meredith said, looking past Marie-Laure up the street.

"Yes, yes, I have always loved those towers. Come by for coffee later this morning and I will tell you all about the history."

"How about nine? I've got to open my shop for my adoring public at 10."

Marie-Laure snorted. "That will be lovely. I will make you some proper coffee – not that gruesome sludge you call coffee."

Meredith rolled her eyes. "Sure. Hey -"

"Yes, ma petite?"

"Have you ever had a recurring dream?"

"Oh, certainly. The one about my poor old Guillaume coming back to haunt me ... it is quite frightening."

Meredith laughed out loud, the sound ringing gratefully along the empty streets. "I'm going to tell him you said that."

"Tell him all you want. You know he is dense as a block of wood."

"You're terrible."

"Perhaps," Marie-Laure smiled.

Meredith sobered. "I've been having the strangest dreams lately..."

"Mmmm...?"

"Are you having trouble sleeping?"

"I'm having trouble staying awake."

"Are you ill? Have you seen Frédéric? He can make a house call..."

"No, I'm fine. Forget I brought it up."

"Meredith –"

Meredith shook her head, a chill shivering up her spine. "It's nothing. I don't want to talk about it."

"Ma chère," Marie-Laure said, grasping Meredith's hand. "We have been friends for –"

"Almost twenty years."

"Yes," Marie-Laure nodded. "You can tell me if there is something wrong."

Meredith nodded absently as she glanced up at the sky, now warming. "Crap – I have to go or I'll lose the light."

Marie-Laure knitted her eyebrows. "I will see you at nine, yes?"

"Huh? Yeah, sure, sure. See you then," Meredith said, giving her a quick kiss on the cheek.

But even as she turned her back on the cathedral and Marie-Laure shuffled into the distance, Meredith's feet betrayed her; a change came over her with bewildering speed. She was pulled into the winding current of the hilly street and drawn inexorably toward the massive basilica. A light mist still hung about its tall Tour St Michel, tremendous and imposing against the gentle sky; she put her eye to the viewfinder and the tower became a mountain eyrie, a quiet refuge for a nesting sparrow. *Click*.

She lowered the camera and waded again up the street. She stopped and raised the camera to her face, framing the winding watery street. *Click*. Framed the lovely rounded No. 10 with its tall, waterfall roof. *Click*. Framed the Tour St-Michel again. *No. Not the cathedral.* She lowered the camera and floated up the street. *I'll just cut through the plaza and down to rue de l'Argenterie.* The swift current emptied into the dark plaza, and Meredith with it. She knelt at the feet of the cathedral, her traitorous limbs betraying her.

The guard at the gatehouse is kindly and shows me the way to the lady's basilica. The morning is cool and still; perhaps I will arrive in time for Prime I stand with the other pilgrims in the nave as the holy brothers perform the offices. The marble is cool beneath my feet and I shiver. I now realize, even in this dim light, it is the eyes of the messenger in the chapel opposite that has chilled me. He smiles and I grip my satchel close.

Prime ends and we move to the holy shrine of the Virgin. I light a candle and pray to holy Ste Marie and the Magdalene to preserve me from the temptation I feel creeping from behind. "Mademoiselle," he says quietly in my ear. I do not turn though I feel his hot breath on my cheek. "It is not wise for a young woman to make pilgrimage without a traveling party to protect her."

I kiss the feet of our holy mother and move to allow the press of pilgrims access to the shrine. I hold my satchel close and walk quickly out of the church. The staircase is warm and I pause to lift my face to the rising sun and give praise to St Jacques.

"It has been many weeks," the voice says quietly. Now I know it is not the devil himself, merely one of his minions. I keep my eyes closed.

"Why have you not come to me?"

"I have had no messages."

I open my eyes and turn to look up at him. I yearn to touch his pale cheek, the scars along his jaw. "You must understand," I plead.

"Your benefactor would not be pleased to find you here," he replied, eyes veiled from me.

"My benefactor is not here," I reply, turning from him.

"Ah, but he is. It is only two days' ride to Cluny, as you well know."

"I am answerable only to God and the saints."

"We shall see." He trails a light kiss along my cheek. I open my eyes to watch him walk back into the dark basilica. May the saints protect and preserve me.

"Huh?" Meredith looked around in confusion. The rising sun had warmed the walls of the town but in the narthex she was shivering. "How the hell did I get in *here*?" she muttered, shaking her head. She hadn't stepped foot in the cathedral for weeks; it was an ongoing point of pride. She gathered her camera and bag and hurried toward the doors leading to the bright plaza. At the threshold, she looked down at her camera and gasped. *Did I roll the film wrong? There's no way I finished off a whole roll.*

The bells began to ring for Prime. She sank down at the doors to the church, her heart racing.

"Meredith?" a quiet voice whispered in her ear.

Heart in her throat, she jumped and turned to find the voice's owner was Dubay.

"Michel," she said, staring out across the plaza.

Dubay quirked an eyebrow. "I am surprised to find you here."

"Me too," she said under her breath.

He offered his hand, and she stood shakily and brushed off her pants.

"Have you been well?" he asked, his long hand lingering on her arm.

"As well as can be expected, I guess."

He nodded and dropped his hand. "What have you been shooting?"

"I – I'm not sure."

"Pardon?"

Meredith shook her head. "Never mind. I think I need some coffee. Yes, definitely. Coffee. I – I need to go." She stumbled down the broad steps then turned to look at Dubay, tall and distinguished and so at home on the steps of the great basilica. "I – " she said, and dropped her camera bag. The street had suddenly become unbearably warm and bright – hot and prickly on her skin and exploding behind her eyes; without thinking, she crossed herself.

"Meredith?" he said, stepping forward tentatively, his hand extended.

"I have to go …" she muttered to herself, and picking up her camera bag, rushed down the still-empty street to her shop, her head pounding.

The key shook in the lock and her hand rattled the worn brass knob. "Come on, come on," she muttered. She won through and slammed the door behind her, shaking the framed photos lining the wall.

She dropped the photo bag on her cluttered desk and hurried into the small kitchen. "Coffee…coffee… coffee…damn! Where is the goddamned coffee?" she said, slamming open and shut drawers and cabinet doors. She leaned against the low counter and hung her head, her breathing ragged. She found the coffee where she'd left it the night before, behind a pile of dirty dishes.

She brewed a pot of extraordinarily strong coffee and sat at her desk, fiddling with the completed roll of film and staring out at the rue St Pierre as it came slowly to life. *Sleep is definitely overrated.*

Three hours later, she awoke with a raging headache. She looked at her watch: 9:42. "Oh no, Marie-Laure!" she muttered. She pulled off her sweatshirt, grabbed her keys, and stumbled to the door of her shop, slamming it behind her. She turned down the hill toward Marie-Laure's house, but an aching throb in her head spun her around, back toward the cathedral. In a moment, without thinking, she crossed herself. Over and over. *What is wrong with me? Stop it!* But the compulsion was overwhelming. She shook her head to clear it, but still her hands would not obey. *Stop goddammnit!* Finally, after what felt like hours, she wrenched herself from the view of the cathedral and with fumbling hands, unlocked her shop and stumbled back inside.

"What the hell was that?" she muttered, slumping into her desk chair. She looked at her watch: 9:47. *I'm losing it*

She picked up the phone and dialed.

"Allo?"

"It's me."

"Hello, my dear. I thought you were coming down at nine?"

"I was – I fell asleep," Meredith said, looking out the window to the café across the street.

"Oh. Did you dream again?"

"Yeah," Meredith replied, distracted. "No, no I'm fine."

"Come down for dinner later, ma chère."

"I - no, thanks, I'm just going to stay in tonight."

"Nonsense. Come down for dinner. I have some lovely lamb."

"Sure."

"What time?"

"I don't care."

"Meredith, shall I send the doctor over?"

Meredith cradled the phone against her shoulder and looked at her shaking hands. "No, I'm fine."

"Really?" Meredith could almost see Marie-Laure's raised eyebrow.

"No. It's been a very weird morning."

"Have you seen Michel lately?"

Meredith's breath hitched. "Yes, this morning. How did you know?"

"I didn't. But it would explain why you are so upset."

"Huh. Maybe. It never gets easier, you know?"

"I do."

Meredith looked out the window at the passing groups of tourists making the trek to the cathedral. She glanced at her watch. "Ooops, it's time. Gotta go."

"What time will we see you tonight?"

"Seven?"

"You will be there?"

"Yeah. See you tonight."

"Take care of yourself today – don't forget to eat."

"I won't."

Meredith hung up the phone and watched Dubay leave the café with a man who looked somehow familiar. As they disappeared up the street toward the cathedral she shook her head and raced up the stairs to her bedroom. She whipped around the small room, searching desperately for a pressed – hell, clean – shirt. Shrugging on an acceptable blouse, she pulled the clip out of her hair and shook her head, running fingers through her hair as she leapt back down the stairs. She unlocked the door to her shop and the first tourists of the day ambled in.

"Bonjour, mesdames, monsieur," she said pleasantly, shoving her still-shaking hands into her pockets.

By four, Meredith had sold scores of postcards and guidebooks and no photos. And had forgotten to eat. She smiled the last customer out of her shop and locked the door. She trudged back to the kitchen, found an apple, and ate it ravenously over the rusting sink. She washed her hands and searched for a towel, and finding none, shrugged and wiped her hands on her jeans.

Meredith climbed the stairs and turned to her small studio. The room was flooded with late afternoon light from the large square window, and the worktable was scattered with negatives and mats, glass and x-acto knives, but also random tarot cards from dog-eared decks. She inhaled – the warm and acrid smell of developing fluid from her makeshift bathroom-cum-darkroom always relaxed her; this was *her*, this was her life now. She looked out over the rue St Pierre, squeezing her shoulders tight and then relaxing. *Everything's fine.* She pulled the first enlargement toward her. *Fine.*

Three hours had passed and the room was silent and growing dark. She leaned back and stretched, throwing her arms wide and yawning. She stood and leaned over the worktable, scrutinizing the framing of the chestnut. Marie-Laure always loved those chestnuts, stately and ancient, fanning just below the chapter house.

Marie-Laure. She checked the clock and realized with surprise that seven o'clock had snuck up on her. *Crap crap crap.* Meredith ran across the hall into her bedroom, pulled on a sweater, and shoved her feet into the first pair of sandals she could find. She attempted to run her fingers through her hair, got them tangled, and gave up halfway down the stairs.

She stepped out the front door and slammed it with a bang that rattled the glass. She ran down the rue St Pierre and skidded around the corner to Marie-Laure's house. She knocked rapidly on the heavy front door and pushed it open.

"Marie-Laure?" she panted, stepping half-blinded into the dark front hallway. "Are you here?"

"In here, ma petite," Marie-Laure called from the front room. "You are just in time."

Meredith turned the corner and found Marie-Laure sitting in her front parlor, holding a book two feet in front of her face, her glasses hanging on a chain around her neck. Meredith crossed the room and kissed Marie-Laure on each cheek.

"I'm sorry I'm late," she apologized, settling into a chair across from Marie-Laure.

"Pffff – it is nothing. I am glad you are here," Marie-Laure replied with a smile, setting her book on the table. "Care for a kir?"

"Are you kidding?"

"As I suspected." Marie-Laure mixed the crème de cassis and Aligoté like an offering, and passed the glass to Meredith.

Meredith took a large sip and sighed. "Thanks. Mmmm, it smells great in here. Can I help with anything?"

"Absolutely not. The lamb will be ready in a few minutes, and there is nothing to do but sit here and chat." Marie-Laure smoothed the front of her dress and sat back, folding her hands.

Meredith took another sip and looked at Marie-Laure. She remembered the first time she'd met her. She couldn't shake the feeling that those light green eyes – almost yellow – could see right through her, or past her somehow. "What?"

"You have had a difficult day."

"That's an understatement."

"Would you like to talk about it?"

"Not really."

"Meredith..." Marie-Laure said. "I am going to call the doctor right now, unless you tell me what is going on."

Meredith sighed and shook her head. "It's just been weird. Weird..." she trailed off and stared out the window into the lavender twilight. "I felt out of control today. And you know how I hate that."

"Was seeing Michel that difficult?"

"Huh? Oh, yes, of course. It always is. But, you know, I never actually talk to him... I see him, walking by, doing whatever he does. But I haven't talked to him in well – weeks."

Marie-Laure squinted at Meredith. "What do you mean 'weeks'?"

Meredith looked into her glass. "I didn't tell you at the time, because I didn't think I was going to do it."

"Do what?"

"Michel sent me a note, asking me to do a series of photos of the interior of the cathedral – for the celebration they're having in a few weeks."

"And?"

"And after a few days, I decided to do it. I mean, I wouldn't have had to spend time with him to do it, and it was good money. But when I went over to the cathedral –"

"You went in?" Marie-Laure asked, putting her glass down on the side table.

"I couldn't believe it either. The place gives me the creeps. But, I went in and met him in the narthex and he gave me a tour, you know, pointing out the shots he wanted, telling me how to do my job," Meredith said, shaking her head.

Marie-Laure smiled. "So what happened? I have not seen any photos –"

"Yeah. Well, we were walking around, looking at all of those weird capitals on the columns, and he was going on and on about them, and I was just nodding and trying to get him to move on. And then this guy comes up from the crypt below the altar – I guess it used to be the altar centuries ago?"

Marie-Laure nodded and Meredith continued. "He said that Michel had to come down into the crypt right away. They had found – something. Michel said he'd be right with him, but the guy insisted – whispered 'glass' and Michel went down there with him. I was pissed of course for being left there – he knows how I feel about that place – but he was gone for a while. I went over and stood at the top of the stairs to the crypt, to maybe hear what they were saying. And then … it was weird…"

Marie-Laure narrowed her eyes. "Yes?"

Meredith took a deep breath. "I put my hand on the iron railing there, and it – I felt like it burned me."

"I am not sure I know what you mean –" Marie-Laure started.

"I turned to leave – my hand was killing me," Meredith whispered. "But I felt like I couldn't. And then – I felt this wave of sadness and… and heat…"

Marie-Laure watched Meredith but said nothing.

"I haven't gone back in there – I couldn't. So I didn't take the job. I hadn't spoken to Michel again until this morning. Maybe I've just been working too hard," Meredith mused, taking a large sip of her kir. "It's just – today I kind of, well –"

"Yes?"

"I think I blacked out, a little."

"How does one black out a little?" Marie-Laure asked, looking at her askance.

"OK, I blacked out. I never made it to the ramparts, at least I don't think I did. Instead of going around to rue l'Argenterie, I went back up toward the cathedral. I was just drawn…"

"Yes," Marie-Laure prompted.

"And then the next thing I knew, I was sitting in the porch, and Michel was there with me."

Marie-Laure looked at Meredith intently but said nothing; Meredith again had the feeling that Marie-Laure could see right into her.

After a few moments, Marie-Laure looked at her watch and stood, feeling Meredith's forehead as she did. "Come with me," she said. Meredith stood, and after gulping down the rest of her kir, followed her into the small kitchen. The room was filled with the smell of rosemary and garlic; Meredith sighed, and Marie-Laure gestured her into a chair next to the stove.

"I do think you're working far too hard. Have you been sleeping well? Eating properly?" Marie-Laure asked, testing the roasting lamb in the oven.

"No and no," Meredith admitted.

"You are exhausted with overwork and overwrought nerves. It is to be expected, given the circumstances," Marie-Laure said, wiping her hands on a kitchen towel and leaning against the counter.

"I guess I am working too hard."

"Up before dawn, taking your photographs all morning, working in the shop all day, framing at night. Seeing Michel again. It is not a surprise."

Meredith nodded, and rolled her head back and forth, tightening and releasing her shoulders.

"Even so," Marie-Laure continued, "you should see the doctor. I really must insist."

Meredith stood and took Marie-Laure's hand. "I am not a teenager anymore. I'll take care of this. You don't need to worry about me. I'm sorry I even brought it up," she said, squeezing Marie-Laure's hand and shaking her head.

Marie-Laure pursed her lips. "I will worry about you if I wish."

"I will be fine. I am fine."

"Pfff. I will be watching you," Marie-Laure said, folding her arms.

"I am fine. You have enough to worry about. Speaking of which, where's Guillaume?"

Marie-Laure dropped her arms and turned back to the oven. "Upstairs, reading. He will be along soon. He has an uncanny knack for appearing exactly when the food is laid."

"What's the infernal noise down here?" Guillaume, lit Gauloises hanging precariously from his lips, shuffled into the kitchen. His watery eyes hollowed in his face, his shirttails hung untucked, and his ratty cardigan was spectacularly misbuttoned.

"We are simply reveling in your idiosyncrasies, my dear."

"Hmmmph. What are you cooking?" he asked, uncorking a bottle of Savigny-les-Beaune.

"Lamb," Marie-Laure replied, pulling it from the oven with a flourish.

"Meredith, my dear," he said, handing her a tumbler of red wine, "you should be very pleased you are dining with us now. She was quite hopeless when we moved here."

"I was not!" Marie-Laure protested. Meredith rolled her eyes.

"You were, and you know it. You were a spectacular teacher, and an abysmal cook," Guillaume said after a long pull on his cigarette.

"It was the bistros! I blame them. Why should I cook when I can get perfectly good food anywhere in Paris? And besides, I was so busy with my students…"

"Yes, I know, I know," he replied, giving her a chaste peck on the cheek. "As I said: spectacular teacher, nightmare in the kitchen. Retirement has had its benefits," he said, dipping a crust of bread into the juices, "though Vézelay is unbearably dull. I learned all of its secrets and scandals within the first six months. The intervening years have been torture."

Marie-Laure rolled her eyes at Meredith, who was no longer smiling but staring into the distance. "Meredith?" Marie-Laure whispered, laying her small hand on Meredith's shoulder.

"Hmmm? Are we ready?" Meredith asked, attempting a smile.

"Yes," Marie-Laure replied. Guillaume raised his eyebrows but said nothing.

Meredith followed them into the dining room; Guillaume held their chairs in turn, and seated himself at the head of the table. They ate in silence for a few minutes, Marie-Laure and Guillaume casting looks over Meredith's oblivious head.

"Meredith, chèrie," Marie-Laure said, breaking the silence.

"Mmmm?"

"I should really take you around to the north ramparts and give you a guided tour myself."

"Excellent idea. You know that was her specialty at the Sorbonne," Guillaume said, mouth full of lamb and asparagus. "Medieval Burgundian art and architecture."

"Yes, of course I remember," Meredith nodded, pushing food around on her plate.

"When are you free?" Marie-Laure asked.

"Tomorrow?" Meredith shrugged, listless.

"Excellent," Marie-Laure said, tight-lipped.

The rest of the meal was quiet, and Meredith took leave of them after only an hour. "Ma chère, take care this evening," Marie-Laure said as she held the front door for Meredith.

"I'll be fine. I'm going to go home and pull the covers over my head and pretend today never happened."

"A fresh start tomorrow, yes? What time shall we meet?"

"Seven, I guess. The light should still be good then."

"Seven it is," Marie-Laure said, squeezing Meredith's hand.

Meredith nodded and watched Marie-Laure into her house. She sighed and trudged up the rue St-Pierre in the cool violet gloaming, exhaustion spreading heavy through her body and mind.

Chapter Eight

HE WAS FAIRLY CERTAIN that his right leg had fallen asleep, though it was nothing compared to the numbness creeping up along his spine or the infernal itch that had erupted just below his ear. He murmured the imprecations and formulae quietly, his back straight and hands clasped loosely. Just a few minutes more, and he would reach that mildly masochistic yet beautifully transcendent place where he was beyond pain, beyond mere physical sensation. Perhaps tonight would be the night he would find perfect stillness, perfect focus. The shadows rustled in the warm breeze of the quiet candlelight and the ancient church sighed as Dubay relaxed into his breath.

"Pardon, Monseigneur?"

Dubay jumped and sighed in disappointment, but hitched up his smile as he looked over his shoulder. He recognized the dark-haired young man as the novice who had brought him breakfast that morning.

"Yes?" he asked, crossing himself and standing creakily.

"Soeur Marie sent me to bring you up to dinner," the novice whispered in the empty, vaulting darkness. "She said you've – uh – been down here long enough, and your dinner is quite cold," he finished quickly, looking abashed.

Dubay straightened and laughed quietly. "Oh she did?"

"Yes. And she asked that I remind you that your calendar is quite full tomorrow, and to let Frère Ignatius see to the Compline service this evening." He looked surprised at his boldness.

"I see. What is your name?" Dubay clasped his hands and smiled.

"Pascal."

"Well, Pascal, you have once again performed your duties admirably. I thank you. Please let the good Soeur know I have received her message and will be along shortly; I need to see to the crypt before I can retire. Ask her to send dinner up to my rooms."

"Yes, Monseigneur."

"Good night, Pascal."

The young novice smiled and his shoulders relaxed. "Good night, Monseigneur."

Dubay watched him through the door to the chapter house, then turned back to the church. The Porter of his order, who had been at Vézelay much longer than he, was to look to the closing of the great cathedral each night. But he preferred to make the rounds himself in the soft light of the altar candles: lingering at the mysterious St. Catherine column, learning and relearning the carved stories of the nave's capitals and bases, venerating the Magdalene in the cool, silent crypt below the main floor.

Taking a candle from the altar, he wandered the long northern aisle of the nave. In his years at Vézelay, he had yet to fully comprehend the two hundred capitals – their blandishments against sin and evil, the victory of the righteous, the Old Testament prefigurations of the coming of Christ and the new law. The symbolism was richly detailed and perhaps more easily understandable by medieval minds; it took a number of nights' study to really capture the meaning of each capital. Certainly, he read Mouilleron's great study of the church; but nothing could compare to craning his neck in the shivering candlelight every night, unlocking the mysteries of the death of Cain or the grasshopper and the basilisk.

Minutes later, he remembered himself and hurried to the narthex to secure the great main doors. He retreated down the long aisle to the altar and crept down the uneven stone steps into the crypt of the Magdalene. In the luminous daylight of the church, the subterranean crypt was dank; at night, lit only by the feeble light of the candle, it was eerie.

He ducked into the long, low room and shivered; he was never sure if it was a susurration of religious fervor or of fear. He bent and stared into the narrow, glassed-in ledge that held the bejeweled reliquary and crossed himself. He knew the good brothers from Saint Maximin had taken the Magdalene's relics in 1220 and returned them to Aix; yet even without the true relics, he somehow felt this rough and unadorned crypt was more spiritual and sad than the rest of the huge basilica, or any church he'd been in.

He knelt on the cold stone floor before the reliquary. Loosely clasping his hands, he closed his eyes and focused all of his energy and mind on the Magdalene. The familiar words of the prayer floated in the empty crypt.

He imagined each event in the story of her life, conjuring them as if he were a player in the action, feeling the power of her conversion and apostolic mission as if he was present. The familiar cold numbness crept up from his knees, and still the scenes flashed through his mind.

A feeling of peace and contentment spread through him, from his mind to his very limbs. Then a new scene, unfamiliar yet oddly resonant: cries and screams, flashing heat and a crush of humanity. His eyes flew open and, heart pounding, he stared around the dark crypt, half expecting a crowd to push in behind him. And in the murk of the far corner, the shade of a familiar face, the damp airs stirring to the echo of a laugh.

He stood and shook his head, hugging himself against the cold shiver creeping along his spine. "Time for bed, I think," he assured himself. "Long days are taking their toll…" With a final look around the small crypt, satisfied that he was indeed alone, he climbed the steps and followed the transept to the heavy double doors of the moonlit chapter house. He climbed the quiet narrow stairs and, exhausted, pushed open the door to his office to find Soeur Marie setting a dinner tray on his desk.

"Ah, a thousand thanks," he bowed, closing the door behind him.

"You need to stop hiding," she replied without looking up, removing the crisp white linen napkin covering the dishes.

He stretched his back and rolled his shoulders. "Oh, oeufs meurette. Bless you. And for the record, I have not been hiding. I have been working."

"Mmmmm."

He sat and pushed his chair over to a small cherrywood cabinet, removing a bottle of Côtes de Nuits. "Care for a glass?" he asked, pulling a wine opener from his desk drawer.

"No thank you, Monseigneur. I do not drink."

He poured a glass of the red Burgundy for himself and downed it. "Ah, such a shame, such a shame."

Soeur Marie shook her head and smiled. "Will you need anything else tonight?"

"That will do. Coffee at the normal time, if you don't mind. I have a very long day in store tomorrow."

"Certainly," Soeur Marie replied, turning to leave.

"And one more thing – leave poor Pascal alone," Dubay said, his energy returning. "I believe he half-expected to find me in my shorts again tonight."

She burst into a high-pitched titter that danced in the air as she shut the door behind her. Dubay snorted and shook his head, smiling. He pulled the eggs toward him and opened the diary with his left hand and a sigh. "Mmm...Frère Marc about the books at 8:00...Soeur Fabienne at 13:30...oh yes, and Flycatcher at 10:00," he muttered, writing Jonas' name in the diary. He stared around the quiet office, a forkful of eggs suspended precariously, halfway to his mouth. "What are we going to do with him?" he muttered.

He poured himself another glass of wine and finished his meal, a scowl creasing his forehead. He pushed the tray away and leaned back in his chair. "And Meredith?" he whispered, staring at the ceiling. He searched his paper-strewn desk for the copy of Augustine's *Confessions* and the creased photo doubling as a bookmark. He pulled it out and stared, not quite at but through it, fingering the edges and humming under his breath.

Dubay sighed and stood, carefully replacing the photo in the book and placing it reverently on the massive bookshelf. He recorked the bottle of wine, setting it back in its cabinet, and crossed to his bedroom door. The rolling parkland and hills of the Morvan beyond the office window were silvery and silent as he turned off the light. He stared at the landscape for long minutes, arms crossed, then turned and opened the door to his bedroom.

Chapter Nine

THE MORNING DID NOT BURST through his window, dazzling and golden. It did not shimmer, dancing off the mottled ancient mirror on the wall. It simply snuck around the corner, obliquely illuminating Vézelay's proud ramparts and the quiet countryside beyond.

Jonas lay on the floor of the workshop, curled under a thin blanket, one bleary eye following the creeping progress of the grey dawn across the sky. He stretched out and groaned then sat up and, yawning, considered the austere room that would be his world for the three weeks. The north-facing windows would provide him steady, clear light and the sturdy wooden table was just about the right size for his work. He pushed his hands through his hair and then stopped mid-way. *Why the hell am I on the floor?*

He stood and shuffled across the rickety hall to the cramped bedroom where he had started the night before. Soeur Fabienne had sent over a cot and linens the previous afternoon and he had tried his best to make the windowless room livable. But the pervasive smell of moldering walls and the shadows groping slowly closer and a sudden fleeting numbness in his hands had at last driven him to the cleaner air of the studio.

He'd leant against the wide window, the blanket around his shoulders, fingering the ragged scars on his arm and watching the stars flash behind veils of high cloud. He'd stared out the window, chain smoking, running through his tools and talents, impatient for the morning and the chance to finally see the glass.

He'd ground out the last cigarette on the windowsill and flicked it out the window into the dark street below. Jonas had stalked into the stifling bedroom, grabbed the musty pillow, and returned to the studio. He'd lain on the hard floor, hands behind his head, and watched the stars shift. It had been late when he'd finally fallen asleep.

He looked around the small room and yawned. *I've got to get out of here.* He grabbed his t-shirt off the cot and sniffed it dubiously. He pulled it on, found his watch shoved in the bottom of his backpack, and discovered that he had two and a half hours to kill before meeting with Dubay. *Why was I such an asshole?*

He finished dressing, grabbed his cigarettes, and headed down the narrow staircase. He hadn't provisioned his kitchen the afternoon before, instead spending his time watching the lazy progress of the neighborhood from his studio window; his stomach gave a tremendous growl as he shut the heavy oak front door behind him.

He looked up and down the empty rue l'Argenterie; the tall closely shuttered houses stood dour against the growing morning. He idly watched the light move and shadow on the steep roof of the house next door; the gathering strength of the morning did not cause the shutters to be thrown wide to meet it. Jonas shrugged his shoulders and set out down the hill toward a café he'd spied the day before.

He reached the small café and tried the door. With a growl of impatience, he continued down the shaded hill. As he rounded the corner to meet the confluence of the rue St-Etienne and the rue St-Pierre, a tiny old lady with dark hair and startling yellow eyes opened her front door and stepped directly in his path. Jonas stopped short with a grunt. "Pardon," he mumbled.

"Oh, mon Dieu, pardon!" she cried. "Est-ce que vous faites mal?"

"Oh. No, I'm not hurt – you?"

"I am fine just a bit startled," she said in English. "I so rarely meet another early riser here. There are only one or two of us."

"Do either of you serve breakfast?" he asked, staring around the empty street, doors locked and windows still shadowy despite the growing warmth.

"Ah yes, you have discovered the secret of life in the country," she laughed. "I cannot find a reasonable breakfast here before nine. Not at all like Paris."

"At least they opened by eight."

"You know Paris?" she asked.

"I was a student there, for a while. About ten years ago," he said, avoiding eye contact.

"Were you really? In what subject?"

"Art – art history," Jonas replied, fidgeting with his lighter.

"One of my favorites. At the Sorbonne, I assume?"

"Yes."

"And what was your specialty?"

"Northern European, eighteenth and nineteenth century," he said, scanning the street over her head for anything that resembled a café.

"I am afraid you won't find much of that here. We seem to be languishing in the dusty High Middle Ages," she smiled. "Are you a teacher?"

"Me? Oh, hell no. I repair stained glass."

"Is that so? Fascinating," she said, narrowing her eyes.

"You know," she continued, "they have discovered a glass up at the cathedral."

Jonas looked again at the old woman, his forehead creased. "Yeah, I know," he replied slowly. "That's why I'm here. I'm doing the restoration. How did you –"

The old woman raised an eyebrow infinitesimally and smiled. "Then it is indeed a pleasure to make your acquaintance, Monsieur –"

"Flycatcher. Jonas Flycatcher," he replied, shaking her proffered hand, but dropped it quickly. *What the hell is wrong with my hand?*

"Marie-Laure Rouchon. I have been here only a few years, but I have learned a thing or two about this town. Please feel free to visit anytime; I would be more than happy to show a charming young man like yourself around," she smiled.

Jonas grinned and relaxed. "Sure."

"Excellent. Good luck on your search for breakfast. You will need it," she said, turning to the rue St Etienne.

"Thanks."

"Au revoir," she called over her shoulder.

He watched her down the street, then turned the corner and climbed the cobblestoned rue St-Pierre. After a block's walk he found the small café facing the photography studio, and tried the door, rattling it unsuccessfully. "Shit," he muttered. His stomach gave another rumble and seeing no other option, he headed for the tabac near the top of the hill. He tried the door and found it unlocked.

The old woman was still behind the counter, enshrouded in a haze of smoke. Jonas nodded at her and scanned the haphazard shelves for anything remotely edible. After five minutes' search, he settled for a hard baguette, a can of orange Fanta, and what seemed to be a Mars bar. "Et deux Gitanes, s'il vous plâit," he said, dropping his breakfast on the counter. The old woman raised her eyebrows in surprise. "C'est pour Monseigneur Dubay," he explained with a straight face.

"Bien sûr," she drawled, disappearing under the counter for the cigarettes. She reappeared moments later and slid the packs across the counter. "Dix–uh–sept Euros."

Jonas smiled and passed her the bills. "Merci bien," he called over his shoulder as he walked out the door.

He tore into the baguette as he wandered through the plaza in front of the church. He stopped and craned his neck to take in the tall towers and façade, backlit and imposing, the intricate sculpture of the exterior tympanum obscured by shadow. He ate his breakfast and silently watched the light turn twenty shades of blue on the face of the cathedral. He crumpled the candy wrapper and shoved it into the pocket of his jeans, then pulled out a cigarette and lit it, never taking his gaze from the façade. *Why the hell didn't I study medieval art?* He blew smoke lazily out his nose and checked his watch – 8:22.

Rubbing his neck, Jonas turned away from the cathedral and sauntered back to the house on rue l'Argenterie for a much-needed shower. As he left the plaza and turned the corner toward the north ramparts, the cathedral released the morning and the town was filled with warm, clear light.

A sharp reflection caught his eye halfway down the street – a small silver car parked in front of his workshop, a surly old man climbing in on the driver's side. Jonas jogged down the street, waving his arms. "Don't leave! Don't leave!" he called. The old man stopped and rested his arms on the roof. Jonas slowed to a walk as he approached the car. "Uh – je suis monsieur Flycatcher. Uh – uh – est-ce que vous avez mon baggage?"

"Oui," the old man grunted, nodding toward the landing in front of no. 23. "C'est tout la."

"You were just going to leave it there? Where anybody could just come by and take it?" Jonas yelled. The old man shrugged his shoulders and shook his head. Without another word, he disappeared into the car, which grumbled into life and tottered up the hill.

He turned to the landing and found piled there his box of tools and his suitcase. "Hallelujah," he muttered under his breath. "Finally." He dug into his jeans pocket and found the old, intricate key and opened the heavy front door.

He pulled the suitcase into the front room and left it leaning against the staircase as he ran up the stairs, box in hand. Jonas set the box on the work table and pushed open the tall windows to catch the cool morning air. "Oh, yeah," he grinned, turning to the box and cutting it open with his car keys. He carefully removed item after item, unrolling them from the chunky bubble wrap, pausing every few minutes to twist the wrap and pop it in a most satisfying way. When his tools were finally laid out with scrupulous neatness, he tossed the box and wrapping under the table and heaved a great sigh.

He took one last glance over his tools, to ensure everything was in place and in working order, and turned to the stairs. He wandered down to the ground floor and out into the small garden. The sun hadn't yet reached the enclosed space, tucked between tall houses. Deep purple morning glories crawled up the pockmarked stone walls, fighting with the ivy. Jonas pulled out a cigarette and put it in his mouth, but did not light it. He turned back into the house and put the cigarette back in his pack.

He checked his watch and hauled the suitcase up to his small room. Holding his breath, he dug through the case, and found, unharmed at the bottom, the framed photo of Ste Chapelle. He pulled it out and leaned it against the suitcase. He sat back on his heels and studied it, chewing absently on his fingernails. Everything started with Ste Chapelle.

THE AFTERNOON HAD BEEN DULL and grey, making the windowed walls glow as if lit from within, as if the alchemy of sand and heat and color had created its own spiritual form that hovered over the long chapel. Jonas emerged from the lower chapel's dark spiral staircase into the shivering glow. "Dear God," he muttered, releasing his breath in a sigh, his eyes wide and an astonished grin spreading across his face. He felt strangely as though his eyes were somehow not created to comprehend this, that he must look everywhere and all at once and still not really take it in.

He stood rooted at the threshold, feeling as though time was moving around him in swirling eddies. And then, the sun had broken through clouds and the world had become glittering and his heart expanded into those eddies of time. Even now, ten years later, he could still remember that moment, when it was all new and wondrous, as if he was seeing colors and shapes and light for the first time.

He walked a few tentative steps into the long space, almost on tiptoe, feeling vaguely as though he should step very lightly. He tipped his head back and followed the lines of the delicate columns leading to the dizzying heights of the lancets.

Working desperately to still his spinning mind, he sat slowly on one of the folding metal chairs lining the ancient walls and closed his eyes.

"Pretty amazing, huh?" his friend Steve had whispered in his ear.

Jonas nodded; he did not open his eyes.

"I've always wondered what it was like, here, with the light streaming in," Steve continued. "It really does feel like a jewel box."

Jonas opened his eyes a fraction. He wanted to take the chapel in slowly. The light fluttering beneath his lashes was all at once blue and then red and green. From somewhere behind the great unused altar, plainsong floated into the chapel, unadorned and pure, standing the hairs on his head on end. His eyes flashed open, and he looked at Steve, who was staring at him intently.

"What?" Jonas whispered.

"I knew you'd like it."

"It's – it's just –" he started, gesturing futilely around the sparkling chapel. "Oh, man. You don't…you just don't even know." Jonas shook his head. "Look – look at the ceiling. It's covered in stars…"

Steve leaned back in his folding chair. "Imagine all the work – Jesus, they had to be on scaffolding or something for weeks – years."

"Look at the glass. My God, how did they do that?"

"Do what?" Steve asked, still staring at the ceiling.

A strange feeling came over Jonas, confusion and elation combining, making him dizzy. "Well, look at it. Look!" he said, his voice rising above the stirring plainsong. "Look how they made that figure come to life – really come to life – more than a painting can really do. Do you know what I mean?"

"Um."

"They're lit from within, they're alive, and it's not just trickery of paintwork and brushstrokes. It's genius…"

"Don't tell me you're swearing off painting," Steve said, looking at Jonas. "Who will I share studio time with?"

"And look at the lines, the forms," Jonas continued, ignoring Steve and gesturing to the north lancets, the stories of Genesis and Exodus.

Steve swiveled in his seat to look at Jonas. "Seriously, you're not going to stop painting, are you?"

Jonas ignored him. "How did they do that?"

"I dunno," Steve replied impatiently. "Faith."

"If you say so," Jonas replied, staring around the chapel.

They sat together without speaking, Jonas taking in the chapel, Steve shooting sidelong looks at Jonas.

"You know what?" Jonas asked finally, his voice hollow.

"Hmm?"

"Nothing will ever be as beautiful as this," he'd whispered. "Nothing."

JONAS SHIVERED AND STOOD up, grabbing the frame. He walked into the brightening workshop and placed the photo on the worktable, arranging his tools around it like an altar.

Minutes later, he folded himself into the tiny, dark bathroom and turned on the shower, leaving the door ajar, steam swirling into the cool workshop. He undressed and stepped into the too-hot water, watching it scald his arms, his scars crimson under the onslaught. *I can do this. I can do this.* The water cooled as he again mentally inventoried his tools and made checklists of supplies and self-assurances.

Half an hour later, Jonas was standing again in the plaza before the church, his backpack slung over one shoulder and a lit cigarette in hand. He looked up at the great cathedral and squared his shoulders. Taking a last, long drag, he flicked the cigarette into the middle of the plaza and plowed through the throng of tourists gathered on the porch steps.

He stepped into the dark narthex and crossed the space quickly without a glance at the intricate tympanum. Pushing open the heavy oak door, he stepped into the hushed stillness, instinctively slowing his step. The great nave towered above him, soaring into a distant ceiling ribbed by round Roman arches, lime and dark stone alternating in a severe pattern, stiff waves rolling heavily toward the altar. The light slanted through the clear clerestory windows, illuminating and austere in the vast echoing space.

Pockets of tourists huddled quietly in the side aisles, gazing at the twisting capitals then at their worn *Michelin* guides, or photographing sculpted marble, holy and lifelike and so cool to the touch. Jonas stood, stock-still, in the middle of the great nave, staring at the ceiling. The arches' swell stopped abruptly at the altar, replaced by the sharply angular chapel, of a cool white stone with a sickly cast, its pointed lancet windows filled with light that did not quite make it to a lowly human level. Jonas shivered, felt as though he could move no further.

He stood transfixed, watching the light make its slow progress along the stone floor, across the rows of stern cane chairs. A decisive footfall echoed throughout the basilica; Jonas looked across the vast space to find Dubay emerging from the cloisters and advancing toward him. Jonas waited, arms crossed.

"Good morning," Dubay nodded, folding his hands.

"Morning."

"I trust you slept well?"

"Yes."

They looked at each other; neither smiled nor made a move.

"If you are ready, we can review the contract in my office."

Jonas took a deep breath. "The contract is fine. Listen, I apologize for how I acted yesterday. It was unprofessional."

Dubay nodded. "You had a trying journey," he said, putting a hand on Jonas' shoulder. "I will do what I can to make you comfortable here. In fact, I ought to phone the airlines again –"

"My stuff got here this morning," Jonas interrupted.

"Excellent. And everything is intact?"

"Seems to be."

"This is good news," Dubay said, taking Jonas by the elbow and leading him toward the gothic choir. "This means you can get started today."

Jonas nodded. "Looks like it."

They walked around the massive altar and into the semicircle of the three-storey choir, the top two levels walled in clear glass.

"Wait here; I will return in a moment." Dubay half-walked, half-jogged back to the cloisters. Jonas stood in the crystalline light of the choir, shifting back and forth and cracking his knuckles. The door to the cloisters opened a few minutes later and Dubay emerged, smiling broadly, carrying a small package wrapped in brown paper.

"I wanted to show this to you here," Dubay said breathlessly, joining Jonas in the choir, "because the light is so pure. It will show the glass to its full effect, I think."

He knelt down and laid the package carefully on the stone floor and quickly untied the knotted twine and pulled at the brown paper.

"You look like a kid at Christmas," Jonas laughed.

Dubay looked up at him over his shoulder and grinned. "You will understand soon enough." He stood and let the paper flutter to the floor.

Jonas made a tentative step forward and gasped as the choir's light burst through the stained glass, shivering it into jeweled fragments on the worn stone floor. "My God," he shuddered, pulse racing. "My God…"

Dubay nodded. "You can feel it –"

"You can feel the color."

"Yes."

Dubay handled the glass by the edges, reverently, shifting and moving it to catch the light and elicit gasps. Though glass was small by medieval standards, the size of a large illuminated manuscript rather than a cathedral-high window, it was rich with sinuous line and glittering color.

"Hang on," Jonas muttered, leaning in closer.

"What?"

"All that's left of her face are the lips."

Dubay nodded. "Yes. And yet…"

"She's …"

"Beautiful?" Dubay supplied.

"Yes," Jonas said, cocking his head to the side. They stood in silence until a cloud shifted past the windows. Jonas shook his head and moved closer to the glass. "No— angry. Righteous. Look at the lines of the leadwork," he said, gesturing at the piece. "The movement feels agitated, almost aggressive."

Dubay looked at him in surprise. "I had not seen it in quite that way."

"Huh. Check out the unguent jar. Yeah, Chevrey was right. It's really amazing – great detail. And the hair –" he said leaning in closely, aching to take the glass from Dubay's reluctant hands. "Look at the detail there – I wonder why so much care was taken on that section… And what's up with this border? Is it the story of the Magdalene's life? Do you have any information on the artist?"

Dubay shrugged his shoulders. "It is not the Magdalene's life; we are not quite sure what the scenes mean, and we know nothing about the artist. Personal glory through art was not part of their make up; the glory was given to God," he said, his hands trembling.

"How can you be so sure it is medieval?" Jonas asked, turning to Dubay. "Maybe it's a reproduction, or a later artist. Where did you find it?"

"It was found in the oldest part of the church – the crypt where the now-empty reliquary for the holy Magdalene is housed."

"Hmmm. It couldn't have been placed there for safekeeping during the le Duc restoration?"

"Unlikely. It was actually found buried underneath the original altar."

Jonas gazed at the glass. "It's just that it's so strong, or – personal. But, based on the damage and wear," he said, finally taking the glass from Dubay's hands, "it is probable it's medieval. High Middle Ages, you think?"

Dubay nodded. "That was my opinion."

Jonas shifted the glass in his hands so it caught the clear light of the choir, now freed from the cloud; a burst of light patterned abstractly on the stone floor. "Wow," Jonas breathed. "Look at the ruby."

Dubay leaned in close. "Spectacular, isn't it?" he whispered.

"There isn't a great range of color – the artist must not have had access to all the supplies they needed. But wow, what colors…" Jonas trailed off, his head suddenly light. He laughed from pure joy.

"It is a magnificent gift."

Jonas and Dubay stood together, peering at the glass and completely unaware of the throng of tourists hovering nearby.

"Can I see where you found it?" Jonas asked, looking reluctantly from the glass to Dubay.

"Certainly. Follow me," Dubay said, walking toward the altar.

Jonas followed, wrenching his eyes from the glass and carrying it carefully. He rounded the altar and watched Dubay disappear down a set of winding, worn stone steps. He approached the crypt's entrance and hesitated. His hands were again numb.

"Jonas?" Dubay's voice echoed up from below. "Are you coming?"

With difficulty, Jonas found his voice. "I – uh – I'm ..." The great basilica seemed to be pressing down on him, oppressive and heavy as God's justice. He could not move.

"Jonas?" Dubay appeared just as Jonas' hands lost control; he caught the glass as it slipped from Jonas' grip.

"What on earth–" Dubay muttered, placing the glass carefully on the floor with shaking hands. Jonas stared at his own hands, turning them over and back. "What happened?" Dubay demanded.

"I guess I tripped," Jonas shrugged, continuing to inspect his hands, which had regained feeling.

Dubay raised his eyebrows but said nothing. The clutch of tourists hurried by, wide-eyed with shock. Jonas looked at Dubay. "I need to watch where I'm going."

"Indeed." They looked at each other for a long moment. "Would you like some assistance? I can certainly have one of the brothers transport the glass to your workshop."

"No, I told you, I just tripped. I'm fine." Jonas knelt down to pick up the glass and Dubay winced. They walked in silence back to the choir and Jonas carefully rewrapped the glass. He stood and found Dubay staring at him intently. "Are you sure you are quite alright?"

"Yeah."

Dubay pressed his lips together, then, shaking his head, walked around the altar and down the long north aisle. Jonas followed, the glass under his arm. *What the hell is wrong with me?*

As they neared the narthex, Dubay stopped, searching Jonas' face. "Take a deep breath."

"You can trust me –" Jonas began.

"I know," Dubay interrupted. "However, I want you to wait here, while I find something more sturdy to carry that in."

Jonas nodded and shifted back and forth, clutching the glass tightly to his chest, recriminations echoing in his head. A few minutes later Dubay returned, a bubble wrap lined pine box in hand. "In here," he said quietly, and Jonas relinquished the glass.

After the glass was packaged to his satisfaction, Dubay handed the box over to Jonas. "I will see you soon," he said, holding the door.

Jonas nodded and hurried through the cool narthex, emerging into the warm brilliant morning. He picked his way carefully through crowds of tourists pressing toward the church, oblivious to him and his frustrated grumbling. "Get a fucking grip on yourself," he muttered, giving a particularly grim and determined looking group with expensive video cameras a wide berth. He walked round to the rue de l'Argenterie, and watched each footfall, clutching the box to his chest. He pushed open his front door with his foot, and, still grumbling, climbed the stairs.

He grabbed the thin blanket from the cot in the dark bedroom and carried it with the box into the workshop. He spread the blanket on the old trestle table and opened the box. With trembling hands, he once again unwrapped the glass, letting the brown paper fall away to the floor.

"Wow," he breathed. He carefully examined the leadwork, the grisalle, the quality of the glass. *This needs more work than I thought.* The glass was completely missing from the ground beneath the Magdalene's feet, and major sections of her still-brilliant rich yellow hair, cascading below her knees, had disappeared as well. Her hands had fractured, yet the unguent jar was completely intact. Her ruby bliaut gown was largely unscathed, including the ceinture at her waist. And the field of deepest sapphire, glittering even in the workshop's indirect light, shivered with spidery hairline fractures.

He scanned the work, making mental notes and plans of attack, and was drawn again and again to the face of the Magdalene. The grisalle showed some wear; he realized with a jolt that he would have to repaint that forbidding face.

Jonas worked late into the evening, cataloging and planning, smoking and staring out the tall studio windows. After the sun had gone down and the evening wind picked up, he closed the windows and passed out on the cot in the cramped bedroom, fully clothed. A whisper swirled into the blue-dark room, jeweled words he could not see but felt like forgiveness. He shifted on the narrow cot. "Must be the wind," he muttered, and fell back asleep.

Chapter Ten

THE ANCIENT MULLIONED WINDOWS were thrown wide to catch the evening breeze, warm and scented with sweet grass. The lights had not yet been turned on in the small front room, and Marie-Laure watched Meredith, the warm setting sun glowing on her face and waving hands.

"...so, I came around the corner, and there was this incredible light. Well of course, stupid me, I didn't have my camera. I have to take that thing with me everywhere now, I swear. Anyway, I didn't have my camera, so I literally ran all the way from the car park down at the bottom of St Etienne up to the shop."

"Did you make it back in time?"

"No. I grabbed the camera and ran back down, but by the time I got there, the shot I wanted was gone, of course. But I did capture that great big plane tree out by the western edge of the north ramparts."

"Wonderful!" Marie-Laure replied, clapping her hands. "I have wanted you to do that tree. How soon can you develop?"

Meredith laughed. "Pushy, aren't you?"

"That is why you like me," Marie-Laure nodded.

"Something like that," Meredith grinned. "And because you've improved significantly as a cook. I think I'd go hungry without you."

"I'm glad you enjoyed lunch. I'm sorry I was so late – Michel and I were chatting after mass this morning and I lost track of time."

Meredith flinched slightly but said nothing.

"Oh, and my dear, I forgot to tell you!"

"What?" Meredith asked idly, rolling the wine glass between her hands.

"There is a most charming new young man in town," Marie-Laure whispered, nearly bouncing in her chair.

"Really."

"Yes. He has been working on the glass Michel found up at the cathedral. I saw him early this morning – utterly charming. And not bad looking."

"I hope more charming than Alphonse."

"What?" asked Marie-Laure, distracted. "I thought you liked him."

"*You* liked him. I thought he was incredibly dull. And boorish."

"But he was a student of mine!"

"Yes, and that's all he could talk about. Don't get me wrong —" she said at the stricken look on Marie-Laure's face. "I love hearing *you* talk about medieval history. He bored me stiff."

"Well, there are academics and there are those who live it. I suspect he never made it beyond mere theory and dates. Though his work on Peter the Venerable would have suggested otherwise..." she said, her eyes scanning her massive bookshelf.

Meredith poured the last of the Muscadet into their glasses and they looked quietly out the window. "I'm so glad you gave me a real tour of the ramparts."

"It is nice to exercise my brain again," Marie-Laure admitted. "I fear I am in the same boat as dear Guillaume, though I will never admit it to him."

"What do you mean?"

"Bored stiff with this town."

"I've had it with this town, too, I think. Let's get the hell out of here. A change of scenery."

"Ma petite, that is a tremendous idea! I would love to spend some time in Paris again."

"Oh..." Meredith said, looking back out the window. "I don't know about Paris."

"Meredith," Marie-Laure said sternly. "You will have to go back someday. Out of respect, at the very least."

A scene flashed across Meredith's mind. Leaving the Sorbonne, a cool evening in early spring. Waving goodbye to

Marie-Laure; she looks so young. Walking to the car on the rue des Écoles, arm in arm with Michel and - . Meredith turned to Marie-Laure, shaking. "No. Fucking. Way," she said. "I am never going back to Paris. Ever."

"But there are still good –"

"No. I don't want to talk about it, all right? How did we get on this subject anyway? Let's talk about something else." She stared back out the window.

Marie-Laure watched her for a long moment, her hands very still in her lap. "Certainly, ma petite."

Meredith gulped the rest of her wine, but did not hear the crack of glass breaking as the glass slipped from her hand and crashed on the floor.

St Christophe and St Jacques are again my guides, providing food and company in the measure that I need. The kindly monk at the pilgrim's hostel provided good bread and a note of pilgrim's passage; I hope I will not need to show it.

I leave the hostel in the morning, shaking the straw from my gown and glad for the rest. I indulge in one more look at the basilica and a candle lit to notre dame before leaving the safety of the walls of Beaune. Another group of pilgrims is leaving this morning for Vézelay and I follow them, at a distance, through the north gate toward the forbidding hills of the Côte. I scan their faces and find none familiar. Pons would not associate with mere merchants, even to act as his spies. I must beware the nobles on the road.

The walk to the base of the hills of Côte is long and solitary. The group beyond on the road are jolly and talkative. No doubt they are from Beaune, and this is their first day. The weariness of the road has not yet taken hold. As I struggle over the hills of the Côte, the sound of their singing guides me and sustains me; blessed Ste Cécile!

We reach the base of the hills and a vast forest spreads before us, unlike anything I have seen in the valleys and vineyards of the Saône. The miracles of the Lord are many. The pilgrims take their rest at the edge of the forest before finding a suitable ford across the Ouche. I rest in the great arms of an oak and listen to the rhythms of their conversation. I remove the offering from my satchel and say a prayer to the Magdalene. Only she can secure my release.

I awake with a start to find the forest has grown dark about me. The group has gone, and I am left alone. In my haste to gather my belongings and move on, the offering slips from my lap and a ruby piece in the corner shatters. I quickly rewrap the offering and place it in my satchel. I pick up the broken piece, knowing I cannot make any repairs until I reach Vézelay. It shall be a reminder that I must be vigilant.

I hurry toward the Ouche, hoping to find an easy crossing. As I pick my way along the bank, I hear rustling in the brush behind me. I have not heard of wolves in this area for many years.

"Meredith. Meredith!" Marie-Laure said, shaking her.

Meredith looked around groggily and found she was sitting on the front steps of a house on the rue St Pierre. "Meredith, mon Dieu, what happened?"

Meredith blinked and looked around the dark street. Then the dream came back to her. "God damn it," she said. "What the hell is wrong with me?"

"Another dream?"

Meredith nodded.

"But so suddenly –?"

"That's how it's been happening," she replied, rubbing her temples. "Where am I?"

"You're halfway to the cathedral. When you passed out, you dropped your wineglass and it shattered –"

"I'm sorry."

Marie-Laure waved her hand. "I went to call the doctor, and when I came back, you'd gone. The front door was wide open."

"It was?" Meredith asked, bewildered.

Marie-Laure settled next to her on the steps. "Yes," she said. "I found you a few blocks back, but I couldn't wake you. You were talking in your sleep – dream – "

"I was?" Meredith looked around the deserted street. "Oh shit. Oh shit."

"Yes," said Marie-Laure, "just snippets of phrases and words. So unlike your voice."

"Like what?" Meredith demanded. "What did I say?"

"St Jacques, and Beaune, and – Pons. And wolves."

Meredith shivered; Marie-Laure put her arm around her shoulders. "She was worried the wolves were following her."

"Why were the wolves following – who?" Marie-Laure asked, turning Meredith's face to hers.

Meredith closed her eyes. "The pilgrim. They weren't following her – yet. I woke up before I could find out...what time is it, anyway?"

"Just after eight."

Meredith groaned. "You're kidding. What time did I – fall asleep?"

"About 7:45."

"I'm getting tired of this," she groaned.

"Your eyes were open, and you were walking quite slowly up the street. You seemed to know where you were going. Do you remember anything at all?"

"I just remember - I remember we were talking about Paris one second and then I'm waking up out here on the goddamned street the next." She turned to look at Marie-Laure. "What the hell is wrong with me?" Meredith asked, eyes prickling with tears.

Marie-Laure took her hand and stroked it. "I – I am not sure. I would say you need a vacation – which you do – but I think it is more worrying than that. Will you at least let Fréderic look at you this evening?"

"No. No way," Meredith said, inching away.

"Why on earth not?" Marie-Laure demanded, narrowing her eyes.

"I – I hate doctors. Forget it."

"You are being obstinate."

"I said forget it," Meredith said, standing up.

Marie-Laure looked at her and shook her head. "Do you know what you were doing just before you woke up?"

"No, of course not," Meredith said.

"You were crossing yourself."

"Oh, shit," Meredith whispered, sitting back down.

They sat together in the cooling darkness, listening to the far-off sounds of the town falling asleep. Meredith stared into the empty street. Marie-Laure stared at Meredith.

"Perhaps you should start with some time off," Marie-Laure finally whispered. "We can go to Aix, we can go to Reims, we can go to Spain if you'd like."

Meredith nodded. "Whatever."

"Come, my dear, let's get you home." Marie-Laure helped Meredith to her feet and led her up the steep street to the dark photography shop. Meredith pulled out her keys and turned to face Marie-Laure. "I'm fine, really," she said. "I just – I didn't get enough sleep last night and I had too much to drink. I'll be fine."

"But – "

"Thank you so much for your help. I'm fine." She kissed Marie-Laure on each cheek and smiled. "I'll figure this out, OK?" She turned and put the key into the lock.

"You can't run away forever."

Meredith's shoulders slumped. "I'm not."

"Meredith – "

"I need to get some sleep," she said, turning and taking Marie-Laure's hands. "Go home and give Guillaume a kiss for me. I'll be fine."

"You can't run away from me. I won't let you."

"I'm *not* running away. I just need to go to sleep."

"I will see you tomorrow."

"Yes." Meredith pulled the door closed and watched Marie-Laure's fragile figure disappear into the darkness. She hesitated at the base of the stairs, then turned and slumped into her desk chair. *I'm fine. I'm fine. I'm fine.* "I'm not fine," she said aloud. She clenched her jaw and picked up a chipped and stained coffee mug, and without preamble threw it against the wall. It exploded, shards flying and old coffee staining the wall and the floor; she grunted with satisfaction.

She reached for another projectile and her hand rested on something cold and metallic. She reached over and turned on the desk lamp. She grabbed the film canister – missing since her last bout with the pilgrim – and bounded up the stairs to her darkroom. With shaking hands, she developed the film and made a contact sheet, waiting, breathless, leaning against the counter in the dim red light.

Time moved slowly while the pictures emerged from the fog. Taking a deep breath, Meredith pulled the contact sheet from the caustic developing fluid, dashed it through the water bath, and hung it on the clothesline. "What is this…" she breathed.

The vast cathedral clutched at the sky, tangling long dark fingers in white clouds. The massive oak doors, earthbound, reached skyward, pleading. *The church?* Her typical work was perfectly sharp and precisely focused, but this – this was fluid somehow, shivering with emotion. Like a daguerreotype, barely capturing the ebb and flow of the world, always a moment too late or too soon.

She pulled the drying sheet from the clip and walked into her bedroom. She flicked on the light, squinting against the shock and sank onto the unmade bed and leaned back, staring at the sheet. *This was taken from the plaza ... from the ground? What the hell was I doing? What the hell am I doing?*

She squinted at the photo, too entranced to reach for the loupe on her nightstand. The photos were off-center, showing a sliver of the street and plaza to the north of the church – a unique composition she would not have considered. Shadows gathered at the edge of the photos, swirling and smoky. She shook her head, and grabbed the loupe. At the edge of the photos, the outline of a woman appeared, grave and beautiful, mouth wide as if calling out.

Meredith threw the sheet aside and covered her face with her hands, shuddering with suppressed sobs. *I'm going insane. Fucking insane.* She rolled over on to her side and pulled a pillow to her chest. *Why did I come back? What was I thinking?* She pulled her knees up and with a shuddering sigh began to cry. She tossed the pillow at the light switch and the room darkened, but she willed herself to stay awake. *No more dreams.*

Chapter Eleven

THE KETTLE LUMBERED slowly to life, a rattling curmudgeon on the tiny stove in the small kitchen. Jonas leaned against the low rough counter, alternately yawning and pulling long drags on the first of his morning cigarettes. Humming, he watched the morning glories creep up the garden wall, grasping and twisting, tugging and writhing in the purple morning darkness.

He stretched, the cigarette dangling precariously between his lips, and grasped his hands behind his back. He stopped mid-stretch as an image from the previous night's forgotten dream floated into view: a crimson-robed figure, fluid yet rigid as glass, grasping him by the arms and twisting him into strange convulsive figures, dangling him over an edge and spinning him, with a sign of blessing over his hands, into a pale morning sky.

Minutes later, the whine of the kettle brought Jonas back to himself. With a grunt, he filled the coffee press with a shaking hand.

An hour later, the sun had risen and filled the countryside below the town with gentle light. Jonas leaned over the glass, inspecting the sapphire field and its spiderweb of fractures, humming along with a CD blaring on the stereo. His tools lay in orderly rows, ready for use on the first major section of the glass, the ground beneath the Magdalene's feet.

He stood and rolled his shoulders then shuffled to the open window. The morning still smelled new; no diesel buses had yet made the journey to the hill's top, no heavy sun or stiff breeze had yet overpowered the scent of sweet grass and summer-bright trees. He breathed deeply and for the first time in days, thought of home.

Jonas made to light his cigarette, and found his coffee cup was empty. Pocketing his lighter and grabbing the mug, he sauntered down to the kitchen. As he set the kettle on the stove, a knock on the front door startled him. He crossed the empty parlor and pulled open the heavy oak door.

"Good morning," Dubay said, a tense smile on his face.

"Morning," Jonas said, holding the door open. "What can I do for you?"

"How are you feeling?"

"Fine. Why?"

"You were rather nervous yesterday."

"Oh, yeah," Jonas shrugged. "I'm fine. That was – weird. I'm fine."

Dubay nodded. "Good. Good."

They looked at each other for a long moment; Jonas broke the silence. "So, what are you doing here?"

"I am here to take you to breakfast."

"Oh," Jonas said, dropping his hand from the door frame. "Well, I'm waiting for my shipment of glass…"

"It will not be here for hours. Come," Dubay said, turning toward the sidewalk.

Jonas fiddled with the lighter. "OK, just give me five minutes," he said with a short sigh.

"Certainly," Dubay said, coming back in and closing the door behind him.

Jonas walked up the narrow staircase and stopped at the landing. "Hey, can you pull the kettle off the stove?" he yelled down the stairs.

"Of course," Dubay called.

Jonas closed the tall windows of the studio and covered the glass carefully with a soft sheet. He turned off the stereo and studied the detailed workflow tacked up on the wall next to the photo of Sainte-Chapelle; three weeks and so much to do.

"Jonas? Are you coming?" Dubay called from the parlor.

He stood, irresolute.

"I am not going to leave without you. And you do not want me to starve, do you? That would be a heavy weight on your conscience."

Jonas laughed. "OK, OK. I'll be right there." He turned from the schedule and crossed to his small bedroom. He found his high-tops under the cot and pulled them on.

Dubay stood in the parlor, hands clasped behind his back and humming. He looked up and smiled when Jonas joined him. "Ready?"

"Yeah."

Dubay pulled open the door and followed Jonas through into the warm morning light. They walked down the hill, towards the rue St-Etienne and the best café in town.

"Have you given any more thought to the border?" Dubay asked, nodding politely to the townsfolk emerging into the bright morning.

"I have, but I can't figure it out yet. It's so intricate, I would almost think it was added later – it doesn't fit with the style of the rest of the glass. But I don't know how that could be – they would almost have to have re-created the entire glass to add that border."

"Is it possible that it was simply the same artist?"

"It is possible, but I don't think it's likely. The styles are too different. The border is so detailed, but the body of the glass is simple and very powerful."

"Ah, yes, but artists are capable of stylistic and temperamental complexity."

Jonas scanned the street, pondering the possibility. "Maybe," he said slowly. "Maybe. But I'm not convinced yet. It almost looks like an illuminated –"

"Monsieur Flycatcher! And Michel! What a pleasant surprise," Marie-Laure said, smiling broadly. She stood at the confluence of the rue St Pierre and rue St Etienne, her morning shopping under her arm.

"Hi," Jonas said, shaking her free hand. Dubay, smiling, also shook her hand and kissed her on each cheek.

"I hope you are well, Monsieur Flycatcher. How is the progress on your glass?" she asked, placing her shopping bags on the sidewalk.

Jonas smiled. "Well –"

"Marie-Laure," Dubay interrupted, "I think you should come have a look at it, right away."

Marie-Laure looked at him askance. "Certainly. But why?"

"There is a most unusual border on which you may be able provide some insight," Dubay said, smiling.

"Ahhh," she said, her eyes widening. "Is that so?"

"I have some preliminary theories," Dubay said, "that I would like to test with you."

Marie-Laure clapped her hands and laughed. "I would be honored," she said. She turned to Jonas and smiled. "What would be convenient for you?"

"Oh –" Jonas said, looking sidelong at Dubay. "How about tomorrow?"

"That would be delightful. I shall see you – when?"

"In the morning – before lunch?"

"Lovely," she said turning to go. "Monsieur Flycatcher, it is a pleasure."

Jonas shook her hand. "Please call me Jonas."

"Then Jonas, I shall see you tomorrow. And Michel, I shall see you this afternoon."

Dubay nodded. "Au revoir," he said. They watched her as she turned the corner and disappeared. They began the climb up the hill to the café, joined by a growing stream of tourists with their ubiquitous digital cameras. Dubay pushed the door open and followed Jonas in and they settled at the same table they'd sat at the day after Jonas had arrived, near the wide window on the street.

"Have you known Marie-Laure long?" Jonas asked, lighting a cigarette.

Dubay nodded. "Oh yes, for many years."

"Lots of energy."

"Indefatigable. And brilliant."

"Yeah?"

The café owner appeared, cigarette dangling from his lips. "Deux café au laits et deux croissants, s'il vous plâit," Jonas said. "Et jus d'orange." The owner nodded and shuffled away. Jonas looked at Dubay expectantly.

"What?" Dubay asked, shaking out his napkin.

"How is Marie-Laure brilliant?"

"Ah, yes. Well, in her day, she was one of the foremost experts in the world on medieval Burgundy."

"No shit."

"Indeed," Dubay smiled, folding his long hands on the table. "She was a well-respected professor at the Sorbonne."

"What's she doing here?" Jonas asked, leaning back and blowing smoke toward the ceiling.

"She retired a number of years ago and moved here with her husband, Guillaume."

"When did you meet her?"

"I was a student of hers at the Sorbonne."

"Really? She taught theology?"

"No, history."

Jonas narrowed his eyes. "But don't you have to study theology to be a priest?"

Dubay turned his fork over and over on the table and looked out the window. "Yes. Yes, of course," he said faintly.

Jonas cocked his head and looked at Dubay, his strong profile outlined against the bright street. "Oh, merci," he said, taking the proffered café au lait.

They sat together in silence, looking out the window, until Jonas ventured another question minutes later. "Did she do any work in art history? I don't remember her name from my program there."

Dubay blew on his coffee unnecessarily and shook his head. "No, she did not teach in the art program, although of course history and art are so intertwined in medieval studies, it is difficult to become an expert in one without knowledge of the other."

"What was your specialty?" Jonas asked, pulling off an end of croissant.

"Winemaking in medieval Burgundy."

"That's one of the reasons I never went for my Ph.D. Jesus, you have to be so obscure, because it's all been done before! What a pain in the ass," he laughed, shaking his head. "So why did you become a priest, and not a professor?"

Dubay choked a bit on his croissant. "That is a long story," he said quietly, looking out the window again.

Jonas looked down at his coffee, stirring designs into the foam.

"So," Dubay said brightly, looking back at Jonas, "is your workshop comfortable enough? Is there anything you need?"

"Yeah, it's fine. It's great," he said, stubbing out his cigarette. "The windows, you know, are amazing and the table is perfect. The cot is a little short but that's OK. I'm not really sleeping well anyway."

"Oh?"

Jonas hesitated. "I've been having crazy dreams," he said in a rush. He groaned inwardly.

"Dreams are rarely crazy; we simply don't understand their messages."

"Yeah, but the one this morning was really bizarre –" Jonas stopped, looking at his hands. Dubay waited in silence. "I was floating," Jonas started. Dubay nodded. "I was floating, right, and fighting I guess with this – thing. Well, not really fighting but grappling – and it had this beautiful red robe and it was spinning me around and it looked like glass but it was moving like I was, and then at the end it held its hands over mine and tossed me out into the sky. It was kinda creepy."

Dubay smiled.

"What?" Jonas demanded, lighting a cigarette.

"You've been given a blessing."

"Huh?"

"Do you not see? Your hands were blessed."

Jonas stopped mid-drag and looked at his ragged fingernails and the small white scars on his hands. "Wouldn't that be nice…" he murmured through the smoke. Dubay watched him, but said nothing. Jonas looked at Dubay with a crooked smile. "Of course, you already knew that. Otherwise they wouldn't have hired me."

Dubay laughed. "Absolument."

They finished their breakfast in friendly conversation and parted ways with a handshake outside the café, Dubay climbing the rest of the hill toward the cathedral, Jonas heading back toward the rue St-Etienne and his own rue l'Argenterie. He ambled up the narrow street, turning his hands over and over. He reached number 23 and pushed the door open. Walking through into the cool darkness, he kicked the door shut behind him and headed straight up the stairs to his workshop. He pushed the windows open and smiled as a gentle breeze curled into the room, fluttering papers. He turned on the stereo and sang along at the top of his lungs.

Jonas stood and stretched an hour later, having successfully removed a small area of splintering glass. He placed the delicate glass, so near to shattering, in a tissue-lined box marked "sapphire field #1", corresponding to the sketch he'd tacked on the wall. The Clash blasted from the stereo and he pulled out his pack of Gitanes. *Damn!* He salvaged the last cigarette, crumpled the pack, and threw it in the open suitcase. It landed on top of the unopened carton of Marlboros.

He walked to the window and started to light his cigarette when he noticed two men pounding on his front door below. He turned off the stereo and stuck his head out the window. "Hey! Hey!"

The man looked up and scowled. "Est-ce que tu es – uh – Flycatcher?"

"Oui, oui c'est moi."

"Nous avons une livraison."

A what? Jonas shrugged his shoulders and held out his hands. "Je ne compr –" The men pointed in annoyance at the large mattresses they were hauling. "Un moment, s'il vous plâit," Jonas hollered. He flew down the stairs and pulled open the front door.

"Que est-ce que c'est?"

"Un lit – du père supérieur Dubay."

"D'accord, d'accord. Come on," he laughed, and led them up to his small bedroom. "Un moment," he said, hastily pulling the cot and the suitcase across the hall into the studio. The twin bed took up the entire windowless bedroom, and after the deliverymen left with a curt "D'accord?", Jonas sprawled on the bed, luxuriating like a feudal lord. He folded his arms behind his head, crossed his legs, and promptly fell asleep.

He woke with a start hours later, his right arm numb and feet sweltering in his high tops. He stumbled across the hall to the workshop, where the light was clear and bright, and found his watch under a pile of drawings – just after one o'clock. He ran his hand over his face and scratched at the three-day beard. *Need. Smokes.* He grabbed his wallet and headed to the tabac.

As he closed the heavy front door behind him, he saw a note pinned there.

M. Flycatcher –

The shipment of glasses are here. They are delivered at the office of le père supérieur.

À votre service – Frère Pascal

About time. Jonas set off up the rue de l'Argenterie to the chapter house. The door of number 21 opened and a small old man emerged, blocking Jonas' path. "Bonjour," he said brightly. "Ça va?"

Jonas smiled. "Oui, ça va. Et vous?"

"Oui, oui, merci. Est-ce que vous êtes un pélerin?"

"Uh – pardon – je ne comprends pas."

"Un pélerin – la Magdalene -?"

"Oh – oui, oui. La Magdalene," Jonas nodded.

"Ah, bien, bien."

Jonas hesitated, smiling uncertainly. "Uh – au revoir."

The old man smiled serenely. "Au revior."

Jonas waved and walked the rest of the way up the hill. He rounded the corner and emerged into the plaza, filled with more tourists than he'd yet seen in the town. He picked his way through the crowd lining up to get into the cathedral and pushed open the heavy gate to the chapter house garden. He saw Dubay on his knees, digging with a trowel and his bare hands in the dirt, containers of purple violets at his feet.

"Abbot Dubay?"

Dubay looked up and grinned. "Jonas!" he said, standing and wiping his hands on a handkerchief. "I see you got the good brother's note. Were you out?"

"No, I actually passed out on the bed you sent over. Thank you –"

"Oh, it is nothing. I had not realized we had been such poor hosts – a cot. What a travesty."

"I've slept on worse. It wasn't a big deal."

"I am sure you have, but not while you are my guest."

Jonas shrugged. "So, where's the glass?"

Dubay chuckled. "Always to the point, yes? The shipment is up in my office." They walked to the chapter house and into its dark coolness. "Why didn't Frère Pascal just leave the shipment on my doorstep?"

"I did not want anything to happen to the glass," Dubay said over his shoulder as they climbed the stairs to his office. "This is a very important project – to the church certainly, and the town most definitely. But to me also. I do not want anything to jeopardize it." He pushed open the door to his office. A large package wrapped in stiff brown paper covered the large desk.

"Sweet," Jonas muttered. "You mind if I check it out here, just to make sure they delivered what they were supposed to?"

"Of course," Dubay said, relaxing into his chair. Jonas ran his thumb under the heavy tape and slit open the paper. Scores of sheets of jewel-bright glass spectrumed together on Dubay's desk – sapphire, ruby, deep orange, and warm golden yellow.

Dubay leaned forward. "So this is how it arrives," he whispered.

"Yeah, I know a guy who does cathedral-quality glass up in Rouen. I love it because – look here –" he said, pointing to a corner of the ruby glass. "See how it bubbles? They're called seeds. Little pearls of air. That way you know it's from a real craftsman, not some crap from a factory. Plus, it refracts the light better – it's more authentic, of course, but it really gives this amazing shimmering quality to the glass."

"Mmm, I see, I see," Dubay murmured, entranced. He leaned closer and smiled. "It looks as if it were lit from within," he breathed.

Jonas looked up. "Exactly. Exactly!" he said triumphantly, banging his hand on the table. He stood back and watched

Dubay peer intently at the glass, investigating its perfect imperfections. Dubay ran his hand along the cool surface of the glass, then his fingers along the ragged edge.

"You probably don't want to –" Jonas said stepping forward, hand outstretched. Dubay looked up at Jonas and then at his hand, which was bleeding freely. Dubay turned his hand over and watched the blood run down his wrist. "Ah, merde," he whispered.

Jonas' stomach twisted. "We ought to –"

"I am fine, Jonas," he said, making no move to staunch the flow.

"No I really think –" Jonas looked desperately around the office for anything to bind Dubay's hand. "Uh – uh –" Finding nothing, he pulled off his t-shirt and wrapped it around Dubay's hand. "Here – hold it up – yeah – above your heart." He looked into Dubay's eyes; they were flat and glassy. "Here – stay just like that and *don't move*, OK?"

He yanked open the office door and leaped down the stairs two at a time. He ran through the chill hallway lining the cloisters and found Soeur Marie polishing a great mahogany door. She looked at him in surprise and quirked an eyebrow.

"Uh – Abbot Dubay - il est – um – hurt. Damn!"

Soeur Marie shook her head.

"Il fait mal –" he tried.

"Eh, oui?" she said slowly.

He showed her his hands, fresh with blood. "Un – doctor – vite! Vite!" At last she seemed to understand and pulled open the door. Jonas watched her disappear down another long hallway. He scrambled up the stairs to find Dubay sitting, as requested, with his hand in the air; a few drops of blood continued to trickle down his arm. He was ashen but smiled; his eyes were no longer glassy. "My apologies. I did not realize the glass would be so sharp."

"Yeah, glass is funny that way," Jonas said. "Here, let me see." He held out his hand and took Dubay's in his own. "I asked Soeur Marie to find a doctor."

"That was not necessary. I am fine. But I am sure you gave Soeur Marie quite a fright. She is accustomed to only seeing me without my shirt."

Jonas nodded absently. He gagged as he pulled back the makeshift bandage. "Ugh," he breathed. The cut was deep along the pad of Dubay's thumb, down to his first knuckle. "It looks pretty deep. That'll leave a nice scar," he said, rewrapping Dubay's hand.

"Scars do not bother me," Dubay said, smiling. "They are stories of your life – the fortuitous and the unfortunate."

"Mmm hmm," Jonas nodded. "Keep your hand up. Thank you."

"Those scars – on your side – they tell a story, yes?"

Jonas stepped back and crossed his arms. "Yes."

Dubay leaned back in his chair. "And?"

"And they're still none of your business."

Dubay nodded and continued staring at Jonas.

Jonas scowled. "Fine. My mom – my mom was an alcoholic. She didn't like me trying to help, so she threw shit at me – usually broken bottles. I particularly like this one," he said, twisting and pointing out a nasty jagged scar on his side. "That's when I had enough and told her she was a frigging lunatic. She actually attacked me. Cut me with the glass," he whispered.

"And your temple?" Dubay asked quietly.

Jonas looked out the window. "Car crash," he whispered.

Dubay flinched, then nodded. "Ah, I see," he said. "I see."

A quiet knock at the door broke the silence.

"Monseigneur?" A small badgerish man with a balding pate and thick hair around and in his ears poked his head around the door. "Que se passe-t-il?"

Dubay waved the doctor in and explained what had happened. Jonas wandered around the office, excluded from their conversation in rapid French, the doctor shaking his head and a smirk pulling at the corners of Dubay's mouth.

Jonas scanned the bookshelf, then came to rest at the window looking out on the distant hills of the Morvan, rubbing his arms.

"Jonas –" Dubay said.

Jonas turned around. "Yeah?"

"You must be cold. My rooms are through that door there –" Dubay said, attempting to point with his injured hand.

"Monseigneur!" the doctor said in exasperation.

"There are shirts in the armoire. Please, go put one on."

"OK." Jonas opened the door to Dubay's Spartan room and walked through to the bathroom. He washed his hands, watching the blood circle in the sink, then dried his hands on the plush white towel. He returned to the bedroom and pulled open the doors to the large mahogany armoire. *Mmmm...priest clothes...priest clothes...priest clothes. Jeez, how many of these dresses does he need? Uh – oh shit, underwear, didn't need to see that. Polka dots?* Jonas sniggered and continued his exploration, but came up empty. "There's no t-shirts in here," he hollered.

"No, no, take one of the collared shirts – they are with the vestments," Dubay hollered back. Jonas pushed aside the heavy robes and found a row of exquisitely tailored shirts – stripes, French cuffs, contrasting collars. "Are you sure?" Jonas called.

"Yes."

With a shrug, he pulled out a plain white cotton shirt, smooth as silk, and shrugged it on. The crest on another white shirt caught his eye. "What is Dubay et Fils?" he called. Hearing no answer, he walked back into the office, buttoning the shirt. "Huh?"

"It is nothing."

"Oh, come on," he said, folding his arms.

Dubay looked quickly at the doctor who was finishing his stitches. "It is my family business."

"Oh yeah? What do they do?"

"D'accord, Monseigneur," the doctor said, closing his bag.

"Merci, Frédéric," Dubay said, smiling.

"De rien, de rien," the doctor replied, nodding at Jonas and pulling the door closed behind him.

"Do you need assistance transporting the glass to your workshop?" Dubay asked.

"What is your family's business?" Jonas asked.

Dubay smiled. "Always to the point. My family is in the wine business."

"Oh, is that all?" Jonas laughed. "Shit, I was expecting you to say they were in the mafia or something."

Dubay looked at Jonas and smiled. "Families are complicated beasts."

Jonas nodded. "I know," he said.

"So, shall I ask Frère Pascal to deliver your glass?" Dubay asked briskly.

"No, I'll take it with me right now. I really want to get going with the sapphire if I can tonight."

"Excellent," Dubay smiled. "I look forward to seeing the progress."

"I'm sure you do," Jonas grinned, rewrapping the glass. "Why don't you come by tomorrow afternoon and I can show you what I'm doing?"

"That would be delightful. The process must be fascinating."

"And tedious. But it's fun. By the way, thanks for the shirt."

"It is nothing."

"Well, thanks anyway."

"I will see you tomorrow afternoon," Dubay said, wincing as Jonas shifted the glass to grab the door handle. "Ah – allow me to get the door for you."

"Thanks," Jonas nodded and gingerly carried his package down the narrow stairs, across the long hallway, and out into the garden and the golden afternoon light. He sidled around the feet of the cathedral and escaped into the quiet of his street.

The sun warmed his face and the golden stone of the tall houses and he breathed deeply. Windows along the street were thrown open to catch the breeze and light; flower boxes on every side spilled with pansies and crimson geranium. Humming, he unlocked the massive door to his house and hauled the glass shipment to his workshop.

An hour later Jonas stood and stretched, admiring the square inch of sapphire glass he had completed. He opened windows and leaned out, watching the quiet progress of the street: the grey tabby skulking toward the café; hopelessly lost tourists; the old man next door serenely smoking on his doorstep. He shoved his feet into his high-tops and headed to the tabac.

The afternoon was golden and warm; Jonas rolled his shoulders and neck, reaching up and stretching like a cat. As he blew out a stream of smoke, the stark photographs in the studio opposite stopped him mid-stretch. The long branches of the black trees seemed again to reach out to him, as they had his first night in town, and, dreamlike, he was pulled across the current to the studio's door.

He pushed it open and a bell tinkled above him in the empty shop. It smelled of photo processing chemicals, coffee, and lavender; he wrinkled his nose and gave an idle turn to the metal racks of postcards and requisite tourist guides to Vézelay in the narrow entryway, but stepped past them, up into the main shop. On every inch of wall, and piled on rickety wooden tables down the middle of the room, were black and white photos – tall narrow streets and geometric trees and the ramparts near his workshop.

"Bonjour." The quiet voice behind him startled Jonas out of his reverie. He did not turn around, but replied "Bonjour" half-heartedly over his shoulder, and resumed his inspection of the photo.

"Nous sommes ouvert pour dix minutes seulement, monsieur."

Jonas turned around. "D'acc-" He shivered with a strong and unnerving wave of déjà vu. A woman, maybe 35, maybe 40, stood between the long tables, wiping her hands on her khakis. Her light brown eyes were almond-shaped, and deep wrinkles scored a tracery from the edges. He stared at her for fifteen, twenty seconds. She cocked her head slightly to the side and narrowed her eyes. "Monsieur?"

"Uh – parlez-vous anglais?"

"Oh, yes, of course."

"Ah."

Another silence.

"Are you OK?" Jonas continued to stare. The woman pushed her dark curls from her face and raised her thick eyebrows. "Did you want to purchase that photo?"

"Huh – oh, yeah, it's amazing. It's so – it's like a dream."

She smiled and nodded.

"I love the form," he said, turning back to the wall. "Does the photographer live around here? I'd love to talk to him."

"I'm the photographer," she said evenly. Her congenial smile disappeared.

Jonas snapped around. "You're kidding! Did you take all of these?" he asked, pointing around the room.

"Yes."

"Wow. Were they all taken around here?"

"Yes."

"So this is your shop?"

"Yes." The woman looked at her watch. "Did you want to buy it or not?"

"I think so. But I can come back tomorrow."

"Suit yourself," she said, folding her arms.

Jonas made no move to leave. *What did I say?*

"So...we open again at ten tomorrow morning."

"Oh, right, right. OK. I'll see you tomorrow then," Jonas said, patting his pocket for a smoke.

"OK."

"OK."

She stared back at Jonas for a long moment, then laughed, an arpeggio that filled the empty room. "So when the hell are you leaving?"

He grinned and shrugged his shoulders. "Now?"

"Are you always a pain in the ass?"

"Yes."

She laughed again and her shoulders relaxed. "Are you staying in town?"

"Yeah, I'm doing some work up at the cathedral."

She walked to the door and turned the handwritten sign around to *Fermé*. "Better you than me. What kind of work?"

"Repair."

"Of what? The chairs in the nave were just re-caned last year. Don't tell me the handrails down to the crypt are broken again."

"No."

"Then what?" she asked, walking back. She leaned against the table and folded her arms.

"They found a stained glass. That's - that's what I do. I repair stained glass."

"Mmmmm. You must be pretty good if you're here all the way from the States."

"I am."

"And they couldn't find anyone locally to do it?"

"They wanted the best."

She cocked her head again, and looked at Jonas. Or looked through him. "Let me see your hands." She reached out and grabbed one of Jonas' hands, not waiting for assent or answer.

He stared at her as she ran her rough fingers along his knuckles and fingertips; he shivered and his eyelids fluttered closed. She stopped tracing after a few moments, and his eyes opened, heavy lidded. He swallowed with difficulty. "What did you find?" he whispered.

"You have beautiful hands – artist's hands," she replied quietly, running her thumb along the side of his hand, almost unconsciously. "Why are you doing repair work?"

He snatched his hand away. "It pays the bills," he said, reaching into his pocket for a smoke. "Listen, I gotta go," he said, heading for the door.

She crossed her arms again, her voice no longer quiet and dreamy. "Do you still want the photo?"

"Yeah, sure," he replied, his hand on the doorknob. "Uh, I'll just come by sometime this week and pick it up."

"Sure, that's fine. Can I get your name? I'll put it aside for you. You can pick it up whenever you're ready." She walked to the small, cluttered desk at the back of the shop.

"Jonas Flycatcher."

"Pardon?"

"That's my name."

"Oh. Right." She scribbled his name on the back of a business card, then walked to the front door. She handed him one of her own: *Salon Meredith Thibault, 40 rue St-Pierre, Vézelay.* Her fingers lingered on his.

"I'm sorry - I didn't mean to piss you off."

"It's no big deal."

They stood in silence; he dropped his hand.

"Good luck with the glass," she said.

"Yeah. See ya."

Jonas stepped into the street and shook his head. He lit another Gitane and looked at the business card. *Meredith.* He shivered and, rubbing his hands, wandered back up the long cobblestoned street towards his workshop.

Chapter Twelve

THE NEXT MORNING Jonas stretched and yawned magnificently, reaching all corners of his new bed at once. He rolled over on to his side and, pulling the pillow under his head, looked at his hands; only one cut from all of yesterday's work. He had returned to the workshop after his time at the photography salon and worked deep into the night, making progress on the sapphire field and plotting the work for the ground beneath the Magdalene's feet.

He rolled out of bed and, scratching his head, shuffled into the workshop. He pushed the windows open and breathed in the languorous morning, gold and sensuous. The street below was empty and quiet; in the distance, beyond the ramparts, a farmer was cutting new grass and as he watched, Jonas imagined he could smell the sweetness from his window. He stretched again and grabbed his smokes from the worktable. He stuck a Gitane in his mouth and lit a match, but was stayed halfway as a glint of something familiar in the glass caught his eye. He leaned close and looked at the grisalle of the Magdalene's face.

An image fluttered to the surface of his mind, of the glass' border writhing and swirling, and the Magdalene speaking to him in a voice he recognized. He gazed at the Magdalene's face, narrowing his eyes, stepping back and then in close. *Angry. Beautiful.* He turned back to the window and took a long, slow drag on his cigarette.

By the time Jonas took his first break the morning had lost its golden hue and the afternoon slept colorlessly outside his windows. He'd managed another cut on his hand, but had completed a small section of the Magdalene's bright yellow hair. A knock at the door downstairs broke the silence; Jonas stuck his head out the window and Dubay waved. "Bonjour, Jonas. Is this a good time to look at the glass?"

Jonas nodded. "Door's open," he said, then leaned down to the stereo and restarted his CD.

Dubay appeared in the doorway, holding up his hand and smiling. "Frédéric said I will have my stitches out in a week."

"Good. Hey, do me a favor –"

"Of course."

"Don't touch the frigging glass anymore."

Dubay laughed. "On my word," he said, placing his hand over his heart. "Show me what you have," he said, walking directly to the worktable and the glass.

Jonas stood back and, arms folded, watched Dubay inspect the glass. "Hmmm..."

"What?"

Dubay looked at Jonas and then at the schedule tacked on the wall. "Will you make it?"

"What do you mean?"

"I assumed – well, I assumed that the progress would be more evident."

"Can't you see the difference?" Jonas asked, leaning over the glass. "Here? And here? Look at how much I got done on her hair – just this morning."

"Oh. Well. I am just the lay person in this instance," Dubay smiled. "I simply assumed the changes would be – more noticeable."

Jonas stood up and again folded his arms.

"I am not doubting –"

"Yeah, you are."

"Jonas – I assure you. I have full confidence in your abilities."

Jonas gritted his teeth. "I'm not so sure."

Dubay smoothed his shirt and breathed deeply. "Yes, of course I do. Yes. You would not be here otherwise."

"Then trust me when I tell you we are on track. Jesus. Here – look." He pointed out the inch of reconstructed sapphire field. "This took just over a day. It normally takes about two. We're on pace to be done right on time, if not early. OK?"

Dubay nodded, but said nothing.

"Abbot?"

"Hmmm? Oh, yes. Yes. She is mesmerizing, isn't she?" He leaned in close, inches from the Magdalene.

Jonas sighed. "Icy, too, though, even with all that bright hair."

"Will you have to repaint her face?"

"I think so. It's just too worn."

"A pity. She's so lovely just as she is." Dubay leaned in closer, while Jonas rested his elbows on the table and ran his hands over one edge of the border. The room was breathless and still, and yet they did not hear the footsteps on the stairs.

"I hope you do not mind, but I let myself in," Marie-Laure said quietly, smiling.

With reluctance, Jonas pushed himself up. "What can I do for you?"

She walked over and offered her hand to Dubay, who took it and kissed her on each cheek. "Do you not remember? You offered to show me the glass yesterday."

"Right, right," Jonas said, shaking her hand. "Well, there it is."

Dubay moved aside to make room for Marie-Laure. She leaned in and surveyed the piece. After a few moments she huffed in irritation and put on the glasses which hung about her neck. "Oh my. What is the presumed date?"

"We believe it is from the early twelfth century," Dubay said, sitting on a spindly wooden chair across the room.

"Hmmm. It is no wonder you have been keeping this quiet, Michel. It is quite revolutionary."

Jonas' eyebrows creased. "What do you mean?"

"Look at the treatment of her hair – and the bliaut gown for instance. So much care went into rendering the folds perfectly. Romanesque is rather stylized, you know – look at the tympanum in the cathedral. Swirls and flat planes represent fabric and motion alike. But this shows care, and detail."

"But that is not enough to mark it as revolutionary," Dubay countered. "Stained glass artists were moving away from the Romanesque at that time – look at Chartres. That was – 1140s, yes?– and the glass was quite detailed."

"Yes, yes, but think about it," Marie-Laure said, tapping the worktable for emphasis; Jonas cringed. "The figures are more detailed at Chartres, yes, but the perspective is still primitive – my goodness, in one of the windows Our Lady's feet seem to be somehow stuck on to the front of her legs!"

Dubay laughed. "Yes, but -"

"But, it is quite amazing," Marie-Laure interrupted. "And you know it, Michel." She pulled out a small notebook and scribbled observations and sketched the border, peering over her glasses at the piece.

"Perhaps," Dubay demurred. He reached out to touch the border; Jonas raised his eyebrows and Dubay withdrew his hand.

"Tell me again when was it found?" Jonas asked, peering at the Magdalene's face.

"A month ago, perhaps?" Dubay said, leaning across the table for a better look. "UNESCO wanted to take it right away, but I insisted the work be completed here. I kept it wrapped and safe until you arrived."

Jonas nodded. "Thanks," he muttered.

"My pleasure," Dubay whispered. "It is a jewel."

Marie-Laure moved Jonas aside and finished her survey of the glass. "There seems to be much to do. When will it be completed?"

"In time for the Magdalene's feast," Dubay said, standing straight.

"Ah, yes, fitting. That is only – three weeks away. Will you make it?"

"I have every confidence that he will make it," Dubay said.

Marie-Laure smiled at Jonas as she closed her notebook, shoving it into her voluminous purse. "You are very lucky to have Michel on your side. I would not wish to have it otherwise. Do not disappoint him."

"I – I don't intend to," Jonas said, surprised.

"Excellent. Then, Michel, I shall –" she stopped and peered closely at the border of the glass. "Oh. Look at this."

"What?" Jonas asked.

"Oh – look – oh my," she said, her eyes bright. "That is very, very interesting. This needs some research, but oh my – if it is the case –"

Jonas looked at Dubay, who shrugged his shoulders.

"Madame Rouchon —" Jonas began.

Marie-Laure looked up. "Marie-Laure, mon chèr, Marie-Laure. This border," she said, tapping the edge of the glass, "is very, very intriguing. Come by for dinner tomorrow night — both of you — and perhaps I can shed some light on it."

Dubay shook his head. "Unfortunately, I have a dinner appointment with monsieur Merimée."

Marie-Laure looked at Jonas, eyebrows raised.

"Uh — sure. Sure, what time?"

"We eat rather early. We will see you at seven," she said over her shoulder, hurrying toward the staircase.

"OK."

Marie-Laure disappeared down the stairs and moments later the front door closed with a bang.

"What was that about?" Jonas asked.

"Marie-Laure. Just Marie-Laure."

"What the hell did she see in the border?"

Dubay joined Jonas at the worktable and scanned the border. "I do not know. But I am certain we will hear about it in detail soon enough."

"I'll let you know what she says after dinner tomorrow."

"Yes, please. And good luck with dinner."

"Why?"

"Marie-Laure never does anything without a reason."

"Maybe she just likes me," Jonas protested.

"Mmm. Yes, that is possible also," Dubay said. "I shall let you return to your work." He smiled, and with a last look at the Magdalene, turned and sauntered out of the studio and down the stairs.

Jonas let out a long, low whistle and rolled his shoulders, then set to work for the rest of the afternoon. At quarter of four, Jonas stretched and admired his handiwork, a sinuous line of bright gold trailing below the Magdalene's knees. He checked the schedule tacked to the wall: one week to finish her hair. One week. He grabbed his smokes and found underneath them the business card he'd picked up the day before: *Salon Meredith Thibault*.

He leaned against the table and took out a cigarette, rolling it back and forth over the backs of his fingers. *I've got too much to do.* He stuffed the business card in his jeans pocket and walked over to the window and struck a match. *Yeah, but I really should get that photo.* He let the match burn down to his fingers and flicked it out the window. He checked his watch and hurried out of the studio and down the stairs.

He rounded the top of the rue de l'Argenterie, and, grumbling, sped down the rue St Etienne towards the photography shop. He slowed as he reached No. 40 and smoothed his hair. He pushed open the door and found the shop empty. "Hello?" he called.

"We are about to close," Meredith's voice called from the back of the shop.

"Yeah, I know."

"So...come back tomorrow morning, and I'd be happy to –" Meredith appeared, coffee cup in hand. "Oh, it's you," she said, half-smiling. "I guess I didn't piss you off completely."

"No, not too much."

"Back for more then?"

Jonas grinned. "I'm a glutton for punishment." Meredith passed by him and locked the shop door. "I actually wanted to pick up that photo," he said.

"Oh. Sure. Yeah, I've got it right here." She pulled the photo from behind her chair and laid it on the desk. "Why did you choose this one?"

Jonas walked over to the desk and leaned over the photo. "I love the form," he said, tracing the tree's spidery winter-bare limbs. "What were you thinking when you took this one?"

Meredith cocked her head and crossed her arms. "Mmm. Good question. You know, I'm not sure. Nothing, really. I saw an interesting form and snapped it before I lost the light."

Jonas looked up at her. "Really? Nothing? It's just instinct?"

"Yeah, I guess. My job is to capture the form, to chronicle. I'm not making any kind of grand statements," she shrugged.

"That's not what I meant," Jonas said, moving around to Meredith's side. "Look at the composition – how this branch arcs across the top of the frame, and these smaller limbs frame the cathedral tower so perfectly in the background."

"The cathedral is just a coincidence," Meredith said stiffly. "So, cash or charge?"

Jonas stood straight and looked at her, shoving his hands in his pockets. "It was a compliment," he said, eyes narrowed.

Meredith shook her head. "I know."

"Well, it was my turn to piss you off anyway. Can we call it even now?" he said, offering his hand.

"Yeah, if you buy me a drink," she replied, grinning.

"Deal," he said, and they shook hands. "Are you free now?"

Meredith nodded. "Sure."

"Cool. Where do you want go?"

"The café across the street isn't bad."

"Works for me." Jonas stepped aside and followed Meredith to the door.

"Sure you don't have other plans?" she asked, shutting and locking the door to the shop. "We can do this another time."

"Nope. I'm done for the day."

They crossed the narrow street, dodging a stream of tourists from the last bus of the day, and settled at a table on the sidewalk. Jonas flopped into a chair with his back to the street; the afternoon sun glanced obliquely, settling in the red in Meredith's dark curls. "So, why don't you take pictures of people?" he asked.

"How do you know that I don't?" she said, leaning back and raising an eyebrow.

"Well, why don't you sell any pictures with people in them?"

"People are, as a rule, a serious pain in the ass."

Jonas laughed.

"Take you, for example," she continued.

Jonas choked a bit and pulled out a cigarette. "Yeah, what about me?"

"I pegged you as a pain in the ass the minute I saw you."

"Mmm hmmm," Jonas prompted, blowing smoke out his nose.

"But you can't be too bad, you're buying one of my photos," she grinned.

"Where's your artistic integrity?"

"Where's yours?" Meredith asked, leaning her elbows on the small table.

"Excuse me?" Jonas said, leaning forward.

"I said, where's yours?"

"Didn't we go over this last night?"

They stared at each other in silence over the table; Jonas grinned. "Now who's the pain in the ass?"

Meredith smiled.

Jonas looked up and found the café owner watching them expectantly. "What'll you have?" Jonas asked, leaning back and taking a drag.

"Un kir, s'il vous plâit," Meredith said to the owner. "And what do you want?"

"Red wine, whatever they've got."

"Et un verre du vin rouge – côte des nuits?"

The owner nodded. "Bien sûr," he said, and wandered back into the empty café.

"So," Meredith said, looking at Jonas.

"So."

"Why do you smoke?"

"Why don't you?"

"How do you know I don't?"

"Want one?" he asked, offering her the pack.

"Hell no," she grinned.

Jonas laughed. "I smoke because it relaxes me," he said, taking a drag and leaning back in his chair, letting his arm trail behind him.

"It doesn't seem to be working."

"Are you always this rude?"

"Are you?"

"Yeah."

"No, I'm not."

Jonas chuckled. "So, it's just me that brings it out in you?"

Meredith looked down at the table and played absently with the coaster. "No, no. Though you are pretty damn rude," she said, glancing up at him with a smile. "No, I've had a – a rough few days. Haven't been getting a lot of sleep lately."

"Mmm. Do you get up early to do your work?"

Meredith sighed. "Sure. Yeah." She stared past Jonas to her shop. Jonas ground out his cigarette in the plastic ashtray and waited, watching her with eyebrows knitted.

"Monsieur?" The owner set their drinks on the table along with the receipt and walked back into the café without a word.

"Why do you shoot black and white?"

Meredith twitched and looked at Jonas as if surprised to find him there. "Oh. Well, I was a photographer for a newspaper, and never got out of the habit, I suppose."

"Have you experimented with color?"

"No. Doesn't do much for me."

"Are you kidding?" Jonas spluttered, setting his glass down quickly. "Do you mean in general, or just in photography?"

"In general, I guess. But especially in photography. You *see* more when you use black and white," she said, sweeping her arms, "it brings out the basic elements of a scene. Strips away all the extraneous garbage."

"Sure, I guess. But I wouldn't call color garbage. That's crazy. Crazy! It's the soul of art—no, really! Why are you laughing?"

"You're so earnest," she said, leaning back and folding her arms. "It's kind of endearing."

"Well, if you can't be passionate about something, what's the point?" he said.

Meredith shrugged. "So," she said, leaning forward. "How long are you going to be in Vézelay?"

"Until later this month," Jonas replied, looking into his wine.

"Just a few weeks, then?"

"Yeah," he nodded.

"Oh," she said, looking into her own drink.

"The project is supposed to be complete by July 22, in time for - "

"For the Magdalene's feast," she whispered.

"Yeah," Jonas cocked his head. "You're pretty religious, huh?"

"No – why would you say that?"

"I don't know. Maybe everyone here knows that date. But I just…I think I saw you last week. Outside your studio." Meredith's eyebrows creased in confusion. "You were…you were crossing yourself."

"Oh… yeah. Well, that was…that was a weird day," she said, looking down again at the table.

Jonas lit another cigarette and looked up at the sky. "I've had more than one of those," he said.

She looked at him quickly and took a deep breath. "Listen, do you want to go to dinner with me tomorrow night?"

Jonas smiled at the sky. "Sure." He blew smoke out the side of his mouth and looked her in the eye. "I'd love to…Oh shit…"

"What?"

"I promised this woman I'd have dinner with her."

"Oh…"

Jonas laughed. "No, not like that. It's an older lady, Marie-Laure. She's doing some research for me on the glass."

Meredith grinned. "I know Marie-Laure."

"Then come too – at seven. She doesn't have a smelly old lady house, does she?" Jonas asked, his glass of wine halfway to his lips.

Meredith laughed. "No. No. It's a wonderful place."

"Then come too."

"OK. I will," she said, looking at her hands.

Jonas checked his watch – nearly five. "I need to get back to work – I've got a shitload to do to make this deadline," he said, crushing out his cigarette.

"Oh, sure. Yeah, I've got a lot to do, too," she said, looking across the street.

"Great. Well."

"Yeah."

"So, I guess I'll see you tomorrow night."

OK. See you then."

Jonas stood and grabbed the pack of cigarettes from the table, smiled, and walked down the steep rue St Etienne, a grin pulling the corner of his mouth. The sky grew golden again as he rounded the corner of the rue de l'Argenterie. *You forgot the frigging photo.* He laughed out loud and hurried up the street to no. 23.

Chapter Thirteen

THE DARKROOM WAS WARM and close in the late afternoon. The pungent chemicals mixing with the rising July heat made Meredith's head swim, but she pressed on nonetheless. The last three afternoons, since she'd developed the first roll, had been a torture of apprehension, confusion, and anger. And curiosity.

One by one, she'd enlarged each frame. Each day, new photos, and a fresh wave of frustration. She slipped the last contact sheet into the developing fluid, turned on the timer, and leaned heavily against the counter. She rubbed her eyes. *Long. Fucking. Day. Week. Life. Whatever.*

She rolled her head slowly from side to side, groaning at the series of cracks and crunches, and waited, head bowed and arms crossed, for the photo to emerge. The timer squealed and, without looking, she silenced it with her outstretched hand.

Meredith sighed heavily, dipped the contact sheet into the stop bath and water rinse, and hung the contact sheet on the line.

"Same damn shot," she whispered, pulling open the door and flooding the darkroom with orange afternoon light. She yanked the still-wet photo off the line and stalked into her workshop. A light breeze from the south-facing windows lifted papers and fluttered strips of negatives littering her table. In a movement, she swept everything but the photos off the table and grabbed her loupe. *Same angle. Same subject. Same light.* "Shit!"

She grabbed the other photos and peered closely at one, and then the next, willing them to be different. Willing them to make sense. But the photos were still exactly the same, identical to the last detail; the woman still floated, ghosting along the edge of the photo, crying out, a phantasm.

She tossed the photos and loupe back on the table and trudged into the bedroom. She checked her watch, then pulled open her closet and stared absently at the piles of shoes and haphazard shelves. *I need that vacation. I need some distraction. I need...* "I need some new clothes," she muttered, pulling out the last clean pair of jeans and a silk shirt, tossing them on the unmade bed. She crossed to the cool, dark bathroom and turned on the shower, then, after a moment's hesitation, turned the light off. She climbed in and sat, knees pulled to her chest, under the shower for nearly half an hour, until the water grew cold and prickled her skin.

Shivering, she stepped out and flicked the light on. She looked at herself in the small mirror, pulling at wrinkles around her eyes and sucking in her cheeks. "What's the big deal?" she asked her scowling reflection. "It's nothing. Dinner at Marie-Laure's."

At six-thirty she smoothed the front of her silk shirt and fought down the impulse to check the mirror. After some searching, she found her keys under the pile of clothes on the bed, and without a look at the mirror or the photos, set off for Marie-Laure's.

The town was serene and the streets empty of tourists as Meredith hurried down the rue St Etienne. The town returned to control of the locals in the slanting evening light, and they filled the cafés and bistros. Meredith nodded to the one or two locals she knew by sight as she passed. She turned the corner and found Marie-Laure leaning against her front door, her eyes closed and a serene smile on her face. The evening light picked out streaks of silver newly shimmering in her dark hair.

"What are you doing out here?" Meredith asked, smiling.

Marie-Laure grinned but did not open her eyes. "Mmm. When it is quiet like this, no buses and cars trundling by, I like to imagine Vézelay in years past."

Meredith suddenly shivered, rubbing her arms.

"At its peak on the pilgrim route, and during its sad slow decline. I imagine I can hear the voices and the animals…and I love to think that the sun shining on us now shone in the very same way then…on another woman, standing on her doorstep, listening to the world go by…" She sighed and opened her startling yellow eyes. "I can almost see that woman, standing out on the street – here – " she gestured to the long sweep of the rue

St Pierre – "can see her crying her wares, or crying her devotions. Hmmm." Marie-Laure closed her eyes again and sighed.

Meredith shivered and stared at Marie-Laure.

"That's why I love history. That feeling," Marie-Laure said, opening her eyes and looking at Meredith in surprise. "Oh, ma chère, my apologies. I am chattering on like an old woman. To what do I owe the honor of your visit this evening?"

Meredith shifted uncomfortably. "Uh, well – didn't – I thought he would have told you."

"Who? Tell me what?"

"Typical guy," Meredith said, rolling her eyes. "Well, yesterday, I had a drink with Mr. Flycatcher – " she rolled her eyes as Marie-Laure raised her eyebrows, "and he told me he was having dinner with you tonight, and invited me to come too. Though now that I think about it, I don't know if it was because he wanted to have dinner with me, or because he was afraid of you!"

Marie-Laure laughed. "I am sure his invitation has nothing to do with me," she said, steering Meredith inside. The strong, woody scent of thyme drifted from the kitchen, and Meredith halted in the foyer. "Ahh. What are you making?"

"Pauchouse," Marie-Laure replied from the parlor, opening a bottle of Mâcon-Villages.

"What's that?"

"Mmm, fish stew with thyme and white wine. But we were not talking about food."

"Sure we were," Meredith replied, taking the proffered glass.

"I believe you were about to tell me how it was you were having drinks with Mr. Flycatcher."

Meredith laughed. "Well…"

"Yes?" Marie-Laure prompted, settling into her chair.

"So…well, he came into the shop night before last, just before closing. He was a real jerk," she laughed. "He had the nerve to ask who the photographer was, and if he could talk to 'him'. Unbelievable. Anyway, I sold him one of the photos – "

"Which one?"

"The chestnut on rue St Etienne."

"Oh, another one of my favorites."

"Yeah, I like that one. I think it's one of my favorites, too. But anyway, he was rude, and I was rude back."

"How unusual," Marie-Laure smiled.

"Enough out of you," Meredith laughed. "But there was just – something – about him. He left in a snit and didn't take the photo. So, he came by yesterday, right before closing."

"I'm sensing a pattern here. He likes to get you alone."

"Oh," said Meredith, surprised. "Oh, I hadn't thought of that." She smiled. "OK, stop distracting me! He came by to pick up the photo…I don't know what got into me, but I asked him out for drinks."

"He is a charming young man."

"Ha. I don't know about that. But he's interesting. And, I don't know…there's just something about him that's intriguing. I can't really explain it. He kind of grew on me, you know?"

"I do indeed. And he is attractive…" Marie-Laure grinned.

"Hmm," Meredith said, looking out the open window. "I guess so. He's all kind of angles though, you know? Too tall, too skinny…and his face is so severe. I don't know if it's attractive."

"Oh, I think you do know."

Meredith turned back to Marie-Laure. "OK, you. You are *transparent*. You and Jonas arranged this dinner thing all along!"

"Me?" Marie-Laure laughed. "Oh no, I would have been much more overt. But you have to admit, he does have lovely eyes," she said, pouring Meredith another glass of wine.

"Yeah, they're OK. Nice kind of grey color. But his hands are really his best feature. It sure isn't his personality," Meredith laughed.

Marie-Laure snorted. "Yes, but it wasn't just his hands you invited to drinks."

Meredith laughed. "Oh, be quiet," she smiled fondly at Marie-Laure, then shivered with the familiar feeling that Marie-Laure could see right into her. "Thank heavens for you. You've made me laugh more in the last year than I have in…in 20 years. I don't deserve you."

"You deserve to be happy."

"I wonder sometimes."

"You have to let it go someday, ma chère. It's been so long."

"I know."

"You simply need closure – why don't we go to Paris, and –"

Meredith stood and turned her back on her, staring at the bookshelves packed with elegant leather-bound volumes and tatty paperbacks. "I can't," she whispered. "I – I'm not ready."

"Of course."

"I think about it every day, you know?" Meredith said, running her finger up and down the gilt edge of a massive book. "And it never gets any easier. Sometimes it fades into the background, and I think I can go on and be happy. But it's always there, eating at me. And then other days, out of the blue, it will just slap me around and it's all I can think about all morning, all day. Sometimes I wonder why I came back to France…it's so hard, you know? But there's nothing really left for me in Chicago, either. I guess this was the only place left to go."

"It was my good fortune."

Meredith turned, tears starting in her eyes. "No, it was mine. I'm sorry. I'm so tired, these dreams are freaking me out. I just feel – splintered," she said, her voice quivering.

Marie-Laure stood and pulled Meredith into a tight hug, patting her back as she sobbed quietly. Guillaume appeared in a haze of cigarette smoke at the door to the parlor a moment later. "When are you ladies –" He stared from his wife to Meredith, then attempted to back out without a word.

"Don't go," Meredith said, wiping her eyes. "Don't go. And don't be alarmed," she laughed at Guillaume's expression, "I'm done."

"Good," he said stoutly, taking her by the arm. "You need to choose which wine we're drinking this evening. Marie-Laure has been no help whatsoever." They headed toward the kitchen, but a knock at the door froze Meredith in place. "I better go wash my face," she muttered, leaving Marie-Laure and Guillaume alone in the foyer.

She pulled the door to the small washroom closed and snapped on the light. She pulled her hair into a quick ponytail and scrubbed her face with icy water; Jonas' deep voice rumbled in the foyer. *OK, get it together. You're fine. You're fine.* She finally looked into the mirror, her face and eyes red. She took a deep breath and buried her face in a towel.

Squaring her shoulders, she pulled open the door and followed their voices down the hall to the small kitchen. Jonas and Guillaume were in the corner deep in conversation over the bottle of wine Jonas had brought, shrouded in a haze of smoke. Marie-Laure stood over the stove, ladling the pauchouse into a serving bowl and grinning. "Guillaume, you're so impatient," Meredith chided, arms folded. "I thought that was my job!"

"Yes, yes, but see what Mr. Flycatcher has brought –" he said, waving Meredith over. "Your friend has excellent taste."

"He does indeed. It's good to see you, Mr. Flycatcher," she said, offering her hand to Jonas.

"Yeah, you too," he smiled, "Mademoiselle Thibault."

She smiled, relaxing. "So what did you bring, anyway? It takes a lot to impress Guillaume, trust me."

"A Les Clos – Domaine Brocard," Guillaume said, handing her the bottle with a flourish.

"Mmm, nice job," Meredith smiled, handing the bottle back. "Clearly *you* didn't pick it out."

"I know what I like when I try it, but I'm no expert. In wine," he said, smiling. "Abbot Dubay suggested it."

"Ah," Meredith said.

Marie-Laure turned around quickly. "Jonas, mon chèr, can you help me with this? It is rather heavy." She handed the serving bowl to Jonas and pointed him across the hall. "On the table would be wonderful. Merci."

"Sure," he said, smiling at Meredith and stubbing out his cigarette in an ashtray.

She rolled her eyes at Marie-Laure's back and felt a smile creep across her face. "Here, I'll help you," she said, following him into the small dining room. "She's always like that," she said, taking bowls from the sideboard and laying them out on the table.

"Yeah, I know," he laughed.

Meredith stopped and watched him place the serving bowl on the long, elegant table. "She is the sweetest person I've ever known."

"Yeah? Don't get out much, do you?" he grinned, leaning against the window and folding his arms. "How did you two meet?"

"We've known each other forever. I knew her when she was a professor at the Sorbonne," she said, folding and unfolding a napkin.

"Did you know Abbot Dubay?"

Her eyes grew wide; after a moment she recovered and said, "Yes. I moved back to France about a year ago, after, God, 19 years or so. And just by dumb luck I ended up here. I didn't even know until – I guess it was a week or two after I got here – that she and Guillaume had been living here."

"Did you know Dubay was here?"

"No," she said, finally looking up.

"So," Jonas said, walking over and leaning over the back of one of the chairs, "I forgot to take the photo home last night. Can I pick it up from you tonight? After dinner?"

Meredith laughed. "You can't wait until tomorrow when the shop's open?"

"Nope," he smiled.

She laughed and tossed the napkin on the table. "We'll see what we can do," she said, grinning.

Jonas opened his mouth to protest but smiled instead as Marie-Laure walked in carrying a large bowl of salad. "Ah, thank you mes chèrs. I think we are ready. Sit wherever you would like," she said, settling in at the head of the table. "Guillaume, we are starting without you," she called.

"Oui, oui," he muttered, shuffling in with the wine and sitting opposite Marie-Laure.

"So, Jonas, how is the glass coming along?" Marie-Laure asked, ladling stew into his bowl.

"Thanks," he said, taking the bowl. "Good. I got another section of her hair done."

"Excellent, excellent," she said. "You really must see the glass, Meredith. It is quite remarkable."

Meredith nodded mid-sip. "I'm sure it is."

Marie-Laure raised her eyebrow slightly and turned back to Jonas. "How is it that Abbot Dubay found you? I don't believe he ever told me."

Meredith leaned forward.

"I have no idea."

"What?" Meredith laughed.

"I don't know. I got a call from some woman at UNESCO –"

"Are you serious? UNESCO?" Meredith asked.

"Yeah. She called about a week ago."

"Well, how did UNESCO find you?"

"No idea," Jonas shrugged, taking a sip of wine. "I guess one of my clients gave me a referral. I used to do a lot of work here. A few years ago."

Meredith smiled. "What's so amazing about this particular stained glass that they had to bring the world-famous Jonas Flycatcher all the way from – "

" – Boulder Creek, California," he supplied.

" – from the boondocks to work on it?"

"It's very – " he started.

"Mysterious," Marie-Laure said.

"Rare, I was going to say. But, yeah, I guess mysterious, too. And it's beautiful. So much gorgeous *color*," he said, winking at Meredith. "Any luck on that research you were doing for me?" he asked Marie-Laure.

"Mmm, I do have some theories but I am not ready to share them quite yet. I need to do a bit more research. I think I will have something substantive to share tomorrow."

"What do you have her working on?" Guillaume asked. "She has been impossible –"

"More than usual?" Meredith asked with a wink.

"Yes, even more than usual, if that can be believed. Up until three in the morning, pulling down books and pulling out old file folders. Chattering to herself in the office all day long. It has been rather tiresome," he said, a fond smile slipping through.

"Yes, yes, tiresome," Marie-Laure said, waving her hand. "But it has been good to use those brain cells again. At least you," she said, pointing an accusatory finger at her husband, "have your book to work on. I am stuck coming up with new ways to mangle a perfectly good lamb recipe."

An hour later, after a dried cherry galette with crème fraiche, strong coffee, and an exhaustive discussion of American photojournalism, Jonas checked his watch. "Is it too late to pick up that photo?" he asked Meredith.

"Nope," she smiled, standing up. "Thanks again for dinner, Marie-Laure. It was wonderful, as always. Can I help you with the dishes?"

"No, you may not. Go on. Have a good evening," Marie-Laure grinned, leading Jonas and Meredith to the front door.

"Thank you," Meredith said, hugging her. "Merci, Guillaume. À bientôt!"

"Au revoir. Je lui aime," he called from the kitchen.

Meredith laughed. "I'm glad," she called back. "Are you ready?" she asked Jonas.

"Sure. Thanks," he said, offering his hand to Marie-Laure. She took it and kissed him on each cheek.

"I shall come by tomorrow with my research, if that is agreeable?" she asked.

"Do I have a choice?" he asked.

"No."

"I'll see you tomorrow," he said.

"Excellent. Have a good evening, mes chèrs," she said, shutting the door behind them.

The town had grown quiet and the twilight blue, save for the silvered stars. A cool breeze swirled down the steep rue St Etienne, hinting at the scent of sweet grass and evergreen from the distant Morvan. Meredith sighed.

"You OK?" Jonas asked quietly.

She opened her eyes and looked up at him. "Yeah, I'm fine. I'm – great, actually."

"Good," he said, leaning against the wall. "I love how the sky is so many shades of blue," he said, gesturing at the sky with his lit cigarette.

Meredith leaned back and folded her arms. "It is nice," she admitted.

They watched the sky darken in silence for long minutes. A door slammed in the distance, echoing along the street, and they were awakened from their reverie. "Are you ready?" Jonas asked.

Meredith looked at him in confusion.

"I was going to pick up the picture, right?"

"Oh, right, right," she said. "No, I'm not ready. Let's go have a drink instead."

Jonas nodded, taking a last drag and crushing the cigarette out under his shoe. "Fan-fucking-tastic idea. Lead the way."

They climbed the street to the small, nearly empty café opposite Meredith's shop and settled in, side by side, at a small table on the sidewalk. "So why did you move back to France? And what were you doing here, anyway?" Jonas asked, gesturing vaguely at the street and the medieval buildings.

"Well, it's a long story," Meredith said, waving the words away.

"I've got time," Jonas replied leaning back in his chair and looking up at the sky.

"Well," she said, looking at her hands. "I lived in Chicago all my life, and moved back when I left France. When my dad died two years ago, I didn't really have anything left there. So, I don't know, I came back here. I don't know why. It just seemed like the thing to do."

Jonas nodded but didn't look at Meredith. "What happened to your dad?"

"He had a heart attack."

"So did my mom."

"Really?" Meredith asked, looking at him. "Did she – die?"

"Yep."

"I'm sorry."

"I'm not."

"What – what's wrong with you? How can you talk about your mom like that?" Meredith demanded.

Jonas turned his head to look at her. "You didn't know her. It was a relief for both of us."

"I'd give anything to have my mom back," Meredith said quietly.

"When did she die?"

"1980. She was only 50. I was 19."

"Of what?"

Breast cancer. It was horrible. It happened so fast…" she said, looking down again at her hands. "I had just graduated from high school. I hardly got to say goodbye. One day, she was helping me with college applications, two months later, she was dead."

"You were close?"

"Sure. Yeah," she said, shaking her head. "I was a mess. I went to college for a while, but you know, my dad was a frigging basket case, so I spent most of my time taking care of him. I couldn't take it anymore after a while, you know? It was too much. I applied to a study abroad program at the Sorbonne so I could escape."

Jonas leaned on his elbows on the table, chin in his hand. "Me too."

"You did a program at the Sorbonne?"

"Yeah, well, it was mostly graduate research right after my B.A. – about ten years ago. '89? '90? Anyway, I came over with my friend Steve."

"What did you study?"

"Eighteenth and nineteenth century art history. You?"

"French literature."

"Really?"

"Yeah. Both sides of my family are French, so you know, it was natural. My family was obsessive about genealogy – I guess we come from around here, actually. Some place out near Beaune, I think. Anyway, I wanted some kind of connection to my past. I met Marie-Laure when I was at the Sorbonne. She was friends with my –"

The café owner ambled over to their table. "Mademoiselle? Monsieur?"

"What'll you have?" Jonas asked.

"Whisky."

"Deux, s'il vous plâit," he said. The café owner nodded and shuffled away.

"So," he said, turning back to her. "What about Marie-Laure?"

"No, enough about me. What about you? What's with your name, anyway?" she said, leaning forward.

"What about it?" he asked, folding his arms.

"It's just, um, unusual."

"Not that unusual."

"Gimme a break."

"My grandfather's name was Ingvar Fiksdalsstrand –"

"Feek- what?" she laughed.

"It's Norwegian," he said, rolling his eyes. "Anyway, my dad got shit all the time when he was a kid so he changed it to Flycatcher when he got older."

"Oh, now that *is* an improvement," she laughed.

"You know, you really are a pain in the ass," he said, lighting a cigarette.

"It's been said," she laughed. "So, where did you grow up? Oh – merci," she said, accepting the glass of whisky from the café's owner. "In Northern California?"

"Yeah, San Francisco– cheers," he said, clinking their glasses.

"A votre santé."

"San Francisco, then I went to undergrad at Berkeley."

"So is that where you learned to repair stained glass? At Berkeley?" she asked.

"No. No, that was after the Sorbonne. I had a business over here, working on ecclesiastical repairs and some reproductions. I moved back to the states after my mom died."

"But I thought you were studying Romanticism."

"I was. But I went to Sainte-Chapelle…"

Meredith smiled and nodded. "Now I understand," she said, rolling the smooth glass between her hands.

Jonas swung back and looked at her, holding his cigarette behind him. "Do you?" he asked.

"It's an amazing place. I used to love going there when I was in Paris – I would just stand on that threshold and let it all wash over me. And I loved watching people's reactions when they first walked in, you know? But of course, I was young – maybe 20 – and that's all that seemed to matter at the time," she said, shaking her head. "How stupid."

Jonas looked at her, intent, then turned away, taking a long drag on his cigarette. "Not stupid. At all." He crushed out the cigarette in the orange plastic ashtray on the small table and looked at his watch. "Can I pick up that photo now? I've got to get some work done tonight to stay on schedule."

"Oh. Oh, sure," she replied.

Jonas drained the rest of his whisky and placed a ten-Euro note under it on the table. "After you," he said, standing.

They crossed the street quickly and stood outside her shop, the waxing moon silvering the narrow street.

"Thanks for tonight. I had a good time," she said, turning around to face him, smiling.

"Me too," he said quietly. Suddenly, he leaned in and kissed her on her neck, just below her ear. "Thanks," he whispered.

Panic and heady excitement chased each other around her brain. "My pleasure," she whispered. He leaned forward again and, twining their fingers, kissed her, quickly, awkwardly. Her fingers tingled with a strange, warm energy.

He pulled back and looked at her, unsmiling. "See ya."

"Yeah. See ya," she said, her voice a wisp in the darkness.

Jonas stared at her for a long minute, then turned and walked up the street, towards the cathedral. She watched him disappear through the deserted plaza, around the corner, and out of sight.

Meredith searched her pockets for her key and, hand shaking, opened the door to her dark shop. She ignored the call of the bookkeeping piled on the desk and climbed the stairs to her bedroom. She flicked on the light and flopped on to her bed, torn between happiness and unmitigated panic. She swept the photos of the cathedral from her nightstand and picked up the lone framed photo that stood sentinel there.

"Am I allowed to be happy?" she asked. The smiling faces, as ever, did not respond.

Chapter Fourteen

"SANCTA MARIA ET OMNES SANCTI..."

Dubay stood still, quiet, waiting for the moment that occurred in every service he offered. Beneath the Latin and the formulae, or perhaps because of it, a feeling would overwhelm him, a word or idea would take over his consciousness. It was his gift from God, and he thought guiltily that he sought to lead the monks in prayer to achieve that transcendence for himself alone. He stood, arms stretched before him, hands pleading, waiting, guilty and expectant.

Remembrance.

The word seemed to float on the soft breaths of the monks and the light streaming through the lancet windows, quietly filling the basilica. "...*et opera manuum nostrarum dirige super nos et opus manuum nostrarum dirige...*" He stuttered to a halt. The brothers looked up expectantly at him, silhouetted by the morning light. The word wreathed in the grey swirls of incense and in the shadows high among the arches: *remembrance*. Dubay squeezed his eyes shut and an image of twisting curls and a lazy dark river appeared. "No," he whispered under his breath. *Not now.*

He opened his eyes and smiled apologetically. "*...et opera manuum nostrarum...*" he continued, breathless. He completed the service, with a whispered "Amen" and passed through the brethren to the doors of the shadowed chapter house. He closed the door behind him and let out a long, shaking sigh. *Remembrance?* He shook his head and pushed away from the door, grasping the narrow iron handrail and climbed the worn stairs to his rooms. Unfastening his vestments, he pushed open the door to his office with a polished wingtip, and, pulling his vestments off over his head, sank wearily into his burgundy leather chair.

An hour later, a sharp knock on the door woke him from his reverie. He slid the photo of the young woman under a book and opened the door to find a smiling Marie-Laure. "Come in, come in," he said, kissing her on each cheek and leading her to a chair by the open window.

"I'm not interrupting –" she said, looking around the room and laboring under the weight of a very full canvas bag.

"No, not at all. To what do I owe the honor?" he asked, settling back into his chair and rolling up his shirtsleeves.

"Research. I have been very busy since I saw you yesterday. Let me show you what I've found." She spread the bag's contents on his desk and he looked through them avidly. "I revisited the Poitiers *Chronicle* last night after they left –"

"After who left?"

"Jonas and Meredith."

"Is that so?" he asked, glancing up from the pile of papers momentarily. "How did they get along?"

Marie-Laure shrugged and sat back. "Quite well, in their own way."

"I'd wondered when they'd meet," he muttered, shifting papers.

"Apparently he purchased one of her photos, and the rest is history," she chuckled. "It's good to see Meredith smiling again. It has been far too long," she said, looking out the window to the leafy park below.

"Indeed," he muttered. "Has she seemed strange to you in the last few days?" he asked, looking up at Marie-Laure.

"Yes," she nodded, playing with the chain holding her glasses. "She – she has been ill, I think. And she refuses to let Fréderic see her."

"What's wrong with her?"

"I – I'm not sure," she admitted. "Exhaustion? I can only guess. She has been working so hard to make a success of her studio."

"She won't tell you?"

"You know her, Michel. Stubborn."

"Indeed," he whispered, turning his hands over absently, tracing the jagged scars with a long, slender finger.

"I will keep an eye on her," Marie-Laure said, watching Dubay with narrowed eyes.

"Mmm," he nodded. "Yes, yes, that would be good..."

"Michel?" she said, resting her wrinkled soft hand on his wrist.

"Hm? Oh, forgive me," he said, shaking his head. "I was far away, I'm afraid."

"Yes," she smiled. "I know. Why don't you join us this evening? Guillaume has been wanting to show you his latest chapter."

Dubay shook his head. "I can't tonight. I'm having dinner with Monsieur Mermiee."

"Tonight? I thought you were having dinner with him last night."

"I was, but he cancelled at the last minute."

"So why didn't you come to our house for dinner?"

Dubay grinned. "I relished a quiet evening. I even led Compline, if you can believe it. The first time in many weeks. It was wonderful. And I led Prime this morning."

"My goodness, what's got into you?" she laughed. "Next, you'll be saying Mass on Sunday."

He smiled. "Ah, no. Frère Ignatius would never hear of it. The dear brothers are quite happy to let me act as administrator. They indulge me on occasion, but..." he said, looking out the window. "But they look to Frère Ignatius for the salvation of their souls."

Marie-Laure reached across the desk and patted Dubay's hand.

Dubay looked at her and smiled weakly. "Enough of this," he said, shaking his head. "What have you brought?"

"Well, since you are so keen, let me show you what I found." She picked up the first folder and pulled out its contents. "The border of the glass is so rich…"

Dubay grinned. "I thought you might uncover the stories."

"Mmm, I'm only just beginning, my dear," she smiled. "There are about ten different scenes, from what I gathered."

"Yes, yes, that sounds right," he said, leaning back in his chair, hands laced behind his head.

"And you would think that they would be scenes from the life of the Magdalene."

"That would make sense."

"Ah, it would…but you see, they're not. Only one of the ten scenes touches on the Magdalene. Which of course is our first mystery," she said, tapping the folder. "The first two scenes at first glance appear to be random images. In the bottom left corner, you recall, is an extraordinary scene of a vineyard."

"Yes, yes," he said, nodding. "Quite rich – the color – "

"And the perspective. It is quite remarkable."

The great church bell rang nine times; they both looked out the window at the green countryside, growing bright with the warming morning.

"Exquisite," he said, nodding. "Coffee?"

"That would be lovely."

The door to the office opened, and Soeur Marie entered, carrying a laden tray of coffee and croissants. "Thank you," he smiled. "Where's Frère Pascal? Have you frightened him away again?"

Marie-Laure laughed. "Don't tell me you've scared away another one, Marie?"

Soeur Marie grinned. "Me? No, not yet. He is at Nones service. Coffee, Madame Rouchon?"

"Thank you, my dear," Marie-Laure said, taking the proffered cup.

"Is your hand feeling better, Monsiegneur?" Soeur Marie asked, handing a cup to Dubay.

"Much," he smiled. "What would I do without you?"

"Be helpless," she grinned. "Will you be taking lunch here?"

"Yes. I have more work than I care to think about to finish before my dinner with our dear Monsieur le maire this evening."

"I'll see you at noontime, then," she nodded, closing the office door behind her.

"Here, hand me your cup," Dubay said, reaching into a desk drawer.

Marie-Laure smiled and winked. "Ah, you are nothing if not a civilized man, Michel," she said as he poured a finger of Drambuie into her coffee.

"So where were we?" he asked, grinning.

"In the vineyard."

"Right."

"I did a little searching, and found this –" she said, pulling a book from her bag and opening it to a scene of a rich vineyard, sweeping in long, tight rows to a wide pale river. "Does this look familiar to you?"

He scanned the photo and shook his head. "Yes, and no. It would be incredible to find the very view...the chance of that happening is astronomical."

"Don't you believe in miracles anymore, Michel?"

He smiled and nodded. "Of course. Now show me your proof."

Marie-Laure laughed merrily. "You always were my best student – you never let me get away with anything." She moved around the desk to stand behind Dubay. "See here –" she pointed at the curve of the river "—see that lazy turn? The artist captured it quite skillfully. And the hills rolling down to the river in two gentle arcs?"

"Hmm...I don't know...The scene is idealized. It could be anywhere."

Marie-Laure smiled and raised here eyebrows. "Ah yes. Yes, you could leave it at that. But I dug a little deeper."

Dubay rolled his eyes. "Yes?" he asked in his best long-suffering tone.

"Look – here," she said, pulling out a magnifying glass. "See just here – yes, there. Do you see that farmhouse in the distance?"

"Yes..." he answered slowly.

"There is a tiny rendering of that same farmhouse in the glass. Very subtle, but it is there."

He sat back and folded his arms. "So perhaps it is the same scene. And?"

"And," she said with a flourish, "it is a vineyard at a turning of the Saône."

"Really…" Dubay finished his coffee and set the cup in the saucer with a clatter.

"I know of only two vineyards – both owned by the Clunaics of course – along the Saône in the twelfth century - one was run by the Cistercians, near the current Batard Montrachet –"

"Not the Clunaics?"

"Surprisingly, no. And the other by – "

"Dubay et Fils."

"Precisely."

"Now that *is* interesting," he said looking out the window and twirling his coffee spoon.

Marie-Laure's face shone and she clapped her hands. "And there's more."

"Hmm?"

"The next panel…well, I thought the crest looked familiar, but I had to pull out the *Chronicle* and some other works to be sure. Thank heavens Guillaume is a packrat; I might have thrown those notes away. After a bit of searching, I'm quite sure it is the crest of the Dukes of Nevers, circa 1120."

"A clue to the artist's patron."

"Quite possibly. Or at the very least, an indication that the artist was local to Burgundy." Marie-Laure sat back in her chair, a satisfied grin on her face. "So? Not bad for a day's work."

Dubay shrugged his shoulders. "Not bad," he smiled.

"So what do you know about the Dubay et Fils lands?" she asked, leaning forward.

He put his hands up in protest. "My specialty is eleventh century Côte d'Or –"

"Yes, yes," she nodded, watching him keenly. "One of the better dissertations I've seen."

"—and now, this church of course. I don't remember anything about Dubay et Fils history," he said, standing and running his hand along the broad bookshelf.

"But –"

He turned around and smiled. "Would you like to see where we found the glass?"

Marie-Laure quirked an eyebrow. "If that is what you'd like."

"It is," he said, grasping his hands behind his back.

"Then lead the way," she said, gathering her papers and books and shoving them into her bag. She followed him out the door and he handed her down the steps to the broad oak door crossed with iron that separated the chapter house from the nave.

They entered the church, squinting in the brightness after the cool gloom of the cloisters. The morning light curled through the tall clear glass, caressing the high rounded arches and intricate Romanesque capitals. Dubay bounced on the balls of his feet, hands clasped behind his back. "Glorious, isn't it?" he smiled.

"Oh yes," Marie-Laure breathed. "The stories are alive this morning," she said, pointing at the River of Paradise. "You are a lucky man."

"Blessed."

"Yes. Blessed."

"Ready?" he whispered.

"Yes, yes."

He nodded at the small crowd of tourists moving forward to gape at the great gothic choir and helped Marie-Laure down the ancient, uneven steps to the crypt.

"We found it here," he said, kneeling and pulling up a stone flag.

"Did it seem to be intentional? Hidden here? Or just lost after so many years of building and rebuilding?"

"It's hard to know. Do you want my guess?"

"Of course."

"I think it was put here intentionally."

"Why?"

"I don't know. Just a – a feeling," he said, looking around the long, low room.

"Intriguing," Marie-Laure muttered.

Dubay nodded. "When I'm here – in the evenings – I can almost sense what it was like to be here, before the great fire. I can almost feel what it was like to pray and lay offerings to the Magdalene…" he said, running his hands along the stout columns and rustic capitals. "In the candlelight, I can see the penitents and priests kneeling here – and here. And swooning with relief and fervor, and the heat. I – I can almost feel the artist - here –" he said, kneeling before what had been the altar a millennium ago, "offering prayers and thanks to the Magdalene and the saints. Sweating with effort and emotion…"

"Does it feel warm to you now?"

"It always does."

Marie-Laure shivered, her lips pale. "I'm cold to the bone down here."

Dubay stood and offered his hand to her. "You should have said something. Let's go back upstairs."

"Yes, yes, thank you my dear." She took his hand and he looked at her sharply; her fingers were like icicles. He took a hand and her bony elbow and guided her slowly up the worn steps and into the bright nave.

He turned to her and rubbed her arms. "Better?"

"Yes, yes, I'm fine, thank you. I forget that I'm an old woman sometimes," she said, smoothing her crisp linen suit.

Dubay narrowed his eyes but said nothing, walking her toward the great narthex doors. "Did seeing the location give you any more clues?" he asked, pushing the massive door open ahead of her.

"Mmm…not yet. I need to let it settle. It will come to me. It always does."

"Why don't I come by for dinner in a few days, and you can enlighten me then?"

"Excellent idea. I'll see you on Thursday. Let's say seven?"

"Perfect," he said, holding the door to the narthex open for her. "See you then. Be well."

That evening, he returned to his church after a contentious and draining dinner with M. Merimée, Vézelay's mayor. The streets were still warm from the day's heat, but largely empty of life in the darkening evening. A faint apricot glow still tinged the sky; he smiled at the twinkling stars leaping overhead. The great basilica glowed warm and Dubay smiled: this was *his* home, this magnificent center of history and art and religion.

He met the order's Porter, Frère Martin, hurrying to close up the church in Dubay's absence. Dubay bowed low to the old man. "My apologies. I was tardy and did not see to my duties," he smiled. "Many thanks for seeing to the doors."

Frère Martin nodded. "Thank you for singing Prime this morning," he said, ushering Dubay into the narthex. "I felt God with us."

Dubay's breath hitched. "I am glad. Truly." He smiled at the old man and, rather than lingering in the aisles to study the capitals and column bases, hurried directly to the ancient crypt and altar. He lit a single taper and trod the well-worn path to the Magdalene's reliquary.

He crossed himself at the ancient altar, then turned back to the reliquary and kissed the cool glass. He sank to his knees and prayed fervently to the Magdalene, his orisons of thanks mingling with the warm smell of stale incense and images of deepest ruby lit from within and the smiling face of a woman idling next to the Seine.

An hour later, he stood creakily and, crossing himself, climbed the stairs to the silent and now-dark church. The limestone was cool around him; he was drenched in sweat.

Chapter Fifteen

THE MORNING BREEZE SWIRLED lazily from the banks of the Cure to the top of the ancient, rounded hill. Jonas leaned, arms crossed, against the sturdy chestnut, watching the swaths of fog and cloud crown the wooded hills beyond in the Morvan. He breathed deeply, the cool air bright in his lungs, the sunrise edging above the swirling hilltops. The morning was his orison and he worshipped with his eyes.

He stretched and rolled his tight and creaking shoulders, feeling both exhausted and exhilarated. In the cold pre-dawn, before wandering down to this empty park, when the sky was still wreathed in darkness, he'd awoken, spread-eagled on his bed. The dream had lingered about the edges of his brain.

A woman in a deep ruby gown spun fervently in the dawn before the great basilica, her dress swirling sinuously, her head thrown back in ecstasy, a dervish. Jonas watched from the steps of the cathedral, a kindling light from behind casting long shadows down the steep, hilly streets. He stood and moved slowly around the square, trying to catch a glimpse of her face; it was crucial that he see her, know her, kiss her hands. He circled, but her wind-whipped hair and swaying arms thwarted him. *If only I had my wings.* The sky grew sapphire as he rose into the air, watching the empty town and the swirling statuary of the tympanum and the dot of whirling red. "Now I will know her," he said, floating toward the ground, "by the curve of her neck." As he neared, his dusty wings fluttering and scarred, the dervish collapsed and wept.

In a moment, the dream had disappeared.

He'd stretched and stumbled into his workshop, grinning sleepily at his handiwork. Cigarette butts overflowed a cheap orange plastic ashtray, CDs and their cases piled on the worktable and the floor next to the stereo, papers strewn across every surface. But he only saw the glass, shimmering somehow with its own light.

He'd left Meredith the night before last, feeling certain. About what, he wasn't entirely sure. But a sense of both calm and energy overtook him, and he worked through that night and last, stopping only in the afternoon to walk to her shop and thank her. "For what?" she'd asked, smiling hesitantly. "Just thanks," he'd replied. "I'll see you tomorrow."

Peering out the window at the quiet morning, he'd detected hints of gold flecking the high clouds. *Maybe she's up now.* He rummaged in his suitcase for a clean shirt and drowsily pulled on his jeans and sneakers. He descended the staircase slowly, listening for each creak, running his hands along the low wooden ceiling. The front room was quiet and dark, and smelled of mold and old fires.

Jonas had pushed open the heavy front door and stepped into the current of the cool morning, rubbing his arms vigorously, watching the twittering songbirds swoop and wheel above the swaying plane trees. Setting off up the rue l'Argenterie towards the cathedral, he skirted the hush of the plaza and the quiet murmuring of the Prime office within, then down to no. 40.

He rapped quickly on the glass and waited, looking up and down the street, windows still shuttered, cobblestones still slick. He knocked again and peered into the dark shop. When there was again no response, he trudged up the empty street, past the still-closed tabac, and drawn to the dawn touching the eastern sky, wandered into the park at the feet of the chapter house, breathing with the chestnuts and welcoming the sun.

"Lovely," a voice whispered quietly behind him.

Jonas jumped in surprise but didn't turn around. "Mornin'," he said, crushing his cigarette in the gravel and blowing the smoke lazily to the sky. "*Hell* of a view."

"I saw you from the window," Dubay said, gesturing to his office with his bandaged hand. "What are you doing out here so early?" He tucked his arms against the cool breeze. "You must be freezing," he said, nodding at Jonas' t-shirt.

Jonas shrugged. "No, I'm good."

They stood together silently for many minutes, watching the golden sun fill the shallow valley. The trees swayed slightly in the breeze, shaking off the night's dewdrops and sprinkling them like jewels along the gravel path, and in their hair. Dubay chuckled and turned to Jonas. "So what are you doing out – mon Dieu, Jonas, you look like hell!"

Jonas laughed and rubbed his arms. "Story of my life."

"No, I am quite serious," Dubay said, frowning, grabbing Jonas' arm. "Those circles are so dark under your eyes – you look as if you have been in a fight. And you are very pale."

"Yeah, it's been a long couple of days," Jonas said, shaking his head and shrugging.

Dubay looked out across the valley. "I can imagine."

"I got the hair done," Jonas said triumphantly, pushing away from the tree and turning to face Dubay. "I really made a lot of progress the last two days. I didn't think I'd have it done for another week, but I just put my head down and –"

"— and had many pots of awful coffee –"

"Yeah, of course," Jonas laughed, kicking at the gravel path. "I just powered through and got it done. And it's so gorgeous –"

Dubay laughed and shook his head. "Always humble," he grinned.

"No, seriously! And it's not me," Jonas said. "It's the glass. There's something about it...it just vibrates. With energy. Or something... It was like I wasn't doing the work at all. The glass kind of told me what to do and...I listened." He turned away and shook his head. "I lost track of time, I guess."

Dubay nodded. "It is easy to do," he said, resting a hand on Jonas' shoulder. "Did you sleep at all?" he asked gently.

"I think so," Jonas shrugged, lighting another cigarette.

"Eat?"

"Do candy bars count?"

Dubay snorted. "No." He dropped his hand and smiled. "As I am the reason for your sleep deprivation and appalling diet – at least at the moment – let me buy you breakfast."

"That's a deal," Jonas nodded, checking his watch. "Though the café doesn't open until eight, right?"

"Ah yes. One does lose track of time…" Dubay turned away from the view and stared at the hulking basilica, the morning light gilding its awkward gothic buttresses.

Jonas followed his gaze. "Why are you up so early?"

"Hmmm? Oh, I am always awake before dawn. It has been my habit for nearly twenty years."

"Every day? What's wrong with you? That's sick."

"Peut-être," Dubay demurred, shrugging his shoulders and smiling. "But it is many, many morning's worth of history I do not think I could shake off." He looked again at the church. "Even if I wanted to."

Ask him why. Ask him why he became a priest. Ask him. "Maybe there's another café open now?"

Dubay looked at him, mildly surprised. "Mmmm? Perhaps we could persuade monsieur Blanchard to open le Compostelle a bit early," he said, taking Jonas by the arm. "And then you can tell me the real reason why you were up all night."

Jonas looked at him and laughed. "You are probably the weirdest priest I have ever met."

"Then you must not have met many," Dubay grinned, leading Jonas out of the small park and around the chapter house. The sun had risen golden and the wall surrounding Dubay's garden glittered with pale roses touched with dew and quiet violets creeping out to meet the sun. As they walked briskly past, Jonas ran his hand along a trail of dark ivy. "How do you have the time to work on the garden? Aren't you supposed to be praying all the time or something?"

"Perhaps had I been abbot five hundred, a thousand years ago. And perhaps not even then."

"Why? Don't you pray?"

Dubay laughed. "Of course. Of course. I pray every day, but prayer takes many forms. We still largely follow the Rule of St. Benedict; we are a community that lives in the world – although abbots and monks historically did too. Particularly the Clunaics that ran this monastery 800, a thousand years ago," he said nodding toward the chapter house. "They were deeply embroiled in the politics of their time – and nowhere more so than here at Vézelay."

"All about the money."

"Absolument," Dubay nodded. "The town wanted the money from the pilgrim trade, as did the good brothers, as did the diocese of Autun. The Dukes of Nevers wanted control of the roads – which, of course, meant control of the pilgrim traffic, and the Abbot at Cluny wanted control of it all. And largely had it. Not only did the townspeople here murder one of the abbots over control –"

"Yeah, I remember you saying that. Hey, where is this place, anyway?"

Dubay smiled. "At the Place de Champs de Foire."

"How far?"

"Feeling winded?"

"Hell no."

"Mmm. It is at the bottom of rue St Etienne. Not far."

"OK. So, we were discussing murder."

"Ah, yes," Dubay nodded. "Yes, the townspeople murdered one of the Abbots in a rather violent tax revolt – it seems they were not pleased that they had to both pay taxes to the abbey and share with them the pilgrim revenue. The tension continued to grow with the wealth of the abbey, and eventually the townspeople burned the church down."

"No shit. Really?" Jonas asked, stopping in the middle of the street. "Burned the whole thing down?"

"Indeed. Well, not the entire church. But they burned the ancient nave to the ground."

"Holy crap."

"Something like that, yes."

Jonas pulled out a cigarette. "Want one?"

"No, thank you," Dubay sniffed. "It was a much different time, you have to understand. They were not doing it for their glory but for the glory of God."

"Yeah, right," Jonas laughed. "You know, that's why religion just sucks."

Dubay shrugged. "It is much different now, to be sure. Though after a thousand years, I find that we are still arguing with the mayor, and the abbot at Autun. Here we are." He rapped smartly on the worn door of le Compostelle, its ornate nineteenth century façade awkward and somehow unseemly in the midst of the medieval town.

A prim old man in his shirtsleeves poked his head out the door. "Oui?"

"Monsieur Blanchard! Bonjour, bonjour."

"Oui?"

Jonas snickered quietly. He watched each man in turn fold his arms, shrug his shoulders, and utter a Gallic "pffff." Somehow however, minutes later, he found himself seated at a small table near a narrow window, Dubay smiling widely. Jonas lit a cigarette and grinned.

"Oui?" the old man grunted, looking anywhere but at Dubay.

"Une tatine, s'il vous plaît, et un café au lait," Jonas said through a mouthful of smoke.

Dubay arched his eyebrow slightly but said only, "Une tatine aussi. Et café, s'il vous plâit."

Jonas leaned back and folded his arms, cigarette hanging from his lips. "So do you, pray or whatever, with the brothers at the monastery?"

"Yes, yes. But my role has largely become an administrative one." Dubay smiled slightly, then gazed out the window.

Jonas took a long drag and sat in silence as the smoke wreathed around them. "Why did you become a priest?" he asked quietly.

Dubay flinched and grabbed his bandaged hand. He did not look at Jonas, but exhaled, his shoulders sagging visibly. "I – it…it is a long story. I do not want to bore you with it," he said, turning to Jonas and smiling brightly.

"Oh no you don't."

"Pardon?"

Jonas leaned forward, looking Dubay in the eye. "I told you about the damn scars," he said. "Your turn."

Dubay held Jonas' gaze, but did not move nor speak. Jonas took a drag and blew the smoke out the corner of his mouth. "Your turn. Why did you become a priest? Why didn't you become a professor like Marie-Laure?"

"I – I had planned to," Dubay replied, turning to the window. He sat silently, flexing his fingers. Jonas pushed his chair back and hung his head, resting his elbows on his knees, waiting and smoking.

After long moments, Dubay said quietly, "I was thoughtless."

Jonas looked up at Dubay, eyebrows knitted. "What do you mean? Do you regret it?"

"No, no," Dubay said, smiling out the window. "My decision was very, very clear. I do not believe it was a decision, actually. It was an inevitability. So, you see, when I consider it now, it was thoughtless. God provides guidance in strikingly literal ways sometimes," he mused.

"Where were you when you realized it was what you wanted?"

"Laying in bed."

"When? Where?"

Dubay turned slowly and looked at Jonas. "Why do you want to know?" he asked gently.

"I just want to know."

Dubay took a deep breath. "I was supposed to have worked with my brothers and father. It was expected – Dubay et Fils, n'est-ce pas? It was understood, it was not questioned. And to my father's great disappointment, I entered the Sorbonne with honors," he said, a slight crease wrinkling between his brows. "Of course, he was looking to me to carry it all on…my brothers…Do you have siblings, Jonas?"

"No," he said, watching Dubay's sharp, closed profile. "No, just me."

"Mmm. My brothers – they have beautiful children…"

Jonas looked at his hands, watching the cigarette burning slowly down.

"I awoke in the hospital. They told me I had been in a coma for three weeks. I did not know my family…of course, I knew their names, their faces, the nervous way Paul plays with his rings and the way Eugène smiles when he is distressed, and Rolf…how he laughs when he does not know what to say. I knew my father would be sitting in the chair in the corner of the room, looking at his immaculately polished shoes.

"But I found...found that I no longer knew them, truly knew them. I looked in their faces and saw – nothing. Nothing I was able to understand. It frightened me. To my core," he said, staring at Jonas.

Jonas nodded.

"It was frightening. I realized in a moment my world had changed. I felt separate in a way I never had in my life – I had always been part of Dubay et Fils, part of the Sorbonne, part of that constructed community that was assumed and reassuring. At that moment, I was set adrift and yet I was calm," he said, a gentle smile tugging his lips. "Hugo saw that I was awake. I watched him reach over and touch my leg – and realized I could not feel it."

"Wait a minute –" Jonas said, sitting up after a moment. "Don't tell me you were paralyzed."

"From the waist down."

"Holy shit," Jonas muttered, eyes wide. "What the hell happened to you?"

Dubay took a deep breath.

"Père superieur," the old man interrupted, setting their breakfast on the table. He turned and left them without a word.

"Merci, Monsieur Blanchard, merci," Dubay muttered. He turned back to the window. "What happened is that in that moment, when I found that I was not my body and not my family and not even my mind, everything fell away and all that remained was me...and an overwhelming sense of gratitude. A wave of love and the world opening to me.

"In that moment, I no longer was who I had been. I was stripped bare and filled with joy. Have you seen Bernini's Sainte Therese?" he asked Jonas suddenly, coffee cup paused mid-air.

"Sure. Ecstasy – painful."

Dubay nodded. "I was pulled open," he said quietly, "and where there had been greed I was filled with God and where there had been pride I was filled with God. I felt as though I would burst, or laugh, or sing. I made a decision – unconsciously – in that moment to dedicate my life to God. I did not know at the time what that meant. But I followed my heart," he smiled, "and here I am."

Jonas breathed deeply, his heart pounding. "Wow," he whispered.

"You asked," Dubay laughed.

"Wow."

Dubay took a sip of his lukewarm coffee. Jonas watched Dubay's long, elegant hand, scarred and white. "Thank you."

"For what?"

"For telling me."

"I believe we are even now."

"Guess so."

Jonas crushed out his cigarette and looked out the window at the awakening street. After a few minutes, he said quietly, "I felt that way once, at Sainte Chapelle…the glass was so alive. Well –" he said quickly, looking at Dubay apologetically, "—probably not the same way…"

"Art can be transformative."

Jonas shrugged. "I became a worshipper. A pilgrim."

Dubay sipped his coffee and smiled. "And what had you been?"

"Confused, and... angry I guess. My mom – well," he said, pulling out another cigarette, "Anyway. After Sainte Chapelle, all the stupid shit with my mom just kind of fell away, and I got very clear very fast about what I wanted to do. There was more than the crap I'd been dealing with."

"Why do you repair, and not create?"

"It's not that simple," he said, flicking the unlit cigarette onto the table, narrowly missing his café au lait. "The work that I do–it's creating. It is. I bring the glass back to life, make it whole again. Where there were jagged edges and broken lines, I–I make sense of it all. Make it whole. Do you know what I mean?"

Dubay nodded. "I believe I do," he said, staring at Jonas intently.

Jonas stared at his hands and laughed. "You know, that's the first time I've put it in words – why I do this. I don't think I've even explained it to my friend Steve in that way, and he was there... You priests are tricky, sneaking confessions out of people."

"It is part of our training," Dubay smiled. "We learn it in the first year."

Jonas snorted, picking up the cigarette again and rolling it between his fingers and over his knuckles. "You studied art history, right? At the Sorbonne?"

"Yes–it is a part of any good medievalist's training."

"Is that why you're so interested in this glass?"

"The glass interests me for many reasons. It has intrinsic value –it is deeply beautiful, to my eyes, and vibrates with energy. So it is fascinating to me in that way," Dubay said as Jonas nodded. "It has rhetorical value for our church. It has monetary value for the town. It has monetary value for the diocese. And the research value is incredible."

"That reminds me," Jonas said, finally lighting his cigarette. "What did Marie-Laure find out about the border?"

"Mmm," Dubay muttered, nodding genially to a couple who entered the small café. "The border. Yes, she uncovered a great deal. From what she has learned so far, we believe the artist is local to this area."

"Really? How can you tell?"

"They have left us some clues – landscapes in the region, and strangely, the crest of the Dukes of Nevers. They never struck me as patrons of the arts–that was the realm of the Clunaics. The Dukes were much more interested in political machinations and taking control of the pilgrim roads."

"Art isn't created only for itself. There's always a political or monetary interest there."

"The uses of art are many–but do you not think art is created at first, in the first birth of the idea, for itself?" Dubay asked, taking a bite of his neglected baguette.

"It depends. I mean, look at medieval art–it was created for God, right? Not for the art itself, not for the pleasure the artist took in the work, but as a devotion."

"That is generally true, yes."

"And as time went on–look at the Renaissance. Look at the influence of the patrons on visual art–and even architecture," Jonas said, thumping the table. "Popes and cardinals and the local wealthy merchant getting painted into Giotto's frescoes and ceilings of Titian and built into the capitals at thousands of churches and cathedrals. Art's never created just for itself–there's always some external influence driving the artist."

"In the case of our glass, I think you are right. There is a story beyond the Magdalene... Marie-Laure is attacking the assignment with zest, as you might imagine."

Jonas nodded, stubbing out his newly lit cigarette. "Are you ready to go?" he asked, nodding at Dubay's empty cup. "I really want to get the hands done in the next day or so, so I can start painting her face."

"Do you mind if I come up and see your progress?" Dubay asked, placing a few coins on the table and standing. "I want to take a look at the border again as well."

"Oh sure, sure. Hey, thanks for breakfast, too," Jonas said, putting his hand on Dubay's shoulder. "I really appreciate it."

Dubay smiled. "My pleasure."

Jonas pushed open the front door and Dubay called over his shoulder, "Merci bien, monsieur Blanchard!" The café's owner grunted in reply.

"Ready?" he asked, and at Jonas' nod, led the way up the rue St Etienne. They hiked the steep hill in silence.

As they neared Marie-Laure's house on the corner of rue St Etienne and rue l'Argenterie Jonas smiled.

"What?" Dubay asked, smiling.

"Huh? Nothing," Jonas shrugged, still smiling. "Hey, you know Meredith, right?"

"Sorry?"

"I thought –"

"Yes, I know Meredith," Dubay answered, nodding to a parishioner across the street. "Why?"

"No reason," Jonas shrugged, watching Dubay's now tense back up the street. "We had drinks the other night. She's– interesting."

"That is an apt description," Dubay said. He stopped and turned back to face Jonas. "Did you have a good time?"

"Sure. Yeah. She's great," Jonas said, narrowing his eyes. "Why?"

"Interesting," Dubay said, turning around and leading the way up the street.

They reached no. 23 and Jonas pulled the ornate antique key from his jeans pocket and ushered Dubay through the door into the dark, cool parlor.

Jonas led him up the narrow staircase to the airy studio. "Have you known Meredith a long time or something?" he asked, opening the tall windows.

"Yes. Yes, she… Yes. Quite a long time," Dubay said, leaning over the glass. "This is incredible work, Jonas. What progress!"

Jonas folded his arms and smiled. "Not bad. You know, I was scared of re-painting her face, but now I can't wait to do it. Weird."

Dubay nodded, peering intently at the border. "Oh! Hmm…that is quite interesting. I had not noticed that before…"

"What?"

"See here—a raven, oh—with an open book. It is the symbol for St. Benedict—the monk who regularized the rules for monastic life. Ah, I am one up on Marie-Laure now," he smiled. "But this – this is very interesting. An illuminated manuscript – I had not noticed the border at all before, I had been so intent on the Magdalene, until Marie-Laure pointed it out. Now look – look how rich it is. And an illuminated manuscript, with a scribe. That is very interesting…the detail is incredible."

"It's amazing," Jonas agreed, leaning in closely. "Was it normal for women to work as scribes?"

"No, not generally," Dubay replied, turning to look at him "What makes you think this is a woman?"

"Well–I don't know. Look at her," he said, gesturing at the border. "Yellow hair, looks like it's bound in a braid. And the hands look very delicate. I don't know, it just looks like a woman to me."

Dubay stood straight and smoothed his shirt. "Very intriguing. Very. Well, carry on. I think I need to look in on Marie-Laure and share this with her."

"Good luck," Jonas said, walking Dubay to the staircase. "And–thanks."

"For what?"

"For trusting me."

Dubay grinned. "I will see you soon," he said, and with a brief nod, headed back down the rickety staircase. Jonas watched him down the stairs and turned back to his workshop. He stretched and yawned, reaching up to the ceiling on the tips of his toes. He walked to his worktable and circled it, investigating the glass from every angle, then reached for his paint, but stayed his hand. *Better finish the field beneath her feet first.*

Checking the schedule tacked to the wall, he grabbed a half-eaten Milka candy bar and threw a CD into the stereo. Jonas methodically laid out his tools as the opening notes of "Lark Ascending" swirled through the workshop. *Making it whole.* He grinned and cracked his knuckles.

The sky spread orange and the Coke can ashtray overflowed when Jonas put the finishing touches on the flowing field beneath the Magdalene's feet. With creaking back, he dragged himself to the small shower stall and stood under the scalding water. *This glass is killing me.* He smiled and shook his head. An image floated to the surface as he dried his face in the tattered navy towel–a swirling red dress and the sensation of flying. And suddenly, the urge to see Meredith was overwhelming.

He pulled on a collared shirt–the one loaned by Dubay–and jumped down the stairs and out into the warm late afternoon. He half-walked, half-ran up the narrow street to the cathedral plaza, rolling his sleeves and pushing hands through his wet hair as he went.

He rounded the corner to the rue St Etienne and nearly toppled an old woman in his haste. "Pardon, pardon," he muttered, rushing past. Slowing his pace, he reached the salon and tried the door. Locked. He checked his watch–well past closing time. He rapped on the window and waited, arms folded. He rapped again.

"Nous sommes fermé," a tired voice called from the open window above him.

"It's me," he called up.

A series of small crashes later, Meredith's head poked out the window. "Oh, you, huh? Where've you been?" she asked, smiling.

"Come down and I'll tell you all about it."

"Gimme a minute. I'll be right down."

Jonas nodded and, smiling, pulled out a cigarette. He leaned against the salon's windows and idly watched the exodus of tourists from the cathedral. Five minutes later, after crushing the spent cigarette under his heel, he stepped out into the street. "Are you coming, or what?" he called up. The salon door opened a few moments later, and Meredith emerged. "You always this impatient?" she asked, locking the door.

"Yep," he grinned. "Dinner?"

"It's a bit early. It's only just after 6."

"Drinks?"

"Now you're talking," she nodded. "Let's go over to the terrace at le Dent Creuse," she said, leading the way down the steep, narrow rue St Etienne. "So where have you been?"

"Working my ass off. I got the hair done, and I finished the field beneath her feet today."

"Is that good?"

"Hell yes, it's good," he said. Very good. I might even get the project done early. But–don't tell Dubay that," he laughed.

"I promise," she said flatly.

"Where were you this morning?"

"What? Why?"

"I stopped by–I wanted to…well, I wanted to see you," he said looking up at the window boxes and tall, narrow roofs lining the street. "I wanted to show you the sunrise."

"Oh," she said, watching Jonas.

"So," he continued, looking at her. "Where were you?"

"I didn't realize I had to check in with you."

Jonas stopped. "That's not what I meant."

Meredith turned back and looked at him. After a few moments, she dropped her hands and said quietly, "I was out shooting."

"Cool," he nodded. They stared at each other, unmoving.

"You know, you're kinda maddening," she said, her eyebrows creased.

"It's why you like me."

"You make a lot of assumptions."

"I'm usually right."

She cocked her head and smiled slightly. "Buy me a drink and shut the hell up, will ya?"

Jonas laughed. "Deal," he said, grabbing her hand, and headed back down the street.

The terrace at Le Dent Creuse was already crowded with locals, but they were able to secure a table along the wall, overlooking the north ramparts and the rolling countryside below. A young waiter with coal black hair and a strong air of ennui appeared.

"Oui?" he asked, looking past them.

"Mademoiselle?" Jonas prompted.

"Un kir royale, s'il vous plâit."

"Et un verre de vin rouge–Gevrey-Chambertin, si possible."

The waiter nodded and sauntered away.

Jonas lit a cigarette and blew the smoke out into the golden evening. "So," he said, smiling slightly.

"So," Meredith replied, folding her arms and leaning on the table.

"I hope I didn't scare you the other day."

"When?"

"After dinner at Marie-Laure's."

"Oh," she smiled. "No, you didn't scare me."

"Good."

They sat silently together, watching the crowd ebb and flow across the terrace, Jonas sneaking glances at Meredith. The waiter returned with their drinks and Jonas lifted his glass. "Skål," he said, looking her in the eye.

"À votre sante."

"So what does scare you?" he asked over his wineglass.

"Oh–oh, I don't know," she said setting her glass down. "Not much, really. I've seen too much."

"There's got to be something."

"Well," she said, taking another sip. "Myself, I guess. And fire. Can't stand it. What about you?" she countered quickly.

"Turning into my dad."

"Really? Why?"

"Shallow. Spineless. Just skims across the surface of life."

"I would have thought you'd say your mom."

"Naw," he said, looking out across the countryside. "I made that vow a long time ago."

Meredith nodded and watched Jonas closely. "What else?" she asked quietly.

"Birds. Scare the crap out of me."

"What?" she laughed. "Are you kidding?"

"No way," he said, leaning forward across the small table. "Seriously. They're disgusting. Those nasty flappy wings...iicch," he shuddered, downing the rest of his wine.

Meredith watched him, laughing, and shook her head. She summoned the waiter over to the table with a look over Jonas head.

"Oui?" the waiter drawled.

"Deux plus, s'il vous plâit. La même chose," Meredith sniffed.

The waiter nodded and disappeared into the crowd.

"Do you believe in angels?" Jonas asked, watching Meredith intently.

"No," she replied, looking at him. No, I think God works his good and evil through us. Why bother with intermediaries when he can screw with us directly?"

"But see," he said, pointing at her, "see, that's where I have a problem. I don't think God is a sentient being, if you know what I mean. I mean, yeah, there's a God—because otherwise, how can you explain the world, the universe, the patterns and beauty in nature? But I don't think God is concerned with our little world here, let alone my particular life. God's beyond that – a different level of consciousness. Set us up, let us run."

Meredith swirled the dregs of her drink. "I can't believe that. There's too much good, and evil in the world. There's too many coincidences. And too many things that are horrible and life-changing that you can only believe that God is trying to teach you a lesson."

"I don't buy it."

"How else can you explain when something horrible happens?" she asked, shaking her head. "Like–like when my mom died?"

"Life and death are random. You can't ascribe some higher purpose to it all."

"Then how do you construct meaning in life?"

"Well, that's just the point, right? You have to construct it for yourself. You can't let religion or God tell you what it is or isn't."

"Oh, merci," Meredith said as the waiter dropped off their drinks. "Cheers," she said, taking a sip.

"Cheers," Jonas nodded. *She's beautiful. God, who does she look like?* Jonas shook his head and took a gulp of wine.

"I think the point is," she continued, "until you've been through something really horrible or terrifying, I don't think you've experienced God or the *real* experience of life."

"Oh, I don't agree at all," he replied, blowing smoke up to the sky. "What about something transcendently beautiful or good?"

"I think God expresses his true nature in tragedy. The good stuff is too fleeting," she said.

"Is that why you don't like churches?" he asked quietly.

"One of the many reasons," she replied, watching the crowd.

"Does your distaste extend to church art?"

"No…no, art is the good stuff."

"Good. Then you won't be averse to coming to see the glass tomorrow."

"You assume I'm free," she smiled, cocking her head. He noticed for the first time that her neck was long and white, and suddenly, found that he was obsessed with it.

"Oh, you will be," he grinned. "There are lots of good things in the world. I'll show you." He could almost feel her soft skin under his scarred fingers, swirling figure eights from her chin to her ear.

He spent the next half an hour in a haze, smoking cigarettes and watching in fascination the angles in her face and throat. He nodded absently when she asked him to join her at the studio to finally pick up his photo. The slightly buzzed walk back in the growing twilight was a blur, and when she pushed open the door he followed her through, watching her rifle through a stack of framed pictures. "I know it's here somewhere. I just saw it. It's got to be here somewhere –"

He leaned against the desk and folded his arms, watching her arms flex through her shirt, waiting for a glimpse of her white throat. "Where do you want to go?" he whispered.

She turned around quickly. "What? What do you mean?"

He pushed himself up and rested his hands on her hips. He looked at her for a long minute but said nothing. Increasing the grip on her hips, he repeated the whispered question. "It's not all tragedy, you know. Where do you want to go?"

She looked at him intently, not speaking for long moments. A flush crept up her throat and into her cheeks. "Follow me." She led him up the narrow staircase to her cramped bedroom. She turned and smiled uncertainly. "It's a mess –"

He surprised her with a kiss–rough and quick, leaving her panting slightly. "I don't care," he whispered. He rested one hand on her hip, and wove the other into her hair, pushing curls away from her ear and neck. His lips ghosted along her jaw, soft and reverent, ending in a pattern of small kisses behind her ear. He stood back and looked at her intently, searching her face.

Her eyes fluttered open and she smiled slightly. "Don't you dare stop."

He nipped at her neck, eliciting a soft groan, then pulled her hips toward his, working his hand to the middle of her back, crushing their bodies together. Twirling a curl around his finger, he sucked gently on her earlobe; her fingers gripped convulsively up and down his back. She pressed herself against him; Jonas bit her neck and sucked hard, moaning. Her hand worked its way through his wavy hair, pushing him harder into her neck.

Meredith groaned and pulled his face to hers, resting forehead to forehead. Their breath came in ragged bursts. "Here," she whispered after a moment, turning around and lifting her hair, exposing the back of her neck. He feathered kisses along her neck and swept his scarred fingers along her collarbones, over her breasts. She turned around in his arms and suddenly kissed the corners of his mouth. "My turn," she whispered, pulling him down onto the unmade bed and sitting next to him.

She took his hand and kissed his palm, his wrist, gentle kisses along his arm. She closed her eyes and kissed each fingertip, then laid his hand on her cheek; she seemed to be shivering. He released his breath in a long, low sigh, then reached up and traced the curves of her face, the lines spreading from the corners of her eyes, the soft skin of her lips. He waited there, expectant, the light of the room somehow gathered solely in her face. Then suddenly she captured his finger, slowly drawing it into her mouth. He threw his head back and groaned as she gently sucked. Before his eyes fluttered shut, he thought he saw a smirk curling around his finger. "You are in so much trouble," he whispered huskily, eyes still closed.

She pulled out his finger and kissed his palm again. "You started it," she said, brushing her lips against his ear. He half-laughed, half-moaned and pushed her back onto the bed, holding her hands above her head. "I guess I'd better finish it then," he said, licking her neck.

Hours later, the park below the chapter house was deserted and cool, particularly for a June evening. Jonas wandered between the chestnuts, searching for glimpses of stars between the waving branches, humming quietly to himself and smiling

The Pilgrim Glass

Chapter Sixteen

IT WAS THE HEAT, sticky and inescapable, that threatened to keep her in bed all day. Lazy warm light filtered in from a crack in the curtains and she slowly opened her eyes.

"Jesus Christ, what time is it?" she mumbled, reaching blearily for the alarm clock. "9:32. 9:32?" She let the clock fall from her hand and rolled back onto her side, burying her face in the pillow and smiling. She could still smell him on the sheets, a strange mix of strong tobacco and turpentine and freshly cut grass. She inhaled deeply and lay back, pillowing her head on her arms. *I guess it wasn't a dream.*

She sat up suddenly, rummaged for a t-shirt beneath the bed, and pulled it on as she walked to her small closet. In the back she found a navy sundress and pulled it over her head. Finding one sandal in the closet and one behind the nightstand, she slipped them on and pulled her hair into a ponytail as she ran down the stairs. At her desk, she wrote a hasty note and posted it on the shop window as she hurried out the door.

Vous voudrez bien nous excuser. Nous sommes fermé aujourd'hui.

She hurried down the rue St Pierre, cursing her sandals and smiling secretly to herself. She reached Marie-Laure's ancient house, knocked on the door and waited, watching the crowds of tourists make their way up the hill. After a minute had passed, she knocked again and opened the door. "Marie-Laure?" she called, edging into the foyer. The tall, narrow house was silent, and the hallway dark and cool after the rising muggy heat outdoors.

"Marie-Laure," she half-whispered, peering into the empty parlor. "Hello?" An acrid smell led her to the kitchen, where an untended coffee press sat gurgling and smoking on the stove. "Marie-Laure!" she cried. "Where are you?"

She ran to the back staircase, taking the steps two at a time. Skidding around the corner, she hastily pushed open doors. "Where is she?" she muttered, pushing open the last door on the left.

The room was tall and narrow, its high lancet windows offering a spectacular view of the Place du Champs de Foire and the countryside beyond. The walls were covered floor to ceiling with bookshelves, piled with books three deep, and in the corner, facing the window, a huge cherry wood desk. Marie-Laure lay face down on a pile of papers and leather books.

Meredith rushed to Marie-Laure's side and shook her shoulders. "Marie-Laure. Marie-Laure!" she yelled. After an agonizing moment, Marie-Laure slowly raised her head off her hands and looked in bewilderment at Meredith. "Oh...oh, Mercedes, my dear. I must have overslept. Am I late for class?"

Meredith stood straight and snatched her hand back as if it had been burned. "Marie-Laure, are you ill?" she whispered, lips and throat tight.

Marie-Laure narrowed her eyes. "No, I am quite well," she said, looking around the room. "I - I – oh dear," she said, leaning back in her rickety desk chair. She looked back at Meredith and smiled, bemused. "Oh ma chère, I must be getting quite old. I thought I was back in my office in Paris."

"What happened?" Meredith asked, folding her arms. "Didn't you hear me calling you?"

"Hmm? I'm not sure. I must have been up quite late...I don't remember going to bed at all," she said, smoothing her dress and attempting to tidy her hair. She looked up at Meredith and stayed her hand. "What is wrong, chèrie?"

Meredith stared long at Marie-Laure. "You called me Mercedes," she whispered, her lips hardly moving.

Marie-Laure's hand dropped. "Did I? Mon Dieu, I am getting old," she said, shaking her head. "I am sorry. Maybe I was dreaming of her."

Meredith sighed raggedly and rubbed her arms, now prickled with bumps. "I was worried about you. When you didn't answer –"

Marie-Laure stood and laid a withered hand on Meredith's arm. "I am fine, petite. Quite well. And I am sorry ..." Meredith turned away, but Marie-Laure took her by the elbow and turned her back. "I am sorry."

Meredith shrugged and forced a laugh. "Please, fall asleep in your own bed next time. What was so important that you fell asleep in your office?" she asked, picking up papers from Marie-Laure's desk.

Marie-Laure watched her beadily, then shrugged. "Research for your dear Mr. Flycatcher," she said lightly.

"Well, he's in a lot of trouble when I see him," Meredith said, tossing papers back onto the pile. She sat on the edge of the desk and looked at Marie-Laure. "Please, don't scare me like that again. Where the hell is Guillaume? Why isn't he looking after you?"

"He left for Paris yesterday—didn't I tell you?"

"No."

"He's meeting with his editor, and then visiting with friends. He'll be back in a week. And I have glorious days on end of silence and solitude," she laughed.

"You have to tell me these things! I could look in on you, keep you company."

"Then I wouldn't have silence and solitude, would I?"

Meredith flinched and Marie-Laure wrapped an arm around her shoulders. "Chèrie, I am an old woman, but I can take care of myself. And I am not ready to die yet, so don't concern yourself there. D'accord?"

"But —"

"Besides, you have other, more interesting things to spend your time on," Marie-Laure said, her eyes twinkling.

Meredith grinned, despite herself.

"Yes…"

"Come on, I'll make you some coffee and I'll tell you–well, most of it," Meredith said, standing and moving toward the door.

"Ah, no, I'll make the coffee, dear," Marie-Laure said, patting Meredith's arm and walking past her out the door.

They settled into the parlor, the clean coffee press on a tray between them. "So he showed up, said thank you, and left?" Marie-Laure asked, laughing.

"Yeah, it was a little weird."

"And then?"

"He's…interesting…" Meredith smiled, looking out the window.

"I know that. Have you seen him since?"

"A couple of times. We went to dinner at le Dent Creuse last night…"

"Ah, very romantic."

"I guess. It's strange," she said, sipping the strong black coffee. "He's not one to hold anything back – you know, he's not very subtle. He does things that surprise the hell out of me."

Marie-Laure smiled and nodded.

"And he's got this weird energy under the surface. In–in everything he does," she said, blushing slightly.

"Ahhh...I was wondering when we'd get to that," Marie-Laure laughed.

"I don't know...he...it...amazing... I don't know," Meredith said, smiling and shaking her head. "I feel like I'm 20 again."

"You deserve to be happy."

"Do I? I don't know...I don't know..." Meredith said, holding the coffee cup gently in her hands.

Marie-Laure stifled a yawn behind her hand then smiled at Meredith. "My dear, I am very sorry, but I need to get a bite of breakfast and clean up a bit."

"Oh, shit. I'm so sorry...here, let me clear this away for you," Meredith said, picking up the coffee tray.

"No, no, go on with your day. I'll look after this later. I'm sure you're anxious to see Mr. Flycatcher – "

Meredith stood up straight. "How did you know that's where I was going?"

"An educated guess."

Meredith smiled. "Please, do me a favor and let me know when you're home alone, OK?" She held up a hand as Marie-Laure opened her mouth to protest. "I know you can take care of yourself. I just want to know when I can come by and bore you with my stories, OK?"

Marie-Laure laughed. "Yes, yes, I will let you know. I promise."

"Good. Speaking of Jonas, do you know what number he's at on rue l'Argenterie?"

"Number 23," Marie-Laure replied, walking with Meredith to the front door.

"Thanks. Take care today. I'll call you later, if that's OK?"

"Certainly, certainly."

"Good," Meredith said, kissing Marie-Laure on each cheek. "Talk with you soon." She pulled open the heavy front door, and they were blasted with hot muggy air from the street outside.

"Ugh," Marie-Laure said, wrinkling her nose. "When did the weather change?"

"This morning. Nasty, isn't it?"

"Mmm," she nodded. "Vile. I hope it passes soon. Otherwise I'll be stuck in here for days on end."

"We don't want that. See you soon," Meredith said, squeezing Marie-Laure's hand and turning up to the rue l'Argenterie. As she climbed the narrow cobbled street, the familiar curve of the northern ramparts shimmered in the oven-like heat and her thin sundress grew wet and clingy and uncomfortable.

She rested for a moment on Jonas' doorstep, leaning against the heavy front door and wiping the sweat from her upper lip. Suddenly, music floated from the windows above her, notes hanging in the heavy air and swirling languidly down the narrow lane. She sighed and suddenly felt cooler, standing in the shadow of no. 23. Taking a deep breath, she knocked on the rough door and waited. And waited. She knocked and quickly opened the door, calling "Jonas?" as she walked in.

The front room was surprisingly cool and dark, unfurnished and sterile. Meredith hurried through and followed the music up a narrow, rickety staircase. She paused at the top, in an open room with wide bright windows, Jonas' name replaced by a smile on her lips.

Jonas was bent low over a large table covered with tools and sheets of glass, a cigarette hanging from the corner of his mouth, muttering to himself and conducting with his free hand the soaring violin notes. A welcome breeze stole in, ruffling the papers pinned to the wall. Distracted, Jonas looked up from the glass and grinned widely when he saw her.

"How long have you been standing there?" he asked, standing, pulling the cigarette from his mouth and stretching his neck.

"Long enough."

"So."

"So." She folded her arms and smiled. He took a drag and leaned against the worktable. "What are you listening to?" she asked at last.

"Vaughn Williams."

"It's beautiful," she said quietly.

Jonas nodded. "I'm glad you stopped by," he said, flicking ash into a plastic cup.

"Yeah?"

"Yeah."

"Good," she smiled, turning to look out the window at the sweltering morning.

"Don't move!" he said suddenly, crushing out his cigarette and rushing around to the opposite side of his worktable.

"What?" she laughed, turning to face him.

"Don't *move*!" he said urgently. "Please?"

"No one talks to me like that," she said, not moving.

Jonas shoved tools and supplies out of his way, and after a minute of furious searching, found a sketchpad buried deep under a pile of paper and sheets of glass. He grabbed a pencil and ran back around to Meredith. "Now, just stay exactly how you are…" he whispered, leaning against the worktable again and starting to sketch.

The room was filled with the sound of swirling violins and the scratching of pencil on paper. Suddenly, he stopped. "No, that's not right…" He dropped the pad on the floor and paced back and forth in front of Meredith, looking at her from all angles.

"What —"

"Shhh."

"Don't you shush me," she gritted, narrowing her eyes and yet not moving her head.

"Here, like this," he whispered, placing his hands on either side of her face and moving it slightly up and to the left. His hands lingered on her cheeks and he smiled. "Just like this." Jonas pulled the band out of her hair and arranged it so it fell behind her shoulders and down her back. He kissed her swiftly on the neck and returned to his sketch pad.

Minutes later, Meredith groaned. "Are you done yet?" she whispered out of the corner of her mouth. "This is killing me."

"Just about–just about–yeah, done."

Meredith slumped and sighed deeply. "This had better be worth it," she said, reaching over and taking the sketchpad from Jonas' hands. "Wow, that's – that's amazing. Do I always look that angry?" she asked, wide-eyed.

Jonas laughed. "You don't look angry. You look haughty."

"Haughty?"

"Yeah."

"Huh," she said, peering intently at the sketch.

Jonas disappeared into his bedroom and returned with a new pack of Gitanes.

"You're really good, you know," Meredith said, nodding at the sketch.

"I guess," he replied, tossing the cigarettes on the table and tracing her bare arms with the tips of his fingers. Meredith shivered. "You want to see –" Jonas began.

"Shhh," Meredith said, leaning in and kissing him, chaste kisses at the corners of his mouth, then deep and sultry. She pulled back; Jonas' eyelids fluttered, his mouth open and expectant. "So," she said brightly, stepping back and looking around the room, "what are you working on?"

Jonas' eyes snapped open and he smirked. "Like that, huh?"

Meredith smiled and moved around to the other side of the worktable. The cross-breeze had died down, and the room grew warm and sticky.

"Well," he said, joining her. "I've just about finished her hands and I'm about to start painting her face—and that scares the crap out of me."

"Why?"

"It's a huge deal, artistically, and I guess for Dubay. Finding a glass this complete and advanced is pretty fucking amazing. And you know, the Magdalene is the center of it all, and if her face isn't right...I don't want to disappoint him," he said.

Meredith looked askance at him but smiled and said, "But I thought you were the world-famous Jonas Flycatcher."

"Shut up," he smiled. "Anyway, I have a pretty good sketch to work from now, so that will help."

Meredith paled and turned to look at him. Not—not what you just did?"

"Yeah, of course," he said, shrugging.

Meredith shook her head slowly. "I don't know..."

"Why not?" he asked, lighting a cigarette.

The final notes of the piece floated away out the windows, and the bright room was silent.

"I just feel uncomfortable with it," she said, rubbing her bare arms.

"Well, don't pass judgment until you've at least seen it," he said, putting the cigarette between his lips and pushing papers away to reveal the small, bright stained glass.

The north-facing studio was not filled with light, and yet the glass shimmered with its own, pulsing in sapphire and ruby and sharp emerald. Meredith's breath hitched and she began to shiver. *Oh my God.*

Jonas smiled and folded his arms. "What do you think?" he mumbled behind his cigarette. "Nice color, eh?"

Meredith leaned in closer and felt as though she might be tipped right into the glass, falling through and fracturing into a thousand pieces. The riot of color made her head swim and she swayed slightly.

"Hey–you OK?" Jonas asked, resting his hand on her back.

She nodded.

"Pretty cool, yeah? Obviously, that's the Magdalene," he said, dropping the half-smoked cigarette in an empty Coke can. "You can tell because she's usually shown with the long golden hair and the–"

"Unguent jar," she whispered.

"Yeah," he said, standing back up. "How did you know?"

Meredith shrugged but did not look up. "I don't know."

"Yeah...so that's the unguent jar. I've got a lot done, but her face is a huge challenge. That's going to take me a while and I've got ten days to finish everything. That's why the sketch is so important."

She nodded absently and stared with narrowed eyes at the ghosted face of the Magdalene. *My face...my face...* She shivered again.

"...and the border—that's what Marie-Laure's been doing research on."

"See, there's a vineyard..."

"I've seen that before," she said, a shiver of recognition prickling her arms and her spine.

"What?"

"The vineyard scene. In-in my mom's genealogy notes."

"What? That's weird. But – this was only found a month ago–"

Meredith trembled but said nothing.

Jonas looked at her sideways and continued. "And here's a scribe with an illuminated manuscript—a woman, I think—and they think this is the crest of some Duke or other."

"Nevers," she said, swaying slightly.

"What?" he said, standing her up and turning her to face him. "Are you OK?"

"The Dukes of Nevers..." A wave of profound cold, grey and icy, washed over her.

I awake with a start to find the forest has grown dark about me. The pilgrim group has gone, and I am left alone. In my haste to gather my belongings and move on, the offering slips from my lap and a ruby piece in the corner shatters. I quickly rewrap the offering and place it in my satchel. I pick up the broken piece, knowing I cannot make any repairs until I reach Vèzelay. It shall be a reminder that I must be vigilant.

I hurry toward the Ouche, hoping to find an easy crossing. As I pick my way along the bank, I hear rustling in the brush behind me. I have not heard of wolves in this area for many years.

Two men emerge on foot from the forest, bearing the insignia of the Dukes of Nevers. I am momentarily relieved; I believed it was Pons' minion again, sent to take me to Cluny.

"Please, where is the best crossing of this river?" I ask them.

They look at my pilgrim's staff and the badge of notre dame on my cloak and exchange looks. "Where is your party?" the tall one asks.

"Just beyond," I motion across the river, hoping they believe me, hoping the saints will forgive this lie.

They smile. "Allow us to assist you," the smaller one says with a smirk, as he reaches to grope my breasts. I scream, and soon they are trying to throw me on the ground. The taller one takes my satchel and, after taking a bite of my loaf of bread, moves to unwrap the offering.

May the good Lord and the saints in Heaven forgive and protect me. The smaller one throws me on the ground and crouches on top of me, working to rip the top of my robes. A fearsome rage comes over me as I see the taller one taking out the offering and laughing. I attempt to throw the smaller one off, but he merely laughs and calls his fellow over. "Hold her arms," he mutters, finally ripping my robe apart, and reaching back to pull up my skirts.

Before his partner can pin my arms, I slash as hard as the strength of my arm will allow with the large ruby shard. The smaller one yells with pain. I cut his cheek deeply and he is bleeding The taller one slaps me across the face, but I yell in anger and fear and slash wildly with the shard. Suddenly the taller one is very quiet. I look up to find that his throat is split. The smaller one jumps off of me and stands back, eyes wide. I struggle to my feet and we look at each other for a long moment. He leans down to take the offering. "This will be payment for his life," he says with a grim smile. I scream and push him away, but he fights back and again, the rage overpowers me and he too is lying crumpled on the ground.

I fall to my knees and cry and pray to the saints and notre dame and our dear Lord for forgiveness until the sun rises again and I pass out from exhaustion.

A feathering of red and yellow swept before her eyes.

"I killed her! I killed her!" Meredith said sitting up, shaking her head, arms flailing wildly.

"What?" Jonas asked urgently.

"I mean," Meredith whispered, "I mean...she killed him." She groaned with nausea, and lay back down. She found she was lying in Jonas' lap; he leaned over her and swept the hair off her forehead.

"What are you talking about? What the hell happened?" he asked, fanning her fevered face.

She closed her eyes and sighed.

"Meredith?" he asked, shaking her slightly. "Jesus Christ, what the hell is wrong with you?"

"I don't know. I..." she shivered.

"Are you sick? Is it the heat?"

"How did I get on the floor?" she asked without opening her eyes.

"One second we were talking about the border, and the next you were kind of swaying. You fainted or something, and I caught you and laid you down here."

"How long was I out?"

"A few minutes. You scared the crap out of me," he said, starting to shake. "I–I don't have a phone, so I couldn't call a doctor, but I didn't want to leave you here so I just sat here with you until you woke up," he said, panic rising in his voice. "And you were talking, so I knew you were still conscious, at some level."

Meredith's eyes snapped open. "What did I say?"

"Something about crossing a river, and then you–you screamed," he said. "Screamed like hell, actually," he muttered. "I thought you were going to hurt yourself. What the hell is going on?"

Jesus Christ. What is going on?

Sitting up, she looked at him and tears started in her eyes. "I've been having these–dream things...I don't know what –"

"Hello? Jonas?" Marie-Laure's voice floated up to the studio from the bottom of the staircase. "Are you there?"

Meredith's eyes widened. "Don't tell her what happened," she hissed.

"What?"

"Please—please, just don't tell her what happened, OK? She's—she's got enough to worry about," she said, standing abruptly and swaying. Jonas stood and steadied her. "I want you to promise me you won't say anything," she whispered.

"But —huh? What the hell is going on?"

"Just promise," she said, grabbing his hand and squeezing tight.

Jonas looked at her, and then past her at the shadowed stairwell. "Why?"

"Please," she pleaded, turning his face to hers. "Please."

"I —" he said quietly.

Meredith collapsed into him. "Thank you," she mumbled into his chest.

"Oh! My dears, I am sorry," Marie-Laure said, smiling from the top of the staircase. "I just wanted to give Jonas an update on the research—but I can come back another time—"

"It's OK, I was just leaving," Meredith said, stepping away from Jonas and pulling her hair back into a ponytail. "Thank you," she said, squeezing Jonas' hand. "I'll call you later, Marie-Laure," she said, kissing her on the cheek and hurrying to the stairs.

"But —" Jonas said, holding his hand out to her.

"I'll see you later," she repeated, and hurried down the worn staircase and back into the cool parlor.

She could hear their muffled voices above and with a small sob, hurried out through the door into the oppressive heat. She ran up the street, toward the cathedral, clenching her fists and swearing under her breath. *What the hell what the hell what is wrong with me I'm losing it I knew it was too good to last goddamn it what an idiot how am I going to face him again he must think I'm psycho maybe I am why did I come back here...* "God damn it!" she exploded, bumping into a confused and apologetic tourist in the cathedral plaza. "Pardon," she muttered and ran down the rue St Etienne. After fumbling with her key, she pushed open the door and was finally safe behind the glass of her shop.

The cooler air prickled the sweat on her skin and beneath her hair and she shivered. "Leave me alone," she whispered, collapsing against her desk and rubbing her damp arms. "Get–out–of–my–head," she sobbed, pounding the desk with her fists.

Pictures. The damn pictures. She stood suddenly and bolted up the stairs to her small bedroom. Pulling off bedclothes, pushing over her nightstand, crawling on the floor, Meredith gathered the photos of the cathedral, the swirling smoky patterns at the edges still identical, still maddening. The smell of developing fluid from the darkroom pervaded the room, thick and close.

Meredith sat cross-legged on the floor, spreading the photos out in front of her. She grabbed the loupe from under the bed and grabbed one photo after the next, searching. *Come on. Come on. There has to be something. Come on I'm not crazy. I'm not* "I'm not!" she groaned, crumpling the last photo in her hand. *I am crazy.* She threw the crumpled photo with all her strength at the framed photo standing on the still-upright nightstand. The frame crashed to the floor. "I'm sorry," Meredith sobbed.

Chapter Seventeen

JONAS LOOKED PAST MARIE-LAURE, listening to Meredith's footsteps echoing away. The room had become oppressively still; the sticky heat crept in through the open windows, and sweat beaded on his forehead and the back of his neck.

"Why did she run away in such a hurry?" Marie-Laure asked, dropping her papers and folders on the work table.

"She—had some things to do down at her shop. Bookkeeping or something, I think," Jonas lied, watching the staircase and rolling a cigarette back and forth between his fingers. The heavy front door closed below, and Jonas turned to Marie-Laure. "What's up?" he asked tensely, tossing the cigarette on the table and avoiding her gaze.

"I want to share some more research results with you—if you have time, that is," she replied, watching him intently.

"Yeah, sure, sure," he said, walking to the windows and sticking his head out. He looked up and down the street, empty save for a tabby cat, skittering from shady doorstep to shady doorstep in her progress down the bright hot street.

"I can come another time, if you would like," she said.

Jonas shook his head and pulled back into the studio. "No, you're here, let's talk now," he said, retrieving the cigarette from the clutter on the worktable and lighting it. "So, what do you have?"

"Ah, I could ask you the same thing," she smiled, picking up the sketch of Meredith from the table. "This is absolutely lovely," she breathed. "Did you just do it?"

"Yeah," Jonas shrugged. "I needed a model for the Magdalene's face."

"An interesting choice," she said, fanning her face with one of her file folders. "How does she feel about being the model for your glass?" Marie-Laure settled onto the spindly wooden chair near the work table and folded her hands in her lap.

"Fine, I guess," he shrugged, leaning against the table.

"I did not realize you were such a fine artist."

"Repairing stained glass is an art," he bristled, dropping his cigarette into the soda can.

"Yes, yes, I know," she said, patting his hand. "What I meant is that I did not know you also had talent in sketching and drawing. This is lovely. It looks so much like...like Mercedes..." she whispered.

"Who?"

"Hmmm?" Marie-Laure said, looking up at Jonas. "Oh, it is

nothing mon chèr," she said. "I have learned some very interesting things about your glass there," she said, reluctantly dropping the sketch on the table. Her hands shook slightly.

She stood and gestured at the glass. "Here is St. Bernard, which is not surprising, given his sermon on the Second Crusade here. What is more interesting is this here," she said, pointing to the border along the top. "A view of the monastery at Cluny, in its earliest state. And here—and this is strange—sinners writhing in extraordinary pain and anguish." Marie-Laure whispered, her hands rigid and shaking above the colorful swirl of agony.

"You OK?" Jonas asked, looking from the glass to her face.

She shook her head and smiled. "Yes, yes, of course. Do you not feel that—ah, never mind. Taken as a whole," she resumed, "the border is quite disjointed. It will take me a few days to put it all together. It seems to be a journey, of sorts…But what it is trying to tell us, I…I…pardon, je fais mal," she said, sitting down suddenly on the low wooden chair. She took shallow, gasping breaths and closed her eyes.

Jonas looked up quickly and turned to her, placing a tentative hand on her shoulder. "What's going on? Are you OK?"

Marie-Laure smiled weakly, though her eyes remained closed. "Yes, yes," she nodded. "I am fine. It must be…the heat. It is not good for old women like me."

"You look like crap," he said, kneeling by her side. "Wait here—don't move," he admonished, hurrying into the bathroom. He looked in the mirror as he filled a small tumbler from the faucet. *What is going on here?.*

He shook his head and returned to Marie-Laure. "Drink this," he commanded, handing her the tumbler of water. She set the glass on the floor and stood shakily.

"I am fine, mon chèr," she said, patting him on the shoulder.

"But–"

"Fine. I must have been up too late last night working on the research. I shall go home and perhaps take a bit of a nap," she said, walking slowly towards the staircase. "Yes, I think a nap is in order. I will start work this afternoon. And this heat...May I stop by tomorrow to give you an update? It is quite fascinating, this glass...enchanting... It will take you over if you are not careful. Yes, I shall take a nap and will see you–did I say tomorrow? Yes, yes, tomorrow. À demain mon chèr," she waved, and disappeared slowly down the staircase.

Jonas stood next to the work table, eyebrows knitted and mouth hanging open. "See ya," he whispered as the front door below closed. "What a weird fucking morning," he muttered, shaking his head and returning to the glass. *I should go check on her...*

An hour later, he put aside his schedule when the sound of his growling stomach drowned out the melody of the glass. *Lunch. Cigarettes.* He stood straight and yawned hugely, spreading his arms wide, stretching to his fingertips. *And I better go check on her.*

Ten minutes later, he was crossing the cathedral plaza, evading weary pilgrims, wheezing and sweaty, miserable heaps clutching their guidebooks and shading their eyes from the burning sun. He headed down the sweltering street, following the sun now westering from its height.

He reached Meredith's salon and found the door locked. *Nous sommes fermé aujourd'hui.* He knocked on the door and waited. He knocked again.

"Nous sommes fermé!" a weary voice called from the window above. "It means 'closed'."

"It's me," Jonas called up. "Can you come down?"

"Can you go away?"

"No." Jonas nodded at the tourists trudging by and looked back up at the window. "Are you OK?"

"I don't know."

"Can I come up?"

After a moment's silence, Meredith replied. "Yes. Hang on a second." She stuck her head out the window. "Watch your head," she said, tossing a key down to him. "Lock the door behind you."

Jonas opened the door and pushed through into the salon, locking the door behind him. He lingered, drawn to the beautiful and stark photos lining the wall, struck suddenly by a painful sense of loneliness. The webs of barren trees and stark, empty streetscapes pulled him on, lost for a moment in the quiet dark.

He jumped suddenly, a knock at the door breaking the reverent silence. A pair of tourists stood at the door, expectantly jiggling the handle. "Oh for Christ's sake," he muttered, stalking to the entryway. "Nous sommes fermé," he said loudly. "Fermé. Closed. Not open." They shook their heads without comprehension and tried the door again. "Closed!" he shouted, pointing at Meredith's hastily penned sign. They remained standing at the door, panting in the heat. Jonas shrugged his shoulders and turned away, taking the stairs to Meredith's rooms two at a time.

She sat cross-legged in her navy sundress on the unmade bed, face blotchy and red, curls straying willfully from her ponytail. "What took you so long?" she asked.

Jonas sat next to her on the small bed. "What happened?"

"When?" she asked, eyes darting around the room.

He looked at her intently. "This morning. At my place. You know, when you passed out and scared the shit out of me?"

"I'm fine," she said, eyes closed.

"Don't lie to me. You passed out. Tell me what the hell is going on."

Meredith's eyes snapped open and she stood quickly. "I don't answer to you, so back the hell off!"

"I *know* you're not answerable to me. That's not what – wait a second. How the hell did this suddenly become about me? Listen. You freaking passed out in the middle of my studio! You scared me."

"Yeah, well… I scared myself."

"So why don't you want Marie-Laure to know?"

"I just don't," she replied, standing and leaning against the bedroom door.

"Don't give me that crap. Why don't you want her to know?" he asked, standing up and folding his arms.

Meredith folded her arms and scowled.

"Fine," Jonas said, clenching his jaw. "Are you going to tell me what happened or what?" he asked, his voice rising.

"Listen," Meredith growled. "I don't know who the hell you think you are. Don't you fucking interrogate me!" she yelled, pushing him away and turning her back on him.

"What are you going to do, hit me with a bottle?" he yelled, his face purpling with rage.

Meredith turned around and stared at him. "What?"

Jonas narrowed his eyes, a curse on his lips, then held his hands up. "Nothing. I'll see you 'round," he said, heading for the stairs. He was halfway down when he heard Meredith's voice, small and shaking.

"Jonas. Jonas, don't go. Please."

He paused.

"Please?"

He gripped the handrail, shaking his head.

"Jonas?"

He ran back up the steps and rounding the corner, came face to face again with Meredith. "What the hell is your problem?" he breathed. "No one touches me like that. Ever. *Ever.* Get it?"

She nodded and collapsed on the bed. "I'm sorry," she said, leaning her elbows on knees and burying her head in her hands. "I'm sorry."

He folded his arms and stood over her. "What is going on?"

"Noth-"

"Stop," he said, looking down at the back of Meredith's head. "Just. Tell. Me. I want to fix-I want to help you."

"I can't explain it," she mumbled, shaking her head.

"Are you sick?"

"No."

"Are you high?"

Meredith snorted. "No."

"Then what the hell is wrong with you?"

"–punished."

"What?"

She looked up suddenly, a strange smile curling her lips, her eyes glassy and remote. "We all have paths to trod."

"Huh?" he said, squinting his eyes.

"And some paths are plagued by demons. And some must carry their chains before them. And some," she said her eyes growing wide, "will die unshriven."

Jonas stepped back. "What are you talking about?" he whispered, shivering.

Meredith looked up and shook her head. "What? I just told you I'm not high. Did I mumble or something?"

"No," he said, rubbing his bare arms, pimpled with gooseflesh despite the heavy heat. "Do you know what you just said?"

"Yes…I think so," she said, looking at him askance. "You asked me if I was high and I said 'no'."

"Yeah. But after that. Something about carrying chains and dying unshriven, whatever that means."

"No I didn't."

"Look, I'm not going to argue with you about it. Are you blacking out?"

"I'm not–"

"Enough, Goddamnit!" he yelled. "Are you on some kind of medication?"

"No."

"Did you hit your head? Do you have a concussion or something?"

"I don't know," she murmured, looking at the floor.

He folded his arms. "You should see a doctor."

"No," she said vehemently, swinging her feet to the floor. "Shit!" she gasped, grabbing her foot.

"What?"

"It's nothing," she grumbled, hobbling away into the bathroom.

Jonas leaned over and looked down. Scattered half under the bed, shards of glass littered the floor. "Do you have a broom or something around here? You must have stepped on a piece of glass."

"Yeah, downstairs somewhere. Don't bother. I'll get it," she muttered from the bathroom.

He grabbed a nearby piece of paper and swept the shards onto it with his hands. "No, I got it." He walked to the workshop and shook the pieces into a trash basket. Wandering back to the bedroom, he turned the photo over–a street scene, worm's eye view, the cathedral in sharp relief. Wispy shadows crowding the edges of the scene. "Where did you take this?"

"What?" she asked, sticking her head out the bathroom door.

"This," he said, showing her the photo.

"Where did you get that?" she asked sharply.

"Under your bed."

"What were you doing down there?"

"Cleaning up the glass," Jonas said, narrowing his eyes. "Thirty seconds ago? What the hell is wrong with you?"

"Nothing," she said, snatching the photo from his hands and shoving it back under the bed.

"OK, I'm just gonna go," Jonas said, moving toward the staircase. "I'll see you later."

"Jonas, I'm–shit, don't go –" she pleaded, grabbing his arm.

"I'll see you later," he repeated, shaking off her hand. *God, not her too. I can't do this again.*

He headed down through the cool salon and out into the oppressive heat of the street. He leaned against the glass door, running his hands through his hair and unclenching his teeth. He trudged back up the steep street, in the direction of the small *tabac* and a pack of Gitanes.

He threw the pack of cigarettes on his worktable half an hour later, lighting a new cigarette with the dying embers of the last. He folded his arms and leaned against the table, cigarette dangling from his lips

He picked at a ragged hangnail and narrowed his eyes, looking at the schedule tacked to the opposite wall. *Ten days left...Jesus Christ, what have I been doing?* He circled around to look at the glass; he stopped and held the cigarette behind him, between thumb and forefinger, and leaned in closely to look at the Magdalene's faded face. "Shit," he muttered.

The sky outside the broad north windows had gone from burning white to deep pink by the time he finally stretched and cracked his neck. The paint mixing had gone well, but he'd stood for nearly a half an hour, brush in hand, poised over the glass, unable to make the first stroke. He'd finally gritted his teeth and gently begun the outline of the Magdalene's lips. Now, as he stood watching his normally empty street fill with locals yearning for the cooler air beyond the ramparts, the lips were nearly complete. He flicked another spent cigarette out the window.

He awoke in the dark of the night and walked slowly to the bright studio, the moon waxing to its full and shimmering in the still-sultry heat. He stretched and leaned out into the darkness, drinking in the silence, thick and heady.

A flickering light caught his eye and he turned quickly, head spinning. Ruby light glimmered from the table, shattering into a thousand droplets of light. He rushed over and gathered the light in his hands, grasping it to his chest. He heard a voice mumbling, chanting, desperate and melodious. He looked down and saw the

Magdalene speaking words he could see, but not understand, the tongue foreign to his lips. It was as the soughing of trees in the cool blue evening.

He let fly the light and grasped the glass, bringing the Magdalene's face to his. "What are you saying? What are you saying?" he pleaded. His eyes refocused and he looked through, rather than at, the glass. In the distance, he saw an explosion of glass and red flames. The smoke overwhelmed him, burning his eyes and choking his lungs. He dropped the glass and it fractured irregularly, a shard of ruby the size of a dagger slipping to the floor.

Jonas awoke coughing, hands gripping the sheets. He squinted at the ceiling and caught his breath. A sudden wave of fear gripped him, constricting his throat. He leaped out of bed in the half-dark and ran into the studio. The glass was quiet and gently glimmering in the early dawn. Jonas sighed and leaned against the worktable. "I'm losing it," he muttered. "We're all crazy." He shuffled back to the tiny bedroom and threw himself onto the bed. He curled the sheets between his legs and was asleep again within moments.

Chapter Eighteen

THE EARLY DAWN was grey and flat; the cloudless sky promised another sweltering day. And after a still, sleepless night, Meredith stood under Jonas' window, fidgeting with a film canister, turning it over and over in her hands and squinting to see any movement in his studio.

She paced back and forth, muttering under her breath. "I have to tell him. I have to tell him. I have to tell him." She stopped pacing and looked back up at the empty window. *I can't tell him. He'll know I'm crazy.*

She shook her head and picked up the photo bag sitting on Jonas' doorstep, rummaging in it for an unused roll of film. *Shit. I am crazy.* She shivered and loaded the camera with shaking hands.

Hours later the sun rose blinding behind the cathedral. Meredith continued to shoot, blowing through rolls of film. She shot wide sweeping overviews, minutely detailed segments of the tympanum, the blood-red doors, until the sun blazed over the

Tour St Michel. She walked the narrow alley on the north side of the church, skirting the graveyard and the ghosts of monks and penitents and sinners. She shot the sturdy buttresses and soaring choir reaching toward the Morvan, roll after roll, switching lenses and f-stops in a fever, alone with the cathedral at mid-day in the intense heat.

As she looked through the viewfinder and focused on the chapter house, Dubay emerged from a side door, silver hair shimmering in the morning light, heading toward his gardens. "Shit," she muttered. She moved to lower her camera and escape around the choir, but a shape caught her eye and she looked again through the viewfinder.

A woman walked at Dubay's side, dark-haired and graceful. "What–" Meredith lowered her camera. "No," she breathed, and the woman was gone. Meredith rubbed her eyes and looked back to see only Dubay striding along the path, long hands clasped behind his back. She brought the camera back to her eye and watched the woman, still at Dubay's side, look over her shoulder, smiling. "No–" Meredith's vision clouded and a wave of nausea threatened to knock her from her feet.

She lowered the camera and struggled to keep Dubay in sight, disappearing not into his sunlit cloister gardens, but into a haze of hot black smoke and violently shattering glass. A woman's scream, somehow familiar, ripped through the quiet of the empty park, echoing in Meredith's head. Meredith dropped to her knees, clutching at her chest and sobbing. "Forgive me…forgive me…"

"Forgive me. Forgive me." It has been my chant, whispered in my heart only, as I pick my way through the dense wood. Their bodies were difficult to bury. I stumbled on, first trying to whisper my sinner's sacramentum exeuntium *over their unshriven bodies, but no sound would come. This is the first of my punishments. I do not think it will be the last.*

I gathered my satchel and the broken offering, and have now reached town walls. How many days it has been, I cannot tell. Perhaps three, four, I do not know. I have been alone in the wilderness, this pilgrim's route deserted, the heat of the day and cold of the night biting my hands and feet. It is as the Lord wills and the saints decree, yet I have no more bread and I am hungry

I crossed the Ouche and the Arroux, past Semur and Flavigny, my feet rent and bloodied like my hand. I heard traders on the road beyond the forest's fence say this is Arnay le Duc. Blessed be St. Christophe, and St. Fréderic, and Holy Margaret.

My sleep is broken and my dreams dark, but not less than the visions of my waking days. Perhaps my brother did not know what fate he resigned me to on the morning he made the agreement with the Cluny monk. Perhaps my brother did not know what fate I saved him from. I was one too many in the household after father died, and the arrangement was easy. A small square of land near the river and vines from which to grow a living, in exchange for my body, my hands, my life.

I have grown accustomed to my solitude. The messenger always prepared me for the Abbot's visits, a grace I thank the Magdalene for. Abbot Pons indulged my interest in illumination and has brought texts and jewels. I endure his whims and oppressive passions.

The messenger tells me the monks grow weary of Pons' splendour. Is he an Abbot or a baron, they ask. A finger of holy St. Stephen and the friendship of Pope Calixtus will not be enough to protect him. I can see the messenger laughing, and I laugh with him. May the saints preserve me. May the Abbot be distracted until I reach my ending.

I unwrap the offering and shudder. He brought me what I needed for the glass, under the guise of relaying the Abbot's messages of affection and rendez-vous. Yet he too demanded his price.

Heavenly Magdalene. My offering is too base. Yet I must lay it at your feet. My heart and very mind are fevered with it, now more than ever. I have sinned, I have sinned, I have sinned. The enemy is ever at the gates of my heart.

The sun is hot and bright this morning, yet I wrap my dark pilgrim's cloak close about. The pilgrim's path now meets with the road; I remain in the shadow of the wood. Each step has become a burden of pain and yet I see your shining hair in the rays of the sun in the forest and continue on. The road climbs and my heart swells, for below is a valley crossed with clear streams and a shimmering lake. Just beyond will be Saulieu, and then the blessed hill of Vèzelay.

What food the Duke's men left me is gone. I now have the holy Magdalene alone to sustain me, and the clear, cool water of the Cousin. I follow its wandering course, away from the crowded road, until it meets with the wide Cure. My wanderings seem a lifetime, yet it has been only days by my count of the sun. I lean on my staff and watch the water slip away westward.

The sun has disappeared behind a wooded rise and I hear the sounds of the road, rejoining the river's bank just beyond. I must make haste to find shelter in the forest off the road before the darkness overtakes me once again. Rounding the bend of the river at the hill, the sun reappears for a moment before sinking behind a hill. I step onto the road and look in amaze. At last. Blessed Holy St. Christopher, I will make offerings in your name every year on this day, and thrice more and thrice again.

The great cathedral. The holy hill of Vézela.y Laudate Dominum.

I am pushed off the road by a merchant, thoughtless in his haste to pay the Duke's toll and reach the city walls before nightfall. I remember myself and pull the cloak close about my face, as to remain unseen, unrecognized. Now is my road truly fraught with danger.

I walk at the edge of the road, the dirt still warm from the burning day. In the distance, I hear the rattling of chains. Prisoners, released from their bondage, bringing offerings of their own. The road is littered with the sick and the weary who, like me, cannot make the city walls this night. It is littered with the dead who could not make their offerings and beg for miracles.

"Please, whose feast do we celebrate today?" I hear a fellow pilgrim ask a passing monk.

"Ste. Margaret."

The Vigil of the Magdalene is a sunrise hence. May the holy saints and blessed Magdalene forgive me my sins.

Meredith shielded her eyes against the burning sun and groaned. She lay on the gravel path at the edge of the cathedral park, skirting the ancient foundations of the original abbey and overlooking the winding Cure river below. *Jesus Christ, what time is it?* She sat up groggily and looked across the wide river valley. Dark shapes seemed to move along the river bank; she gasped and scrambled to her feet. She spun around, searching the ground around her. *Where's my Goddamn camera?*

She stumbled up the path, tripping over gnarled roots and slicing open her feet. "What-?" *Where are my shoes?* Her camera and bag were piled near the chapter house; her shoes were nowhere to be found. She gathered her equipment and stumbled back to the edge of the empty park, straining her eyes to find the pilgrims gathering at the riverside. Holding her breath, she twisted on a telephoto lens and searched the swaying stretch of silver.

"Where is she?" she muttered, lowering the camera and wiping the sweat from her forehead with the back of her hand. She dropped her hand suddenly and groaned. *What the hell am I saying?* Slowly, she repacked her equipment and limped on the cool grass beside the graveled path toward Dubay's gardens. "Develop these photos..." she muttered. "Pack my things, call Air France. Marie-Laure can work it out with the landlord. See Jonas—no."

She reached the weathered gate and stopped short with the remembrance of the vision of the young woman with curling dark hair. She pulled out her camera and attached a lens. Warm sandstone. Trailing roses. Cirrus clouds. Chestnuts. Warm sandstone. Trailing roses. Cirrus clouds. Blue sky. Hot sun. She pulled the camera away and slumped against the wall. "I have to get out of here," she whispered, shaking her head.

Meredith again repacked her camera equipment and made her slow way back across the baking cathedral plaza, the pain from her bare and bruised feet making her head swim. Keeping her head down, she passed small groups of tourists and locals, huddling under black umbrellas and the meager shadows of midday.

Slamming the door to her studio, she hobbled up the stairs to her bedroom, still with the heavy heat. She crossed to the bathroom and turned on cool water, filling her tub, discarding equipment and clothing as she moved around the small space. Meredith sat on the edge in her underwear and immersed her feet in the cool water, sighing. *Train station...Everything should fit in the backpack and camera bag. Or maybe I should just leave that here. Leave it all here. Start over again. Always starting over.*

Minutes later, she had grudgingly abandoned the bath, bandaged her feet, and began to process the photos. "Twenty rolls? Jesus Christ, is that even possible?" she muttered. She developed the film, and while waiting for the negatives to dry, she rummaged through her closet, throwing clothes into a pile in the middle of the floor. "Sandals, sandals," she muttered, digging through the pile on the floor of the closet.

She gave up and lay flat next to her bed, pulling from under it bras and t-shirts, old newspapers and half-read books–and a photo of a smiling young woman with curling dark hair and a man with piercing blue eyes. She turned it face down and lay still for nearly an hour, her head resting on her folded hands.

The light creeping through the chink in the drapes was glancing and oblique by the time she sat up, a headache piercing behind her eyes. The timer went off in the darkroom and she dragged herself to her feet, rubbing her temples. She opened the door and pulled the negatives from the clips, cutting them and making scores of contact sheets.

Church Church. Church. Normal. Normal. Normal. Tower Buttresses. She's not here. She's not here. Meredith squeezed her eyes shut, the world gone red, and gulped steadying breaths. She opened her eyes and peered closely at the contact sheet? *When did I take this one?*

She pulled the still-wet sheet from the line and stepped out into her bedroom. She held the image in front of her and shivered. A view of the chapter house, yet somehow–transparent. Flames licking the sky. Cloudy smoke around the edges.

"I'm outta here," she muttered, dropping the photo and grabbing a bag from the top shelf of the closet. A knock at the door stayed her hand.

She dropped onto the bed, clutching the bag, twisting its handle around her shaking hand. Another knock at the door made her jump.

"Meredith? Are you there?"

Shit. Jonas.

"Hello?"

Just let me go. She dropped the bag and walked slowly to the open window, staying close to the wall and away from view. "I'm here," she said, leaning forward slightly. Jonas shifted back and forth, flicking ashes on the sidewalk. "What do you want?" she asked.

He looked up. "Can I come in?"

Meredith shrank back against the wall.

"Meredith. I saw you."

"What?"

"This morning."

She banged her head against the wall. *Damn. Damn. Damn.* She looked around the room, at the pile of clothes on the floor and the getaway bag waiting on the bed.

"Please?"

"Just a minute," she whispered, clenching her fists.

"Meredith?"

"Yeah, just a minute," she called. She pulled on a pair of stained grey sweatpants and a "Taste of Chicago 1999" t-shirt from the top of the pile and hobbled down the stairs. She found Jonas leaning against the door, his forehead stretched and white against the cool glass.

Her breath hitched and she stopped. *I can't do this.* She turned to go back upstairs; he rapped on the glass. She turned slowly and he mouthed, "Please?" She took a deep breath and pulled open the door.

"I saw you," he said, stepping through and shutting the door behind him.

"When?" she asked, backing up awkwardly against the desk.

"This morning. Why didn't you knock?"

"I–"

"What's going on?" he interrupted.

"It's a–I thought you were pissed at me."

"I was. I am."

"So why –?"

"Why were you at my place this morning?" he asked, folding his arms.

She looked around the room, grasping the edge of the desk for balance. The photos lining the walls, shadowy and remote, offered no answers. She took a deep breath. "Have you ever seen someone die?"

"What?"

"Have you ever seen someone die?"

"You mean in real life?"

"Yeah."

"No."

"Good. Good," she nodded. "You're lucky," she said, standing suddenly and walking toward the back of the salon. "Coffee?"-

"Uh –"

"Yeah, me neither. Never mind." She stopped in front of a shot of the rue des Écoles, trees angular and grasping in the dark.

"What does dying–" he asked, following her.

"Jonas, would you shut up for a minute and let me get this out?" she yelled, slumping against the wall.

He nodded.

"I've seen people die. Not just a dead body. The actual last breath being drawn. You wait for the next exhalation, and you hold your breath too. Maybe there's only so many breaths to go around. Maybe if I hold my breath long enough, they'll get the one I didn't breathe. Something like that. And then they do–die–and you let that breath out."

He nodded.

Tears pricked the corners of her eyes. She slumped into a heap on the floor, covering her face with her hands. "And I've seen people die…" she mumbled.

"What?"

She shook her head. "She killed them. I mean, they deserved it…she just slit their throats and it was like I was right there. It was like I–like I was there, like I dropped the–the–"

"Who killed–"

"She did!"

"Who?!"

Meredith looked up at Jonas suddenly. "It's–never mind. Never mind."

"Don't do this to me again," he whispered.

"You really should get away while you have the chance," she said, gesturing wildly. "Seriously. Just run as fast as you can out of here and back to your studio," she urged, voice shaking.

Jonas sat on the floor next to her, saying nothing.

"I'm leaving," she said, shaking. "I have to leave here. That's why I came by this morning," she lied.

"Where are you going?"

"I don't know."

Meredith looked at the ceiling; Jonas looked at his hands.

"Who is 'she'?" he whispered.

Meredith stared at Jonas and opened and closed her mouth. She looked back around the room and then with a growl of impatience pointed at her head. "Her.I don't know who the hell she is. She's coming to Vézelay. A pilgrim. She tells me her story…dream by dream. But…but, it's not really dreaming anymore," she said, smacking her head with her open hands.

"Stop," Jonas said, grabbing her hands. "Stop! What the hell are you talking about?"

"Never mind," she said, wrenching her hands away.

"Are you sick?" he asked, feeling her forehead.

Meredith's empty laugh echoed in the dark salon. "Sure."

"Screw you. Seriously. Are you sick?"

"No."

"Why are you hallucinating?"

She turned to him. "How the fuck should I know?" she whispered, gritting her teeth. She looked at the ceiling again. "Maybe I'm not hallucinating."

Jonas pulled out a packet of cigarettes. "Want one?"

"Yeah."

He pulled two out of the packet and lit them, handing one to Meredith. "Jesus, how can you smoke these things? They're nasty."

Jonas shrugged. "They taste like France."

Meredith started sobbing and laughing at the same time, blowing smoke to the ceiling.

"I saw a ghost once."

Meredith nearly dropped the cigarette. "What?" she asked faintly.

He nodded as he blew out a lungful of smoke. "Yeah. Scared the shit out of me. It was right after my mom died. It wasn't her, though–thank God. It would be just like her to fucking haunt me."

"Who was it?"

"I don't know. It was just a glimmer of blue in the corner of the room–I was sitting at the kitchen table, and I just felt – freaky, you know? The energy of the room shifted–like all the air was sucked out of my lungs. And it was weird – it was like all my thought, my consciousness was there in the corner. The room didn't go cold, I didn't see some spectral human figure or any of that bullshit. Everything just–shifted. We're all just energy, you know. We don't disappear when we die."

"Why did you tell me that?" Meredith asked, her eyes wide.

"I don't know," he shrugged. "I'm freaked out. I didn't know what else to say," he said, rolling the cigarette between his fingers.

"I need to get the hell away from here."

"Is that going to make any difference?"

"I don't know."

"I really want you to go see a doctor."

"No."

"Meredith, please…"

"No!" she yelled.

Jonas shook his head and changed tack. "So, who died?"

She took a deep breath. "These men…they just appeared out of nowhere in the forest. She was stupid, getting so far away from the rest of the group…arrogant…"

"Not in your dream," he said, shaking his head. "I mean who did you see die—in real life?"

Meredith bowed her head and shuddered on a repressed sob. "Mercedes," she whispered.

"Who is she—was she?"

She stubbed out her cigarette on the stone floor. "My sister."

"That's horrible."

Meredith nodded.

"How—"

"No," she said, shaking her head.

They sat together silently, the smoke from their cigarettes hazing the ceiling and curling around the edges of the room.

"When did the hallucinations start?" Jonas finally asked, looking out the window.

"I don't know. A week ago? Last year?"

He placed a tentative hand on hers. "Do you pass out every time?"

The sun rises gently behind me, gilding the walls of Vézelay…

"No!"

"What?" he asked, grabbing his hand back.

"I mean, I have…lately." *Not now Not now.*

Today I shall come at last to the journey's end…

Stop it. Stop it. Stop…

"Meredith! Stop it!" Jonas grabbed her hands and held them close to her sides. "Jesus, you're giving yourself a black eye."

"Oh my God," she moaned, shrinking away from him. "I am losing my mind," she whispered. She stood, shaking off his hands and raced through the salon, heading for the stairs to her rooms.

"I don't think so," Jonas said, jumping up and following her. "Come with me."

"What?"

"Come with me," he said, holding his hands out to her.

"Why?"

"Just trust me."

"No," she said, looking past him to the street. "I–I have to get out of here."

"Where?"

"Uh–Chicago," she said, nodding to herself. "Chicago."

"I don't think that's a great idea."

"And?"

"And I don't think you should go."

"I don't know what else to do," she said, slumping against the wall.

"I don't know either. Just–I want to help you," he said with some effort. "I don't think you should run away."

"I'm not running away."

"What else would you call it?"

"Listen," she said, folding her arms. "You don't know."

"Running away doesn't fix anything. Trust me."

"I'm not fucking running away," she yelled.

He shrugged. "Go to Chicago. Don't go to Chicago. Fine. I have to stay here and finish the glass," he said, blowing out the smoke. "But I think it would be better for you to stay here and figure this out than run away."

"Got it. Thanks. Bye."

"What about Marie-Laure?"

"What about her?"

"Why don't you ask her for help?"

"She doesn't need to save me again."

"What?"

"Never mind."

"Why am I bothering with you?"

"Good question." *Get out while you can.*

Jonas shook his head, then leaned in and kissed her quickly. "Good luck," he whispered. He turned and walked out the front door, the glass rattling as he pulled it shut.

Meredith sat on the bottom step and held her head in her hands. *You brought it all on yourself. All of it. So deal with it.* With a half-growl, half-sob, she stood and slowly climbed the stairs.

Chapter Nineteen

JONAS PULLED THE DOOR SHUT, the glass rattling in the frame. "Enough of this shit," he muttered. "What the hell was I thinking?" The sun cast long shadows, climbing and grasping towards the cathedral behind him. He lit a cigarette and wandered down the street.

He leaned against the door of Atelier Marie-Noelle and wiped the sweat from his forehead with his thumb. *She needs my help.* "It's not your job," he whispered, shaking his head. *Maybe Marie-Laure–* "No!" he said, pounding on the door.

"Monsieur, s'il vous plâit!"

Jonas stumbled backwards and dropped his cigarette as the door opened into the shop.

"Quel est le problème?"

"Pardon," he mumbled, righting himself. Pardonnez-moi. I just lost my balance." He picked up the cigarette and flicked it, still lit, into the street.

He shoved his hands in his pockets and headed down the hill. The street finally met up with the rue St Etienne halfway down and he hesitated. He looked at Marie-Laure's door, then up and down the street. *I can't. Did my time. Not my job anymore.*

He pulled out his lighter and flicked it on and off, on and off. "Shit," he said, knocking hard on Marie-Laure's door. He flicked the lighter again and waited, watching the flame dance in his hand. Flipping the lighter closed, he knocked again, harder. He tried the door and found it unlocked. Glancing up and down the street, he pushed open the door. Marie-Laure?" he called. "Guillaume? Are you guys here?" He walked down the hall, poking his head in at the salon, the dining room, the kitchen. "Helloooo?" he called up the stairs, receiving no answering call. "Damn," he said, leaning against the handrail.

He tiptoed out of the silent house and into the burning street. In minutes he found he was at the car park at the base of the hill, his car waiting patiently for him to return. He pulled the keys out and slid into the front seat. The car was oppressively hot, the steering wheel burning his hands, the smell of leather mixing with stale cigarettes and old coffee. He slammed the door and gripped the steering wheel harder, the pain prickling his hands and sweat rising on his scalp and neck. He unclenched his teeth and rolled down the windows.

Jonas revved the engine and set off, navigating the narrow cobblestoned streets slowly and cruising down the hill and out of Vézelay in neutral. The narcissus and daffodils, so lately bloomed in the green edges, now lay brown and broken in the heat. He cruised down to the small town of St Père Sous Vézelay and pulled over next to the bank of the Cure. A small café stood next to the tabac he'd visited on his way into Vézelay.

Pushing open the door, he was hit with a lungful of smoke that made him splutter. The denizens of the café, exclusively old men, did not stop their low, murmuring conversations when he entered; they merely watched him enter from the corners of their eyes.

He stood at the end of the bar and added to the smoke. After a few minutes, the bartender finished his conversation and nodded to Jonas.

"Un verre du vin rouge, s'il vous plâit," Jonas said, leaning against the bar.

The bartender nodded again.

"Gevrey-Chambertin, si possible," Jonas added. The bartender walked away, returning a few moments later with a glass of red wine.

He looked around the bar, grinning inwardly at the old men. *Jesus, is that how I'm going to end up?* He looked down at his pack of cigarettes and glass of red wine. He sighed into his glass and drained it.

"Un autre plus, la même chose," he said, pushing his glass across the bar. After a moment, he said, "Pardon, pardon – une bouteille, s'il vous plâit." He sat down at a small table near the front window and put his feet up on the sill, fully intending to leave the bar stinking drunk. He lit a cigarette and rubbed his right temple with his fingertips, tracing the thin scar slicing up from his eye.

He dropped the cigarette into the ashtray and sighed deeply, leaning back in his chair. *You can't fix her. She doesn't want your help.* He nodded as the bartender placed a bottle of red wine on the table. He poured a glass and drank it in a single pull, pouring another close on its heels. *It never works. Don't bother. You don't have a brilliant track record.* He drained his glass and grabbed the bottle.

An old man sat down at the small table near Jonas', pulling out a newspaper and lighting a pipe. He nodded affably at Jonas and puffed on his pipe, the sweet smoke curling and rising to the ceiling. Jonas emptied the bottle and again downed the glass in a few gulps.

Jonas lit a cigarette and twisted in his seat to get the bartender's attention. The bartender assiduously avoided eye contact, pouring himself a glass of dark red wine and nodding in amusement at a murmured joke. Jonas waved his hand, the tip of his cigarette weaving figure eights in the darkening room. The bartender took a sip of his wine and leaned on his elbows on the counter. "Bastard," Jonas murmured, moving, somewhat shakily, to stand up.

"Adrien," the old man said into his newspaper. "La meme chose pour mon ami, et un café pour moi." The bartender looked over but did not stand up. "S'il vous plâit," the old man said, chuckling. Moments later, a fresh bottle of Gevrey-Chambertin was set on Jonas' table. He muttered a thanks and turned back around in his seat. The bartender walked away and he poured himself a new glass. "Bastard," he muttered again.

"Vous êtes un Américain, oui?" the old man asked from behind his paper.

"Oui."

"Q'est-ce que vous faites en Vézelay?" he asked, neatly folding his paper and laying it on the table.

"Ah," Jonas nodded. "Je suis un artist. Pour Abbot Dubay," he said, pointing toward the hill of Vézelay with his glass.

"Un artist? De quoi? Peinture?"

"Stained glass."

The old man shook his head in confusion.

"Uh...verre," Jonas said, pointing at the window, "avec couleur."

"Ah, oui?"

Jonas nodded. "Je fais le–uh–restoration."

"Mmm, mmm, oui, je comprends. Ah, merci Adrien," the old man said, taking his coffee from the bartender. "Mais – ça c'est l'art aussi, oui?"

"Yeah, yeah it is," Jonas replied, nodding and swirling the wine in his glass.

"I remember you."

Jonas looked up. The old man was looking at him over the rim of his coffee cup.

"You do?"

"Oui," the man nodded, taking a sip. "Le pélerin – avec les Gitanes," he laughed as Jonas took a long drag.

"You have a good memory. What's a pélerin?"

"Uh..." the old man said, pointing to the hill. "Pélerin. Pélerin. Pilgrim."

Jonas poured another glass and downed it quickly, watching the lights blossom on the hill. "Maybe," he muttered. *Why did I come here? Really? And why can't I feel my upper lip anymore?* He laughed and the old man raised his eyebrow expectantly. "Why aren't you drinking wine? Here, have a glass with me. No, I insist. Adrien," Jonas turned unsteadily in his chair and called to the bartender, who looked over in surprise. "Un autre – le meme chose - et un verre pour mon ami. S'il vous plâit, s'il vous plâit." He leaned over to the old man and whispered, "You have to say please. That's the trick."

"Monsieur, non—mon café c'est—"

"No, come on. Let me buy you a bottle. I mean a glass. Whatever."

"D'accord, d'accord," the old man nodded, pushing aside his coffee with a look of some regret. "Where—eh…where en Amérique do you live?"

"Hmm?" Jonas asked, emptying the dregs of the bottle into his glass. "Oh –California. California. San Francisco. Shit," he mused, looking out the window, "I can't believe I haven't thought about it this whole time…I wonder if that bastard Steve is watering my plants like I asked him." Jonas turned back to the old man. "You know, you just can't really trust people, can you? I mean, you can, but you can't really. Does that make any sense?"

The old man shook his head, trying to follow the one-sided conversation.

"No. Me either. Merci, Adrien. Merci, merci, merci." The bartender placed the bottle and the bill on the table and walked away, shaking his head. Jonas filled the glasses and handed one to the old man. "Salut!" he said, raising his glass.

"Salut. Êtes-vous marié?"

"Hell no."

"Pourquoi?"

"Parce-que…it's just…it's because you can't fix people, and they're always broken. Always. Completely screwed up. Why put yourself in that position? My dad was completely miserable because my mom was such a wack-case.He just gave up. Seriously. He tried for a while and then just gave up. And I'm not even going to start in with Meredith because…" Jonas shook his head and lit a new cigarette from the embers of the old. "It's just better to live your own life and fix what you can and let people deal with their own lives. You know? I have more than enough to worry about. Fuck it. Don't you like your wine?"

"Pardon, mon anglais est très mal. Je ne comprends –"

"It's nothing," Jonas said, waving the question away. "Like your wine?"

"Ah, oui, oui. Merci bien."

"Sure." Jonas poured them both glasses, splashing some onto the table. "Ah, shit," he said, rubbing it out with his fingertips. "Are you married?"

"Moi? Non, non," the old man laughed. "Je suis trop– eh–je suis un perfectionniste. C'est un idée mal pour moi, bien sûr!"

"Are you happy?"

"Oui, oui. J'ai mes amis –" he said, gesturing toward the bar, "–et mon tabac. Je suis content."

Jonas nodded but said nothing. He leaned back and blew smoke to the ceiling. They sat together in silence, smoking and finishing the last of the bottle of Burgundy. After the last drop had been consumed, the old man stood and tucked the folded newspaper under his arm. Jonas stood unsteadily to take the man's proffered hand.

"Merci pour le vin," the old man smiled. "Bonne chance, monsieur pélerin."

"Et vous. Merci. Au revoir."

The old man nodded and shuffled out the door into the darkness. Soon thereafter, one by one, the men at the bar also drifted away and out into the night. Jonas was left alone in the quiet café, standing with his hands in his pockets, staring through his reflection in the window toward the top of the hill and the illuminated cathedral.

With a grunt he grabbed the crumpled pack of cigarettes from the table and dropped some euros on the table to cover the bill. "Merci bien, Adrien," he called, swaying as he opened the door. The bartender made no response.

Jonas stepped out into the darkness, squinting to see beyond the yellow light from the café's windows. *Where the hell is my car?* After five minutes' wandering, he found the car where he'd left it, next to a bend in the dark river, overhung with spreading elms.

The car was stale with the captured afternoon heat. Jonas got in and rolled down the windows, slumping in the driver's seat. After a minute, he grabbed the wheel and pulled himself up. *OK, we can do this.* "Oof," he murmured, his head swimming. "Maybe not." He got out gingerly and crawled into the back seat, curling up and looking out the back window.

The trees waving above were somehow both comforting and grasping in the darkness, their long fingers stretching toward the car and the black sky. He pulled his knees in and hugged himself, shivering in the cool. A memory floated to the surface, of long road trips with his parents when he was seven or eight, watching the summer trees pass and imagining he was flying low and fast along their green tops. He turned over, groaning with a wave of nausea. He fingered the scar on his temple and fell asleep almost immediately.

Swaying in the darkness, a rising wind pushed and pulled and swirled the trees. A young woman emerged from the bushes at the river's edge, clad in a rippling inky cloak. She leaned against the bole of a nearby tree, shimmering silver in the full moon's light. She was panting heavily, as if in fear or passion, her breath white and jagged in the cold.

With effort, she pushed herself away from the tree and limped toward Jonas' car, hugging her cloak close about. "Do not let fear be your master," she whispered urgently, icing the window. "That is the enemy's work. The holy hill is just beyond–" she said, motioning to the dark mass beyond the river, lit by the pearl moon. She raised a bandaged hand and knocked on the window.

Jonas sat up, gasping. He held the back of the driver's seat for support, his heart racing, as he looked around in the darkness. He opened the car door and stepped out into the dark street. He squinted into the blackness, holding his breath and listening. He edged around the car, toward the riverbank. "Who's there?" he whispered.

A shout of wind shook the trees, and a long branch reached out and tapped the back window of the car. Jonas slumped against the car. *Fucking dreams.* He dug the keys out of his pocket and, with a deep sigh and an unaccounted shiver up his neck, settled into the driver's seat. With a last look in his rearview mirror, he picked his way slowly along the road by the riverside, focusing carefully on the lines illuminated by his headlights.

Vézelay glowed gently with its scattered streetlamps. Jonas finally pulled in through the town's main gate and drove through the silent streets to rue l'Argenterie. He parked outside his flat and dragged himself up to his bedroom, making a stop first for two Advil and a large glass of water. He dropped onto his bed and fell fast asleep, fully clothed.

The room had grown less dark, and he rolled over onto his back and grunted. He didn't have a hangover, so much as he felt as though an industrial grader had rolled over his tongue. He smacked his lips, then opened his eyes and heaved himself with effort onto his elbows. He sat up and quickly swung his feet to the ground.

He stood and steadied himself on the doorframe, then stepped into the bathroom and turned on the shower. The steam filled the small room and he inhaled it with gulping breaths. He sat on the toilet and pulled off his sneakers and socks, then his shirt, tossing them into a pile in the corner. He shook his head and stood to kick off his jeans. He stopped mid-kick. *You can't fix her. Let. It. Go.* He shoved the jeans in the corner and stepped into the scalding shower.

A few hours later, he sat alone in the café across from Meredith's shop, sipping a café au lait and watching people drifting up the street, caught in the cathedral's current. He'd considered knocking on Meredith's door, but instead settled into his chair at the café, shielding his eyes against the morning sun. The café owner set a plate of runny eggs in front of him; he stubbed out his cigarette and leaned back in his chair. Meredith's salon showed no signs of activity.

He picked at his breakfast, grimacing at the oily eggs and lighting three cigarettes without smoking them. When his second cup of coffee had gone cold, he tossed some euros on the table and, shoving his hands in his pockets, trudged up the rue St Pierre.

He wandered past the cathedral, headed toward the draughty chapter house, pulled by a feeling that, somehow, he was being directed there. As he passed the worn, ancient doors, sonorous voices floated out to meet him in the cool morning. He stopped and turned back, straining to catch the words sneaking through the cracks of the massive oaken doors. He climbed the stairs and pushed through into the narthex. The room shivered with light, pushing under the ancient doors, an echo of the sunrise. Voices ghosted into the room, murmuring and melodious. Jonas, without a look at the writhing tympanum, pushed open the far left door.

He stumbled over the threshold, blinded. The great nave was flooded with golden light, the rising sun refulgent behind the raised altar. Dubay stood in front of the small congregation, hands outstretched, his silver hair illuminated by the morning sun. *He has a halo.* Shaking his head, Jonas sat down on a nearby cane chair in the empty back row.

The vast, soaring nave was filled with light and chant, and he was transfixed by the shadows and valleys of the deeply carved capitals. Dubay, or perhaps the small choir of monks, sang *Agnus Dei...miserere nobis...dona nobis pacem*; it sounded sweet and relieved, as if at the end of a very long journey. He shook his head again, trying to clear the swirling rhythms. The massive rounded arches, impossibly high, rolled on, wave after wave, into the light and dissolved. Dubay's voice echoed in the nearly empty cathedral, filling the spaces left behind by the waves.

Jonas jumped as a hand rested on his shoulder.

"I'm surprised to see you here," Dubay said quietly.

Jonas looked around. The basilica was empty, and the rising sun gone beyond the vision of the gothic choir's pointed windows.

"Hey," Jonas said, sitting up and shaking his head. "That was amazing."

Dubay smiled. "Why did you come?"

"It wasn't intentional."

Dubay laughed. "Well, I am glad you did," he said, sitting down in the seat in front of Jonas, twisting around to see him.

"Is it always like that?" Jonas asked.

"Like what?"

"Like being swept away?"

Dubay looked at his hands and nodded. "Every time. For me, at least."

Suddenly, the memory of the previous night's dream returned, the chill and an uncanny feeling of foreboding washing over Jonas. He looked up at the altar and shivered.

"Are you ill?"

"I–no, I'm OK," he said, staring around the cathedral. "I had too much wine last night. Not feeling so hot."

"Ah," Dubay nodded, a smile on his lips. "I understand."

Jonas nodded absently and looked up again at the rows of carved capitals. "This place is so overwhelming. Oppressive. There are so many memories, if that makes any sense. They just crowd in on you, like you constantly want to look over your shoulder to see who's looking at you. And it feels like God is watching and judging every move I make."

"I don't know that God judges. God watches, yes, God puts us on a path. But God doesn't judge. How could he?"

Jonas shook his head. "Meredith wouldn't say that."

"Why do you say that?" Dubay asked, cocking his head.

"She's angry. With God."

"Meredith has had a great deal of misfortune in her life."

"So have you, though."

"We all have lessons to learn in this life, Jonas. Her path is unique from mine, from yours. We can't judge her."

"We can't fix her either."

"There is no way to fix people, Jonas. You can only offer your support, if she will take it. Meredith is—complicated. And very stubborn," Dubay said, a slight edge to his voice.

"Yeah. Yeah."

Dubay narrowed his eyes but said nothing.

"I can't find her," Jonas said, looking out across the expanse of oppressive openness.

"What do you mean?"

"She and I—yesterday—" He shook his head. "I looked for her this morning and she wasn't home."

"Perhaps she is out shooting? She often works in the morning."

"Maybe. I don't know. It just—it doesn't feel right."

"I am certain she will turn up. She always does."

"Shit," Jonas muttered, his mouth set and grim. "Shit." He sighed and ran his hands through his hair.

Dubay's eyebrows creased slightly, but he did not say the words that seemed to be at the tip of his tongue. Instead, after long moments, he suggested, "Since you're here, perhaps you can give me an update on the glass."

"Oh. Sure," Jonas replied, folding his arms and shivering. He looked around the massive nave and sighed. "Most of the major work on the different sections is done. We're on track to be done on time."

"That is wonderful news," Dubay said.

"Right now I'm working on painting her face."

"How is that coming?"

"Nerve-wracking. But so far, so good."

"Good."

"What are you going to do with it once it's done?" Jonas asked, watching Dubay closely.

"Well, there's a contingent coming from the diocese at Autun, and the UNESCO people–"

"Madame Chevrey?"

"Quite possibly. And various officials from the arts ministry. One of the brothers shall say mass for the Magdalene, and we will have an official ceremony to present the glass."

" UNESCO'S not taking it, though, right? I mean, you get to keep it, right?"

"Certainly. Most certainly. It was found here, and it will stay here. No one is going to take it from me–us," he said. He looked up to the rounded vaulting of the ceiling, and with a sigh, looked at his watch and said, "I am afraid I must go."

"Yeah, I should get back to work, anyway."

"Would you care to have dinner tomorrow evening? I can give you an update on my meeting with Merimée," Dubay asked, standing.

"Sure."

"Then I shall see you tomorrow evening. Seven?"

"Sure," Jonas nodded. "See you then." He turned to walk back to the cathedral's front doors, Dubay heading the opposite direction. Suddenly, Jonas stopped and turned around. "Hey," he called. "Did you know Mercedes?"

Dubay's shoulders stiffened and his steps faltered slightly, but he continued his purposeful stride toward the chapter house.

Maybe he didn't hear me. Jonas shrugged, giving the cathedral a last, searching look, and turned back toward the town. He stood on the broad stairs of the cathedral and looked down the winding streets of the town. *Where the hell did she go?*

Chapter Twenty

DUBAY PUSHED OPEN the heavy doors into the shadowy cloisters and leaned against them, his breath coming in erratic gasps. "Mercedes," he breathed. He dropped onto the bench and covered his eyes with his shaking hand.

"Abbot. Abbot?" Soeur Marie shook his shoulder gently. "Are you unwell?"

Dubay smiled stiffly. "Yes, yes, I am quite well, thank you."

Soeur Marie folded her arms. "As you please."

Dubay stood up. "If it's not too much trouble, can you send up a bite of lunch in about an hour?"

"Yes, of course. You look very pale, seigneur."

"Dear Marie," he smiled, clasping her hand. "Please believe me. I am quite well. I shall see you in an hour?"

"Yes."

He walked down the long corridor and up the stone stairs to his rooms. He shut the door behind him and collapsed into his desk chair, leaning back and rubbing his temples with a sigh. After a few moments he sat up with a start, the hairs tingling on the back of his neck. "Mercedes," he pleaded in a whisper. He moved aside his paperwork and correspondence, finding the worn photo of the dark-haired woman. "What do you want?" he whispered. The woman smiled back prettily, silent. A moment flickered at the edge of his memory and he dropped the photo back on the desk.

"Michel. Michel!"

He looked up, startled, from his note-taking. "What?"

Mercedes stood in front of him, arms crossed. "We have to meet Meredith for dinner in 10 minutes. Are you ready?"

"No."

She shook her head and looked around the cramped book-lined room. "Don't do this to me," she said quietly.

"What?"

"I promised her we'd go," Mercedes said, sitting across from him.

"I know, but I promised Marie-Laure I'd get her this research before tomorrow morning," he replied, opening another book.

"She'll understand. How much do you have left?" she asked, flipping through a book.

"At least another hour or two," Dubay replied, prising the book from her hand.

"What?"

"Well, I went down another path that seems much more profitable..."

"Can't you just give her what you have and finish the rest tomorrow morning?"

"I have to teach tomorrow morning."

"Well, we can't keep putting Meredith off."

"Ask Marie-Laure to babysit her," he said, pulling a tattered book toward him.

"Michel," Mercedes said, pulling up a worn wooden chair and sitting down. "We've put her off twice this week already."

"Petite," he wheedled, taking her hand. "I have so much to do…"

"So do I. My defense is in a few weeks. But we have to take a break once in a while. Please? I'm all she has right now."

Dubay sighed and closed the book with a snap. "Yes, yes. I have to drop this off with Marie-Laure first," he said, standing and patting the pockets of his sport coat.

"Thank you. You won't regret it."

He lit a Marlboro red and put an arm around her shoulders. "You can make it up to me after dinner," he whispered.

"Good," she said, leading him by the hand out of his small office.

Two flights of worn stairs and one long corridor later, they reached Marie-Laure's office, which was ringing with laughter.

Mercedes pushed open the door and grinned. "What the hell is this?"

"Hey!" Meredith smiled, leaning back in her chair. "You guys ready?"

"You are not taking her from me, are you?" Marie-Laure smiled impishly, pushing a wisp of light brown hair from her face. "She was telling me the most fascinating stories from your youth, Mercedes–"

Dubay sniggered and took another drag from his cigarette. "I am glad I came. Please, do not let us interrupt you," he said, standing behind Mercedes and running his hands along her bare upper arms.

"Oh, we've got plenty of time to dish the dirt. Right now, I'm starving. Come on, you guys," she said, pulling Mercedes by the arm out the door. "I'll see you tomorrow, Marie-Laure!" Meredith called.

"Ah, to be 20 again," Marie-Laure smiled.

Dubay ran a hand through his hair. "I am afraid my research is not yet complete. I will bring you the rest of the information after my class tomorrow morning."

"Michel, relax, please. You are going to turn all that lovely hair silver with worry. Come see me tomorrow afternoon and we will review the rest of the research. Tonight, enjoy yourself."

Dubay hesitated. "You do not mind – "

"Michel! Where are you?" Mercedes called, echoing down the long corridor.

"Tomorrow afternoon," Marie-Laure repeated. "I can manage tonight. I'll walk down with you. I could use the air."

He kissed her on each cheek and they sauntered down the hall. "Yes, yes, here I am," he called lazily.

They emerged into the early spring evening, chill and fresh. Mercedes and Meredith were sitting on the steps, laughing.

"There you are! Come on," Meredith said, jumping up and tugging Dubay away from Marie-Laure and twining her arm with his, and with Mercedes'. "I know exactly where to go. I'll drive."

They turned and waved to Marie-Laure and then disappeared into the blue twilight of the rue des Écoles.

A knock on his door startled him out of his reverie. "Seigneur Dubay?"

He sat up quickly and again hid the photo under a pile of papers. "Come in," he gasped, heart racing.

Soeur Marie pushed open the door with her foot, her hands busy with the lunch tray. She quickly set it on the desk, not bothering to move papers or books aside. "Now you are quite flushed. Are sure you are not ill?" she asked, putting the back of her hand on Dubay's forehead.

"Yes, of course," he said, waving her hand away. "I am just warm." He stood and quickly pushed open the windows, returning to his desk and pulling the lunch tray haphazardly toward him. "Ah, you have outdone yourself. Thank you."

Soeur Marie watched, arms folded, as he picked at his salad and sipped his Chablis. "Do not let me keep you," he said. "I know you are keen to return to your devotions."

"I will send Pascal to collect your tray," she said, opening the door. She hesitated on the threshold but said nothing. After a few moments, she turned and stepped into the hallway, closing the door behind her with a quiet click.

He listened for her steps retreating down the worn stone staircase, and when they disappeared, let the fork drop onto his plate. He pulled the photo out again and fingered its now-tattered edges, head tilted, lips pursed. The Sext bell sounded; he dropped the photo onto the desk, smoothed his vestments, and walked down to the cloisters and through to the nave and his duties.

The next morning, a few hours after an unremarkable breakfast and another highly entertaining interaction with Pascal, the phone rang insistently in his office.

"Yes?" he said, cradling the phone against his shoulder and flipping through his diary.

"Abbot Dubay?"

"Yes."

"One moment, please."

Dubay dropped the diary and took a deep breath.

"Dubay?"

"Good morning, Bishop. How is the weather down in Autun?"

"Fine, fine. Will you have housing for us for the feast day festivities?"

"Of course, yes, Soeur Marie is looking after all of the arrangements."

"The UNESCO people will also be there."

"Yes, we will make certain they are–"

"Dubay, will we be ready in time?"

"Yes, of course."

"Who is supervising the restoration?"

"I am."

"This is an important project for the diocese."

"I am aware of that," Dubay said.

"There is interest by the Cluny in Paris in purchasing the glass for their collection."

"What?"

"It would be most welcome revenue."

"It belongs in Vézelay."

"It belongs where I say it belongs."

Dubay took a deep breath. "Yes, your grace."

"You are fortunate that the brothers still have the power to choose their Abbot."

"Yes, your grace. We have been fortunate to exercise that perquisite for over a thousand years." Dubay stood, clenching and unclenching his free hand.

The bishop was silent for a moment. "I will remind you that Vézelay is no longer answerable only to the Pope, Dubay. You are answerable to me," he said, voice rising.

Dubay said nothing.

"Though I do not have the power to appoint, I do have the power to have you removed. Do not disappoint me."

"I will see you on the feast day eve, your grace," Dubay said shortly.

The bishop grunted and the line went dead. Dubay dropped the handset onto the phone and rubbed his temples, hoping to stave off the prodigious headache threatening to overwhelm him. *It is my glass. By heritage. By right.* His fingers stopped and he dropped his hands. *What is wrong with me?*

An hour or so later, Soeur Marie knocked on the office door. "Seigneur, do not forget your appointment with M. Merimée," she called through the door.

Dubay looked at his watch and stood creakily. "Yes, of course. Thank you." He crossed himself and took a deep breath.

He found Merimée at their usual table at Restaurant Saint Etienne, pouring over paperwork and running a hand through his wavy black hair.

"Good afternoon, Jean," Dubay smiled, settling into his chair.

"Dubay," Merimée nodded. "You're late."

Dubay smiled. "A pleasure as always."

Merimée snorted and poured Dubay a glass of Domaine Menand Mercurey. "I just spoke with Paul and Bernard. They are nearly at capacity for next week – and an entire congregation from Toulouse has booked le Poste et Lion d'Or. Thank God for the church," he chuckled nasally, sipping his wine.

"Indeed," Dubay nodded. "Salut."

"Salut. How is your artist coming along? I promised the UNESCO people they could have a preview of the glass on the 20th."

Dubay lowered his glass slowly. "That was not our agreement."

"It's only a day," Merimée said, waving the words away and nodding his thanks to the waiter for his plate of noisettes d'agneau.

"That was not our agreement."

"Dubay, it's only a day. Is there a problem?"

"Of course not. But I expect you to hold to your agreements, as I do."

"There is a problem!" Merimée, said, striking the table with his fist.

"Jean, I assure you –"

"I've heard about your artist, you know. Wholly unsavory."

Dubay laughed. "What does that have to do with his ability to repair the glass? He will be ready next week."

"All I'm saying is – are you watching him?"

"He is UNESCO choice. Have you lost faith in their discernment?"

"No, of course not. Don't change the subject."

"How long have we known each other?"

"What?"

"How long have we known each other?"

"Nine years? Ten years?"

"Trust me."

"I trust you to look out for the good of your cathedral. And you have to know I have to look after the good of this village. If that means the UNESCO people get to see the glass a day early to keep them happy, then damn it, that's what we'll do."

"Fine."

"Excellent," Merimée replied, wiping his mouth with a crisp white napkin.

"But you have to help me keep the glass here," Dubay said, wineglass paused mid-air.

"Where else would it go?" Merimée asked, eyes narrowed.

Dubay put the glass down and raised his eyebrow. "Musée Cluny. And I must say, that the irony of that name in this situation is too rich."

"What? Cluny? Where did you hear that?"

"They have made a bid to the Bishop, and to my great disappointment, he is entertaining it."

"That's insanity. It's ours! It was found here. It should stay here!"

Dubay nodded and pulled off a piece of crusty bread, pointing it at Merimée. "It is not ours, it belongs to God," he corrected. "Work on Chevrey. She is very persuasive."

"As I know all too well," Merimée laughed, shaking his head.

"Set a meeting between her and the bishop on the 20th– dinner at la Dent Creuse, hmmm? The views from the terrace will certainly put him in a more amenable mood. And the wine, of course. She would not stand for the glass to be moved from its location–and UNESCO has a stake in the success of this village. Yes, this is the best plan," Dubay smiled, chewing happily on his bread.

"It will only work if you give her the first viewing on the 20th," Merimée said, pouring them both another glass.

"Yes, of course, of course. I am certain it will not be an issue." *Please, Jonas.*

Dubay and Merimée shared four more courses in the quiet dining room and parted with a genial handshake on the narrow sidewalk in front of the restaurant. "We shall expect you and the contingent at 1600 on the 20th," Dubay said, edging down the street.

"Just make sure it's done," Merimée said, exasperated.

"On my word," Dubay said, palm flat on his chest, bowing slightly.

"See you next week."

Dubay nodded and turned down the rue St Etienne. He rounded the corner and knocked lightly at Marie-Laure's door. He waited a minute, then knocked again. As he reached for the door handle, the door swung inwards.

"Ah, Michel, it's you. Come in, come in," Marie-Laure said, beckoning him into the foyer.

Dubay closed the door behind him and kissed her in greeting. He knitted his eyebrows as he pulled back. "You do not look well. How do you feel?"

She waved his question away and walked, rather slowly, to the front parlor. "I am fine, fine. Just tired. The research on the border has been a wonderful jolt for my synapses, but I must admit, my old eyes are growing weary," she said, offering him a chair. "Care for a glass of wine?"

"No, I just left Merimée."

"Ah," she smiled. "I hope he paid this time."

"Yes, fortunately."

"Good," she said, closing her eyes and resting her head against the velvet of the wing-backed chair.

Dubay leaned forward. "Where is Guillaume?"

"Still in Paris," she said, opening her eyes. "He is due back tomorrow."

"In that case, would you like to join me and Jonas for dinner tomorrow?"

"It is a tempting offer. I think, though, I will likely catch up on my sleep. I have been having the most unusual dreams lately; they have disturbed my sleep for quite a few nights now."

"What have you been dreaming?"

"Of Mercedes, of all things."

Dubay sat back in his chair. "She has been haunting my dreams as well."

Marie-Laure cocked her head. "Is that so?"

Dubay nodded. "It has been many years since I thought of–that night. But yesterday, it came back to me, at first like a half-heard whisper," he said, looking out the window.

"Mmmm. Yes, she flits in and out of my dreams like–is that Meredith?" she asked, leaning forward in her chair to get a better view of the street.

"No," Dubay replied, shaking his head.

Marie-Laure sat back again and templed her fingers against her chin. "With the troubles she's been having–"

"What now?" he sighed.

"She passed out last week, after we had dinner together. And she was acting quite strangely when I met her coming out of Jonas' studio the other day. I just have a feeling that something is wrong. Do you think you could look in on her? I have been so tired…"

Dubay swallowed. "Certainly. For you, anything."

Marie-Laure closed her eyes again. "Thank you, my dear," she said. Then, taking a deep breath, "Would you like to see the rest of the research? I believe I have the rest of the mystery solved."

"Yes, of course, if you feel well enough –"

She pointed at a pile of papers on a nearby table. "Please bring me those files there–and my glasses, yes, that's perfect, thank you."

"Marie-Laure…perhaps I should call Guillaume. You are not looking well," he said, reaching for her hand. "I can send Frédéric to see you–"

"Nonsense," she replied, smacking his hand away. "I am perfectly well."

"Marie-Laure –" he pleaded, eyebrows creased.

She ignored him and pulled out a paper with line upon line of closely written notes. "So, we have a most unusual story, starting with the image of the vineyard–your vineyard–then the Dukes, an illuminated manuscript, Cluny, and now–here–this wooded area depicted here. I believe this is the story of a journey–because, you see, next is an inexact rendering of this very hill we sit on, and then," she said, her eyes shining, "here we have a smaller rendering of the Magdalene, and then something–consumed by fire."

Dubay sat back and folded his arms. "Interesting theory, but what makes you think it's a journey?"

Marie-Laure put the papers down in her lap and considered Dubay for a long moment. "To be honest, it is simply my best guess. I am following an intuition, which as you know, I believe is the historian's most valuable tool. I believe the border was an offering to the Magdalene here, and the artist was desperate to tell their story."

"But artists were focused on giving the glory to God, not themselves."

"Yes," she said, pointing at him with the papers, "yes, that's true. Which is why I believe this is a highly unusual artist. An amateur, not a professional artisan employed by the church."

"The level of skill is rather high."

"Yes, which makes me think they also had skill in other arts –illuminating manuscripts, for example."

"Ahh...I see your point," Dubay said, taking the papers from her. "Hmmm..." he said, forehead wrinkling. "The fire in the last panel makes me think that perhaps the glass should be dated later –after the 1120 fire."

"Ah, I thought so, too! But–look here," she said, taking the papers back. "Her hair is long and braided, but with no crespine or even a circlet. I believe this puts it squarely in 1120s," she said triumphantly.

"I wonder who he was..." Dubay mused, looking out the window. "He needed the cleansing of the pilgrimage. But why?" He shuddered, his scalp and spine prickling.

"That I have not yet figured. You will give Jonas this information when you see him tomorrow?"

"Of course," he said quickly, checking his watch. "I must get back. That interminable pile of paperwork awaits. And the weekly meeting to hear the brothers' grievances."

"And Meredith," Marie-Laure said, arching an eyebrow.

"Ah, yes, of course. I will look in on her, I promise."

"Thank you," she said, standing with his help. "When did I get so old, Michel?"

"You are fresh as a rose," he smiled.

She smiled and shook her head. "Have a nice evening with Jonas."

He nodded and pulled the door closed behind him. He hurried up the street and stopped at the Salon Meredith Thibault, dark and lifeless. He stepped into the street and glanced first at the cathedral, and then up at Meredith's open window. "Meredith?" he called, half-heartedly. "Are you there? Meredith?" he called again, with more volume.

Dubay checked his watch and turned to walk up the narrow street to the chapter house. *Confiteor Deo omnipotenti...* The words, whispered and yet silent in the bright street, floated tingling along his spine. He turned slowly back to Meredith's door. *Not Mercedes; I hope I have not forgotten her voice. A confession? Meredith?*

He pounded on the wooden frame, the door's glass rattling nervously. "Meredith," he called, peering again into the dark salon. The vespers bell called to him from the cathedral; he checked his watch and scowled. "Where are you?" he whispered, turning reluctantly from 40 rue St Pierre and hurrying up the street to the chapter house, crossing himself as he went.

The nave was flickering with candlelight and the anticipatory breaths of the gathered monks, the sun's westerly course having passed the ancient hall by. He approached the altar and, kneeling, crossed himself and then settled in the first row of cane chairs.

The service, led by Frère Ignatius, whispered in the background. Dubay held his breath, the words and chanted song filling his head.

The service slowly wound to its quiet end. As if sleepwalking, he found his way down to the crypt, oblivious to the looks of his monks. He knelt at the reliquary of the Magdalene and a great smile of relief spread across his narrow face.

The proscribed words fell from his lips in grateful waves, murmured and reverent, and a feeling of peace and calm, cool and welcome as a draught of water, spread through his being. *Confiteor Deo omnipotenti*...the image of–the Magdalene?–floated into his mind, a young woman with flowing golden hair, eyes pleading. *I must have confession before the vigil. Please.* His eyes flew open involuntarily and he swung around on his knees, peering into the dim crypt behind. *No one is there.* He shook his head and returned to the reliquary. *Blessed Magdalene, I am your tool, but I do not understand.*

Dubay emerged from the cathedral into the lilac-sky evening hours later, bleary eyed and aching. He walked down the narrow street, heading towards rue l'Argenterie. The tall houses caught the last glancing rays of the setting sun, gilding their pointed roofs and warming the limestone. At the last moment he swerved and made his way to Salon Meredith Thibault.

He crossed himself and closed his eyes. *Was that you, dear Magdalene? What am I to do? Guide me.* His eyes opened, but no burst of light or great awareness enveloped him. He simply stared into the dark and silent shop, at sea for the first time in many years. *Meredith. Where are you?*

Chapter Twenty-One

THE STUDIO HAD GROWN DARK and silent around Jonas. The red light on the stereo shone across the room, the only light save the glowing end of his dangling cigarette. The sky beyond had grown dark as well, an unlikely violet and satisfying deep indigo. The last notes of the CD had floated away a half an hour before, and yet he did not move from the spindly wooden chair next to the window, his bare feet propped against the casement.

He leaned back further and nearly tumbled over, and with a grunt slammed the front legs of the chair firmly back on the floor, the crash echoing around the studio. He stood and tossed the cigarette out the window into the empty street, watching it spin and tumble.

Jonas pushed away from the window and circled his work table, eyeing the glass, but not moving to pick up his tools. He picked up the sketch he'd made of Meredith, glowing in the darkness on the white paper. *Where the hell are you?*

He had spent the previous day searching the town for Meredith, up and down the narrow streets, in every shop and café. Marie-Laure had been no help; she had been napping in her chair in the front parlor, and no amount of inadvertent door slamming or knocking over of decanters could wake her. Out in the warm mid-July sun, he felt the skin on his neck and scalp prickle as he made his way around the holy hill, asking after Meredith.

He dropped the sketch back on the table and shuffled into his small bedroom, flopping onto the unmade bed. *Fucking wasted day.* He'd picked up his tools a hundred times during the last 24 hours, but despite the work yet to be done on the border and the Magdalene's face, each time put them down and rambled idly around the room, listening to the garbled music of a band playing somewhere down by the Place du Champs du Foire, smoking, starting sketches and then savagely ripping them to shreds.

Where the hell is she? Jonas sat up and felt for his cigarettes and matches. An explosion nearby made him jump and drop the lit match on his bare foot. "Fuck!" he growled, shaking the match off and hurrying to the studio's window. *What the hell was that?* He stuck his head out and looked up and down the street. Another explosion and the night sky filled with emerald and ruby and golden stars. *Aw, shit. Frigging Bastille Day. How did I miss that?* He shook his head and lit a cigarette as faint cheers and notes of what could have been the Marseillaise drifted up the street from the place du Champs de Foire down the hill. *Oh shit. Only a week to finish. Damn. Why was I so damn lazy –*

"Hello? Jonas, are you unwell?"

Jonas looked down to see Dubay, standing on his front doorstep.

"Why aren't you down at the celebration?" Jonas called.

"Are you ready for dinner?"

An explosion sent a shower of blue sparks over the town. "What?"

"Have you eaten?"

"No. Why?"

"There is no food to be had, my friend. All of the cafes are closed. And I suspect you did not lay in stores."

"Not really, no."

Dubay waved him down. "Come, Soeur Marie has been kind enough to leave me dinner - enough for both of us. We can eat it pique-nique in the park, if you would like."

Jonas looked around the room, the work schedule flapping gently in the breeze. "Yeah. Hang on." Without a look at the work left undone, he pulled on his shoes and bounded down the stairs. He found Dubay waiting in the street, hands behind his back.

"Why aren't you down at the fireworks?" Jonas asked as they walked up the rue l'Argenterie toward the cathedral.

"It is a peculiarity of mine."

"One of many."

Dubay smiled. "I love France, yes, wholeheartedly. The Revolution? I simply despise what those barbarians did to the churches – the artwork, Jonas. The history. It was not liberation, it was not enlightenment. It was deplorable, obscene," he said, stepping into the street to give Jonas room on the narrow sidewalk.

Jonas glanced at him but said nothing.

"So," Dubay said, sighing, "I spend Bastille Day in prayer and..." He looked up at the cathedral and then quickly at Jonas. "And studying. I pull out all of my old notes, the books I used when writing my paper at the Sorbonne. It gives me comfort to immerse myself in medieval France. The era is just as complex, and in its own way as violent as the Revolution, but more-satisfying."

"Doesn't it feel weird, though?"

"What?"

"I mean, the accident meant you never got to finish your doctorate. Right?"

Dubay nodded.

"So why pull out your notes? Isn't that a little masochistic?"

Dubay stopped and folded his arms, tapping his lip with the tip of this thumb. "Hmmm. I suppose one could view it in that way. But I view my own history much like I view the history of this church or this country. With love, but with an historian's eye–passion for the mystery, interest in the people, but with the comfortable detachment time affords."

"But it was the defining experience in your life–"

"Yes, but I have experienced so much that is good since–and it was simply an inevitability."

"You're not angry at all? No regrets? I can't believe that. I mean, you're nice and everything, but you're not a saint."

Dubay dropped his hands and stared at Jonas for a split second, then burst into laughter. "No," he said, wiping tears from his eyes, "no, I am not a saint. Far from it. And thank you for reminding me," he said, snorting.

"No problem."

Dubay started walking again toward the cathedral. "Why should I be angry about God's plan for me?"

"That's crazy. Seriously. Sitting in the hospital, you must have been pissed."

Dubay was silent as they walked past the cathedral's doors and around the corner to the garden gate. *Jonas, why can't you shut the fuck up sometimes?* Jonas followed him through into the garden, still warm from the day's heat and redolent of roses.

Dubay stopped suddenly halfway down the path. "I was angry," he said, absently fingering a lavender rose. "I did not understand at first. I had plenty of time to come to understand," he said, turning to Jonas. "What has Meredith told you about Mercedes?"

"Not too much. Just that she died," he replied quietly.

Dubay nodded and continued to the doors of the chapter house. He stepped in and found the picnic basket Soeur Marie had prepared for them, then returned and led Jonas through the gate to the spreading park. Dubay selected a spot looking across to the wooded Morvan and they settled in.

"Meredith was quite young then, just 20," Dubay started, pouring Jonas a glass of Sancerre. "She was in Paris visiting her sister—it was directly after their mother died, I believe."

Jonas nodded.

"I found her terribly annoying," Dubay continued, laughing quietly. "I was a self-important doctoral candidate and she was just a child. But she clung to Mercedes, and Marie-Laure doted on her.

"Mercedes was brilliant," Dubay continued, eyes closed. "Fluent in three languages, a rising expert in the role of women in medieval Burgundy. And beautiful, but different than Meredith. Meredith had a wildness in her eyes, where Mercedes had wisdom. Perhaps that was just the difference in their ages. I was taken with Mercedes the day I met her—of course, I did not let on for weeks."

"How long did you know her?"

"Hmm? Oh, a year, perhaps two," Dubay replied, opening his eyes. "We always had the intention to be married, but I never asked. I was too caught up in my research, my teaching. Marie-Laure chided me for months before…before the accident."

"Abbot…"

"Michel."

"Michel," Jonas said, looking into his wine glass. "Mercedes wasn't with you in the car, was she?"

Dubay jerked, then looked over at Jonas. "Yes."

"Shit."

"I was unconscious on impact, so I do not know what happened to Mercedes. It was God's gift to me."

They sat together quietly, watching the stars and sipping the wine, snatches of music drifting up the hill, the fireworks exploding at the far side of town and lighting them in a soft red glow. After a time, Jonas lowered his glass. "Why aren't you close to Meredith?" he asked quietly.

"Mmm, it is strange," Dubay said, shaking his head. "When she moved to Vézelay last year, I had not seen her since the time she came to visit me in the hospital–nearly 20 years."

"Did she know you were here?"

"No, no, and Marie-Laure did not tell her."

"Why not?"

"Meredith and I–it is a complicated story. She–well, it was not a lack of desire on my part to see her. But she had to deal with what happened in her own way, I suppose," he said, shaking his head. "You know," Dubay said quietly, looking out across the silvery valley, "despite the differences in temperament, Meredith and Mercedes were amazingly alike."

"Yeah?"

"Lovely–beautiful girls, at least to my eyes. The same thick hair, the same tilt to the chin and lovely long arms. Independent and intelligent," Dubay said, swirling the wine in his glass. "Beautiful…"

Jonas nodded. "Her eyes, and that crease she gets between her eyebrows when she's angry, the curve of her neck," he said.

"Ab–Michel," he said, looking up into the tracery of branches entwined. "You haven't seen Meredith today, have you?"

"No, I have not. But it was not for want of trying."

"Huh?"

"Marie-Laure asked me to check on her. Apparently she has been unwell."

"That's an understatement."

"And..."

Jonas looked at Dubay, pulling out a cigarette. "What?"

"And I had a very strange feeling," Dubay said, lying back on the grass, hands behind his head. "A feeling that she was somehow looking for me as well. That there was some-I do not know how to describe it. Something that needs to be said or done."

Jonas hugged his knees, cigarette dangling from his mouth. "Like what?" he mumbled.

"I wish I could tell you," Dubay whispered. "I do not understand. Perhaps I am also unwell." He sat up and poured himself, and Jonas, another glass of wine.

"I'm worried. I'm actually kind of freaked out and I don't know what to do," Jonas whispered, his hand shaking around the wineglass. "But–shit," he said, shaking his head. "I can't. I can't go around fixing people. I tried and it didn't work. I have to let her go, if that's what she wants."

Dubay took a deep breath and closed his eyes. He opened them and said, "Trust that God is keeping her safe."

"I don't know," Jonas mumbled, taking a drag off his cigarette.

They sat together, watching the smoke drift away from the fireworks, caught in the westerly breeze, pulling it like a veil over the night sky.

Jonas lit another cigarette and tossed the spent match into the cool grass, where it hissed. "You know, I never went to church as a kid. My folks didn't think it was necessary."

Dubay nodded.

"They figured I would find my own way somehow, which I guess I have, kind of. But I'm still as confused as shit most of the time."

"About?"

"Myself. People," Jonas shrugged, taking a drag.

Dubay placed a hand on Jonas' shoulder. "This is why it is called spiritual practice, Jonas. One must work at it every day."

"But didn't you say God had a plan? Seems pretty cut and dried to me."

"Yes, yes, I do believe there is a plan," Dubay replied, pulling off a chunk of bread. "But I must struggle every day to understand. To give thanks. To keep myself focused on what is important. So many temptations, Jonas," he said, shaking his head. "Anger. Guilt. Even hate. It is easy to lose your way."

Jonas nodded and drained his glass. "I've never understood, so I guess ignorance is bliss."

"I do not believe that. You know. You could not have your deep connection to art without some transcendent feeling of God. When you are working, you understand."

"Maybe," Jonas said, stretching his legs out in front of him and resting on his elbows. "Maybe so."

Meredith's face floated into his memory. Standing on Marie-Laure's doorstep, her face turned up to watch the stars. "Huh," Jonas muttered.

"Hmmm?"

"Just thinking about Meredith," Jonas said, shaking his head. "She must have been a mess after Mercedes died."

"Yes. From what I understand."

"I mean, what did she have to hold on to? She obviously didn't turn to God."

"I do not know what sustained her. wish...I suppose her father, and Marie-Laure. Her art, perhaps."

"She's so fucking stubborn. She probably just figured she could handle it herself. God damn, she is infuriating," Jonas said, throwing his cigarette into the darkness.

They silently watched the moon break through the veil, yellow and warm in the dark night, rising in a slow arc across the sky.

"Thank you."

"For what?" Dubay asked.

Jonas shrugged. "I don't know. Just—thanks."

Dubay smiled and sat up. "Thank you for listening to my

rambles. I will bore you no more this evening," he said, standing and gathering up the picnic basket. "I have some business to attend to before I turn in."

Jonas stood as well. "I'll walk with you."

They followed the gravel path back to the enclosed garden next to the chapter house. "By the way, I spoke with the mayor yesterday," said Dubay.

"Oh. And?"

"The glass must be finished by the 20th."

"What?" Jonas said, stopping.

Dubay turned and walked back to him. "He made a deal with Madame Chevrey–"

"That only gives me six days to finish!"

"Is there a problem?"

"Well–no, not really. I just–every day helps."

"Yes, I know. I tried to explain, but we have no choice in the matter. "

"But–"

Dubay smoothed the front of his vestments. "Dinner tomorrow?"

"Sure, I guess."

"I will gather you at seven?"

"Fine."

"Good night," Dubay said, turning back to the door.

"'Night."

"Jonas?" Dubay said moments later, his hand on the door.

Jonas turned. "Yeah?"

"Thank you. For listening. I am very grateful."

"See you tomorrow," Jonas nodded.

He walked down the dark rue St Pierre, shaking his head and edging along the sidewalk opposite Meredith's salon. The last fingers of smoke from the fireworks worked their way up the deserted street, veiling his view. As he looked up, a light seemed to flicker in her bedroom window.

His breath caught and he stepped into the street. "Meredith?" he half-called, half-whispered. He stood in the middle of the street, unable to move, straining his eyes for another flicker of light. Five minutes of uninterrupted darkness later, he turned and walked back up the rue St Pierre and around to the rue l'Argenterie and his silent studio.

With effort, Jonas climbed the narrow staircase and dropped onto his bed, struggling with his high tops and finally, with a huff of impatience, leaving them on. Within minutes, he fell asleep, tossing and muttering throughout the night.

A sound out in the studio woke him in the quiet of the early morning, heavy thuds and the horrifying sound of breaking glass. He leaped out of bed and skidded into the studio to find Meredith standing, barefoot, in a pile of splintered glass, hands and feet bleeding.

"Meredith–" he choked, walking cautiously toward her, his hands out, welcoming and pleading. "What–are you OK?" She stood mute, her eyes fixed on her hands. "What the hell happened?" He grabbed her hands, covered in blood, and turned them over. Shards of glass stuck out in odd angles from her palms, strange and beautiful in shimmering emerald and sapphire.

"Jesus Christ!" he yelled, looking at the work table to find the stained glass gone. He dropped to his hands and knees and found her standing in the wreckage of his work. He stood, shaking violently. He grabbed her by the shoulders and screamed into her face. "What the fuck did you do? What the fuck? What – Jesus Christ, what happened?"

"I'm sorry," she whispered, looking at a spot just over his shoulder.

He pushed her away and she stumbled against the window casement, trailing blood. He dropped again to his knees and picked up the bloody wreckage, splinter by splinter. "Jesus. Dubay is going to kill me. Oh my God. Oh my God," he said, tears starting in his eyes. He looked up at Meredith and suddenly sat back on his heels. "You don't have blond hair," he said as she faded out of sight.

Jonas shook his head and found himself on hands and knees next to his bed, tears pooling on the hardwood floor beneath him. He sat back on his heels, heart pounding out of his chest. "Jesus Christ," he whispered, wiping his eyes. He stood shakily and walked out into the studio, half-lit in the grey pre-dawn. The glass lay undamaged on the work table, ready for his final touches; Meredith was nowhere to be seen. Jonas slumped against the wall and ran an unsteady hand over his face. *This place is killing me.*

He fished a nearly broken cigarette out of his pocket and lit it carefully, the end shivering with each tremor of his hand. He stuck the cigarette into his mouth and leaned against the table, peering close at the glass, and then at the portrait of Meredith he'd sketched only a few days before. *You're both killing me.*

AFTER SIX DAYS spent in a haze of intention and sullen inertia, Jonas had not yet completed the glass. Each morning, he arranged his brushes and prepared the paint; and each day, when Dubay arrived to take him to lunch, the glass had gone untouched; Dubay did not press him for details. Despite Dubay's calm assurances that Meredith would return, the only glimpse Jonas had was the hastily sketched portrait; every day, he pounded on the Salon's door, and searched for her face in the ever-growing crowds of pilgrims pouring into Vézelay for the Magdalene's feast.

Jonas' eyes flew open before the alarm, his heart pounding. The stains and cracks on the ceiling seemed to converge, a pattern that always seemed to take the shape of the lines of the glass. He shut his eyes with a groan. *Today. I'm never going to get it done in time. What am I going to tell him?*

He rubbed his eyes with his knuckles and sighed. *God damn, I hate that fucking glass.*

He dropped his hands and his eyes flew open, wide and surprised. He threw off the covers and ran into the studio, past the work table and to the framed photo of St Chapelle. He pulled it off the wall and walked with it to the tall north-facing windows, tilting it to catch the early grey light. He ran his scarred fingers along the frame, caressing the photos, shaking his head slightly.

He turned back to the work table and lay the photo down, circling around to the glass. He leaned in close, planes of ruby and sapphire and gold as broad as the sky filling his vision. The swirl and whorl of the blown glass pulled him in, spinning and lightheaded. His breath caught as waves of emerald washed over him, and in a distant corner of his mind, a melody emerged and he began to hum.

Jonas smiled broadly and stood up, a crash of energy racing through him. He quickly lit a cigarette, ran into his room, pulled on his jeans, and skidded back into the studio. He kicked on the stereo and turned up the volume; the Chili Peppers blared. With shaking hands, he lined up brushes and paint, and took a deep breath. He held his hands out, willing them to be steady.

Another deep breath. He pushed Meredith's portrait under a pile of papers and picked up the brush.

The CD had nearly reached its end and Jonas completed the face and put the finishing touches on the Magdalene's eyes, solemn and haughty. He put the brush down and stretched his back, curving over the table. Standing straight, he rolled his neck, taking pleasure in each creak and pop. He checked his watch–only eight o'clock. *Plenty of time to let everything dry before the preview this afternoon.*

Singing under his breath, he ambled into his bedroom in search of a new pack of cigarettes. *Oh come on. There's no way I'm out already.* He pulled the sheets off the bed, checked under the pillows, dumped the contents of his suitcase onto the floor. "Shit," he muttered, standing up. "Fucking cigarettes."

He pulled on his shoes and checked his pockets for cash. He shifted from foot to foot, shaking his head. The music ended and shook Jonas out of his indecisive reverie. He walked into the small hallway and started toward the stairs, but a prickling feeling on his neck stayed him. He turned and walked quickly into the studio. In the cool light, a figure hovered near the glass.

"Meredith!? Oh my God. Thank God. Mer–don't touch the glass!" Jonas yelled, running to the table. He grabbed her hands as they hovered over the glass, offering a benediction.

She turned her head and looked at Jonas. "I have heard I may seek shelter here," she whispered, looking past him.

"Where have you been?" he asked, holding both of her hands in his. "Jesus, you're covered in dirt–is that blood? Where have you been?" he demanded, shaking.

Meredith stood away from the table, backing against the wall. "I have been on the road. Is this not the hostel for pilgrims? It is more elegant a lodging than I had hoped for these long days."

Jonas' heart thudded and he closed his eyes. "What are you talking about?" he whispered, shuddering.

He opened his eyes and smoothed leaf-strewn hair away from her filthy face. Meredith pulled away, a look of abject terror in her face. "You should not take such liberties," she whispered hoarsely.

He dropped his hand and folded his arms, stepping away. "What the hell are you–"

Meredith shrunk further against the wall.

"Oh Jesus Christ," Jonas muttered. He took a deep breath. "This is–this is not the-the hostel," he said, looking around. He eyed the nearly complete glass with longing and regret. "I will help you find it," he whispered, shuddering.

"Many thanks," she whispered, eyes darting around the room. "First we must go to the cathedral and be confessed."

"No, I think we better find your–hostel," he replied.

Meredith edged away, trailing blood from her hands along the wall. Her t-shirt and jeans were torn and dark with mud, and she had lost her shoes. "No, I must find the priest. I must find the priest. I must be confessed," she cried. "You must help me! I must be confessed," she wailed.

Jonas let out a small sigh of relief as Meredith moved away from the glass. "OK, OK, OK. We'll find the priest," he said, shaking hands open toward her. "We'll find him. But first we have to get you cleaned up."

"No. No, we must go now."

Jonas stopped and considered her. "When did you eat last?"

"I need food no longer. The Magdalene is my sustenance."

"Jesus Christ," he muttered. "Here, sit down. No, sit down," he said, grabbing the rickety chair and placing it on the far side of the room. He pushed her down into it. "Wait right here." She sat uneasily in the chair, legs splayed unnaturally and head lolling.

With a glance over his shoulder, he bounded down the stairs two at a time and into the still-dark kitchen. A coffee cup, a crusty coffee pot, and a half-eaten and likely stale bag of chips comprised his entire provender. "Shit," he muttered, grabbing the cup and bag of chips and hurtling back up the stairs.

Meredith was again standing over the glass, her hands excruciating inches away from the fresh paint on the Magdalene's face. "Meredith," he said, edging towards her. "Meredith. Meredith!" he yelled. She looked up and her eyes seemed to focus. "Are you here to confess me?" she asked.

Jonas shoulders sagged. "No," he said, taking her by the elbow and leading her back to the chair. "Here, eat this," he said, turning her filthy palms up and pouring the chips into her hands. "Eat. And then we'll go find the priest."

She chewed, mouth open, the vague look returning to her eyes. "Wait here–don't move," he said, grabbing the coffee cup and jogging to the bathroom. "Don't move," he called as he filled the cup from the tap. He looked in the mirror; his eyes were wide and forehead lined. *Be careful what you ask for.* He took a swig of lukewarm water from the cup, and refilled it, walking carefully back to the studio.

Meredith was on the floor, curled into a ball, chips crushed tightly in her palms. "Jesus. Jesus," he said, running to her side, water sloshing on the floor. "Meredith. Hello, wake up. Hello?" he said, shaking her at first gently, then with force. She groaned slightly but did not wake.

He stood and paced the studio, arms folded, blood and dirt now smeared across his white t-shirt. *God, did she hit her head?* He raced back and knelt next to her, gently moving her head and pushing away curls to look for blood on her scalp. Finding nothing, he sat back on his heels, rubbing his temple's scar, familiar and reassuring.

I can't just leave her here. It's not safe. Shit, it's not safe for the glass. Michel won't be here for hours...Maybe I can take the glass with me. He stopped and looked closely at the glass. *Eh, it's not dry, it'll get screwed up.* "Ah, shit," he gritted, folding his arms again.

Meredith twitched and cried out; Jonas, with one last look at the glass, crossed to her side. "Hey. Hey, it's going to be OK. I'll fix this," he whispered in her ear. She continued to twitch and he closed his eyes. "OK, I can do this," he said, reaching under her and raising her to a sitting position. "Here we go, here we go," he said, awkwardly half-dragging, half-carrying her across the studio and into his room. He lifted her onto the bed and she rolled onto her side, curling again into a ball, smearing his sheets.

"Wait here," he said, smoothing her hair. "I'll be back soon." He climbed down the narrow stairs, catching his breath at each step. *This is a bad idea. This is a bad idea.* By the time he reached the front door and stepped into the glittering hard July sun, he was gulping for air, desperate for a clean breath. He looked up and down the empty street, searching for an answer.

I need a fucking cigarette.

Chapter Twenty-Two

THE DRY HAY in the room smelled of many days and many previous occupants, musty and sour. The makeshift door—no more than a tattered blanket—was pulled to, and she could see into the main room, strangely empty. She turned to her side for a better view and groaned; the road up the hill to the town had been arduous, shredding her feet and trying every muscle. "Where is the hostel keeper?" she wondered. "Where are the other pilgrims?"

The silence was uncanny; she shivered. "Holy Magdalene, protect me." She pushed, groaning, into a sitting position and her head reeled. "I—strength. Need my strength. Vigil tomorrow," she whispered, rubbing her eyes and smoothing her long blond hair into a plâit. She stood and shook the hay out of her black cloak and repinned her pilgrim's badge. She looked around the room and groaned. "No chamber pot," she muttered, and walked gingerly across the small passage into the main room. "Not even a slop pail."

The ceiling was high, with small glassless windows lining the north wall along the roof line. The glancing, shabby light made the room more dim, and threatening. She looked around the empty room, shaking her head. "Where are the rest of the pilgrims?" She could find no trace of any other travelers: no packs, no staves, no cloaks hung to make a private space. A moment later, her heart constricted, a thought rushing to her head like a flame. "And where is my offering?"

She dropped her filthy cloak onto the filthier hay and searched the room, muttering and crying, turning over hay and pushing aside benches. At last, in the far corner, she found it, still wrapped in its grubby blood-stained linen. She moved the worn cloth aside and the glass glittered, as if of its own volition, in the dank room.

She sighed shakily and closed her eyes. The border had been damaged, the ruby shattered, but it no longer mattered. She would be confessed, kneel vigil, and make her offering on the Magdalene's feast. "And after that?" she whispered, rewrapping the glass and clutching it to her chest. "And after that," she repeated, sinking to the floor, "I do not see."

She curled into the corner, cradling the glass protectively. Her stomach gave an immense growl and she groaned; her last meal had been days ago, out in the woods, before she met up with the last road. As she had expected, the monks had taken all the best of everything in the town by the time she had arrived, leaving scraps for the pilgrims to quarrel over. She pushed a stray wisp of hair from her face. Her eyebrows knitted and she touched her hair again, frowning. She reached back and pulled her hair out of the plâit, and found it was no longer smooth and golden, but kinky and brown.

She shook her head and stood up, the brightness of the room blinding her. She stumbled backwards into the wall, panting. "What?" As her eyes gradually adjusted, Meredith found that she was in the corner of Jonas' studio, the afternoon sun lighting the north ramparts and the narrow street outside the large, bright windows. "Oh no," she sobbed. She looked down to find her hands and feet dark with dried blood, her t-shirt ripped and filthy.

"I–" she sobbed, shaking her hands and head. "How did I get here?" She hobbled back and forth in front of the work table, muttering and crying, pulling at her hair. She stopped in front of the glass and folded her arms, tapping both sets of fingers on her upper arms.

The colors seemed to move in waves across the glass, peaking and swirling, dazzling bright; Meredith leaned in close, drawn by the eyes in the Magdalene's face. "She–I–" she muttered, stepping back and leaning spread-eagled against the sturdy, solid wall.

The light flickered. The windows grew dark, and in the next instant, disappeared, replaced by rough-hewn walls. The musty scent of hay filled her nose, and the warm, close heat drew beads of sweat out along her forehead and the nape of her neck. She shook her head again. "No. No," Meredith said, clenching her fists, squeezing her eyes shut. "God," she pleaded. "No more.

No." She opened her eyes, and the room had again grown bright, the windows in place and shimmering clear.

She slid down the wall and curled in on herself, hugging her knees and rocking. A few moments later the reverberations of an explosion filled the room, rattling the glass. She shrank against the wall, covering her head as the windows exploded and flame and smoke filled the room. Meredith lay on her side and whimpered, pulling at her hair and beating her head with open hands. "I'm sorry, Michel. I'm sorry I'm sorry I'm sorry I'm sorry…"

Hours later, she awoke curled around the offering, the room grown darker and more lonesome as the sun disappeared, replaced by the cool evening breeze. The sounds of the busy city wafted in: the quarreling of the merchants in the street below, the creaking of carts, the squealing of the pigs, the tolling of the cathedral bells.

"Why does he not return?" she whispered, laying the offering aside and stretching. *It would be foolish to go alone. I have no wife's veil; I will surely be detained after curfew. But what if he does not return? I am out of time.*

She stood and again shook the hay out of her hair, her cloak. *The Duke's men could not know what happened. It is too soon. They did not detain me at the toll way. I do regret the loss of my bowl and spoon to them, though. Pilgrims are to be exempt. Pons…he looked so kingly, passing in procession with his monks. The Abbot here will not be pleased to see him…*

She shivered. *He will find me; his messenger saw me, I am certain of it. He looked so well, I regret...* She shook her head and made tentative, creaking steps across the still-empty room toward the stairs. *I must be confessed, I must confess my sins and kneel vigil. I can wait no longer. My sins weigh heavily. Dear Magdalene, they are so heavy I fear I will not go on...*

She clutched the offering to her chest and made her way, step by step, down the staircase, and through the cool, empty main room of the hostel, leaving bloody footprints on the dirty hay. She hesitated at the threshold, heart thudding in her chest. She took a deep breath, pushed open the door, and was caught up in the current of the street, pulling her on to the great cathedral of Vézelay.

Chapter Twenty-Three

JONAS CLENCHED HIS JAW and with a last steadying breath, jogged up the rue de l'Argenterie toward the cathedral and Dubay's office. The late afternoon sun was still hard and bright, shafting between the tall, narrow houses, throwing angular shadows on the cobblestones. He wiped the sweat from his forehead with the hem of his blood-stained t-shirt as he jogged up the street. *This is a bad idea. I shouldn't leave her alone.* "Shit," he muttered, turning the corner to the confluence of rue l'Argenterie and rue St Pierre.

The cathedral plaza was crowded with people, wave after wave pushing and jostling their way to the cathedral doors. Nuns stood together in small groups, silently saying their rosaries, eyes squeezed shut while tour groups following brightly colored umbrellas flowed around penitents crawling on hands and knees toward the basilica.

Jonas edged his way slowly through the crowd, the crash of voices and shifting groups maddening. "Pardon, pardon," he muttered, gritting his teeth. He finally stumbled out of the press and leaned against the gate to the cathedral's walled garden, sweaty and shaking, then pushed open the gate into the blissfully empty gardens. He sprinted through, the crowd now just an echoing murmur behind him. He pushed open the heavy door to the chapter house and stood blinking in the darkness of the ancient building, hands on his hips and breathing heavily.

When his eyes adjusted, he found that a group of men and women in dark suits stood at the other end of the cloisters, arms folded and lips pursed. He jogged down the long hall, making for the staircase to Dubay's office. "Pardon, pardon," he mumbled as he approached. Their quiet discussion stuttered to a stop as he passed through. He reached the staircase and found the door locked. An older woman with perfectly groomed silver hair shook her head. "Ce n'est pas la peine," she said.

Jonas shook the handle and turned to the group. "What the hell is this?" he asked angrily.

"Abbot Dubay apparently is not to be disturbed," replied the woman in heavily accented English, rolling her eyes.

Jonas narrowed his eyes at her and turned back to the door, banging on it with his fist. "Michel! Michel! Open the frigging door—I need to talk to you!" he yelled. The group behind him gasped and retreated half a step as Jonas' yells echoed down the long hall.

A pale young man with dark hair and a monk's habit appeared from a side gallery, darting nervous glances at the door and then at the group as he approached Jonas. "Monsieur, s'il vous plâit," he whispered, wringing his hands. "Abbot Dubay—"

"Let me in," Jonas said, clenching his fists.

"Monsieur—"

"This is an emergency. Let me in!" he repeated, his voice rising.

"Je ne peux pas —"

"Yes, you can. Open the door," Jonas gritted, stepping close to the young man. "Ouvrez la porte. Now!" he yelled.

The young man flinched and stepped back. Silently, he pulled a key from his pocket and unlocked the door. Jonas pushed through and slammed the door on exclamations of protest and anger behind him. He locked the door and took the stairs two at a time.

He ran down the hall and pushed the door open. Dubay was standing at the window pointing his finger in the face of a small dark-haired man. "C'est mon vitrail!" Dubay said, shaking with anger.

Jonas knocked on the open door and Dubay stepped away from the man and dropped his hand. "Jonas, I did not know you were here," he said, folding his arms. He glanced at Jonas' shirt and dropped his hands. "What happened?" he demanded.

"Meredith."

"Where is she?"

"In my studio—I hope. She's asking for—" Jonas glanced at the man standing at the window and backed away from Dubay.

"Ah, yes, Jonas, allow me to introduce Monsieur Merimee. Jean, this is Jonas Flycatcher."

Jonas nodded at the mayor but ignored his proffered hand and turned back to Dubay. "We gotta go. She needs help."

"Dubay," Merimee started, stepping between Jonas and Dubay. "Madame Chevrey–"

"Oui, Jean. Oui," Dubay said, his mouth a thin line. "Jonas, is the glass finished? We have a preview with Madame Chevrey in two hours."

Jonas stepped back and folded his arms. "Yes, it's done," he said angrily. "Tell Madame Chevrey–and this asshole," he said, pointing at Merimee, "to piss off, though. For Christ's sake," Jonas said, shaking slightly, patting his pockets unconsciously for his cigarettes. "Meredith is really sick. She needs your help," he whispered.

"I–" Dubay said, hand on his hip, rubbing his forehead.

"Dubay?" Merimee interrupted, eyebrows raised. "J'attends…"

Dubay dropped his hand and turned to Merimee. "Plus tard, Jean, plus tard," he gritted, ushering him to the door.

"Non. Maintenant," Merimee replied, folding his arms and standing his ground in the doorway.

"Jonas, please excuse us for a moment," Dubay said, conducting Merimee into the hall and shutting the door. Jonas paced back and forth across the office, straining to understand the loud, rapid French in the hallway. Dubay returned a minute later, flushed and shaking.

"What did you tell him?" Jonas demanded.

"I asked him to give my regards to Madame Chevrey and give her my regrets that the preview has been postponed to tomorrow morning," Dubay replied, folding his arms.

Jonas' shoulders sagged. "Thank you," he said.

Dubay stopped and pointed at Jonas' shirt. "Is that blood?"

"Yeah. Yeah. Come on, we have to get back there—" Jonas said, standing up.

"You left her at your studio?" Dubay asked.

"Yeah, I didn't know what else to do. I wish I had a freaking phone in there," Jonas replied, halfway through the door. "She's hallucinating. She kept asking if I was the hostel-keeper, and she kept insisting that she had to be confessed. Are you coming? Come on, we have to go!"

The color drained from Dubay's face. "Say that again," he whispered.

"What?" Jonas asked angrily, turning back. "Come on!"

"No, no—what did she say about confession?"

"I don't know. She said I had to find a priest and she needed to have confession. Come on, let's go!"

Dubay ran his fingers through his hair, took a deep breath, and followed Jonas out the door.

They ran down the stairs and stumbled into the echoing cloisters, nearly knocking over the young monk still lingering near the door. "Pardon, Pascal," Dubay said, steadying him by the shoulder. "D'accord?"

"Oui, d'accord," he replied quietly, drawing back.

"Michel! Michel!" a voice called from the passage from the cloisters to the cathedral. "Un moment, s'il vous plâit." The woman with the perfect silver hair emerged from the shadows, eyebrow arched.

Dubay stopped and turned. "Ah, oui, Geneviève, je vous en prie. Dubay smiled, grabbing Jonas by the arm and walking toward her. "Jonas, this is Madame Chevrey."

Her eyebrow arched further and she looked him up and down again, lingering on the filthy shirt. "We met earlier," she chuckled. "Precisely as I had imagined you."

"Yeah," Jonas nodded, looking past her toward the door to the gardens. "Well, nice meeting you," he said, shaking off Dubay's hand and running down the hall.

Madame Chevrey quickly stepped between Dubay and Jonas, her heels clicking sharply on the worn stone. "Michel – the preview? Where is my glass?"

Dubay clenched his jaw and smiled stiffly. "We shall preview the glass tomorrow morning–I think you will agree, the glorious morning light in the nave will do it the most justice. My apologies, I must attend to an urgent matter. Dinner tonight-at seven?" He kissed her on both cheeks and hurried after Jonas.

"Michel!" Madame Chevrey called, folding her arms.

Dubay nodded impatiently and waved, then pushed open the door and joined Jonas in the garden. Jonas broke into a run and after a moment's hesitation, Dubay chased after him. They skidded to a halt at the gate and Dubay whispered, "Oh no."

"What?"

"The bishop of Autun. My boss. That is his car," he said, nodding to the black sedan crawling toward the cathedral. "He cannot see me. I will be stuck for hours with him. Come, we must go around the other way—his car will be parked just outside this gate." Dubay turned and ran back across the long garden, Jonas trailing behind.

They reached the southern gate, near the chapter house, and broke into a run through the chestnut-lined park, around the massive flying buttresses, past the ancient graveyard. They slowed as they edged along the plaza. "What time is it?" Jonas asked, panting.

"Almost two," Dubay gasped.

"Shit. Jesus, I've been gone too long."

Dubay nodded and with effort they raced off toward rue des Écoles and across to No.23 rue de l'Argenterie.

Jonas pushed open the door and paused, letting his eyes adjust and tenting his sweaty t-shirt to cool off. Dubay stepped in behind him and whispered, "Where is she?"

Jonas nodded towards the stairs. "Up in my room. She was asleep when I left."

"I will follow you," Dubay said.

Jonas ran across the empty parlor and up the stairs, Dubay a few steps behind. "What the hell?" he yelled, rushing to the bed and pulling off the soiled sheets. "Where-oof!" He collided with Dubay at the top of the stairs.

"What ?"

"She's not there," Jonas growled, rushing into the studio. "No!" Jonas yelled, running to the window. He stuck his head out and looked up and down the street, but saw no retreating form, no trace of Meredith. He slammed the window shut and threw his head back, eyes tingling.

"We will find her," Dubay said, squeezing Jonas' shoulder. "She could not have got far."

"God damn it," Jonas shuddered, holding his head. "Damn it."

"It is not your fault, Jonas."

"It is. I failed again, I failed. I failed her, I failed you—"

"You have not failed anyone—"

"I'm trying to fix it, I am. I am," Jonas said, shaking off Dubay's hand. "But I always screw it up. God damn—" Jonas turned toward the work table and stopped. "No," he whispered. The room drained of color, monochromatic and flat. Jonas rushed to the table and suddenly doubled over with a wave of nausea. "No. No way. No way," he cried, shaking his head.

Dubay joined him at the table and his eyes widened. "Oh no..."

"SONOFABITCH!" Jonas yelled, picking up a lead spool holder and throwing it against the wall. He paced back and forth, alternately patting his pockets and pulling at his hair. "No fucking way. No. No. No!" he gritted, pounding the work table with his fists.

"You do not think she took it?" Dubay asked tentatively.

"Where the hell else would it be?" Jonas snarled. "Oh shit," he said, tears running down his face. *How could I be so stupid?* He picked up the spindly wooden chair and smashed it against the wall. He dropped the last splinter and pounded his own head against the wall.

"Jonas. Jonas!" Dubay said, shaking him. Jonas turned to Dubay, eyes clouded and red. "God, I'm sorry, Michel," he sobbed. "I'm sorry."

Dubay put his hands on each side of Jonas' face. "Jonas, listen. Listen to me! We will find the glass. We will find her," he said.

Jonas shrugged Dubay off and slid down against the wall. "There's no way. The way she was walking…she passed out right in front of me. She's probably dropped it already. It's probably in a million pieces in some alley. Oh God," he said, gagging. "What if she cuts herself with it? All that glass…oh Jesus Christ," he cried, squeezing his eyes closed.

Dubay knelt in front of Jonas and put his hands on his cheeks, lifting his face. "We will find her. The glass is fine," he nodded.

Jonas held his breath, looking at the strange gleam in Dubay's eye. "No way," Jonas protested. "There's no way. Maybe find her, but the glass–"

"Trust me."

"But–"

Dubay stood and smoothed his shirt, then held out a hand to Jonas. Jonas stared long at the elegant, scarred hand. He took Dubay's hand and was pulled up.

"Stay right there," Dubay smiled, walking toward the bathroom. "Do not move."

Jonas looked around the studio—the shattered chair, gaping holes in the wall, papers scattered all over the desk and floor. *My career is over. And Meredith...What the hell am I going to do?* He started shaking again, and a wave of nausea overcame him. He rushed to the bathroom, where he found Dubay filling the coffee mug with water, and retched into the toilet.

"Here, drink this," Dubay said. "You are in shock. Breathe. Yes, good. Breathe. Good," he said, taking the glass back from Jonas. "Sit down." He guided Jonas and sat him on the toilet and stood back, arms folded.

"I'm sorry—"

"Jonas, be quiet," Dubay said sharply. "We are going to look for Meredith. She still has the glass, and it is still whole."

"But—"

"Jonas, shut up!"

Jonas flinched and nodded.

"It is still whole, but I do not know if she is. We must find her—you must master yourself. Go down to Marie-Laure's and that part of town; it is possible familiar footsteps took her there. I am going up to the cathedral. I will meet you back here in an hours' time, yes?"

Jonas nodded.

"Excellent," Dubay smiled, backing out of the bathroom. "Splash some water on your face."

Jonas stood and turned on the small shower, sticking his entire head in the cold spray. *Please, God.* He shook his head and scrubbed his face raw with the ratty towel. He turned off the water and walked back out into the studio. "How do you know?" he asked, his voice scratchy and thin.

"Can you trust me?" Dubay asked.

"Yes."

"I will see you here in an hour." Dubay nodded and ran quickly down the stairs. The front door slammed shut moments later, shaking the walls and the glass in the windows.

Jonas took a steadying breath and stumbled down the stairs, across the front rooms, and into the fading sunlight of the rue de l'Argenterie.

Chapter Twenty-Four

HE SLAMMED THE DOOR behind him and broke into a run up the shadowy rue de l'Argenterie. He paused for breath at the edge of the cathedral's plaza, still crowded with pilgrims and dignitaries and merchants setting up stalls around the periphery. The pull of role and appearances was strong; it was his duty as Abbot to make his guests welcome, to ensure the merchants and townsfolk did not clash too strongly with the bishop and his entourage, as it had been the abbot's role these thousand years and more.

Dubay recalled Jonas' face, tear-streaked and hopeless; he scanned the crowd for Meredith's curly dark hair and moved on past the plaza to the park behind the cathedral.

Visitors and pilgrims wandered the leafy park in twos and threes, watching Dubay reverently and casting each other quizzical looks behind his back. Dubay nodded at each, distracted, beyond the reality of their existence when they proved not to be Meredith. He covered the park, the ruins of the old chapter house, the gardens, the dark familiar scriptorium with its rows of carels. He paused at the door to the nave, catching sight of Soeur Marie.

"Abbot? You look unwell again," she said.

"I am well, and am in haste," he said quickly. "Do you know Mademoiselle Thibault? She has a photography salon just down St Pierre?"

Soeur Marie narrowed her eyes. "I believe so. Dark hair? Never comes to mass?" she said, folding her arms.

Dubay nodded. "Yes, that's the one. Have you seen her this afternoon?"

"There have been many, many people in and out today, Abbot. The pilgrims are thick as flies out there," she said, jerking her head toward the nave.

He closed his eyes and sighed. "But did you see her?" he asked, exasperation creeping into his voice.

"No."

"Please keep your eyes open, my dear. It is very, very important that I find her. In fact," he said, taking her by the arm, "in fact, I would be most grateful if you could alert Frère Pascal and the others that I am looking for her, and to bring her to my office–and keep her there–if they find her."

"And what about the bishop?"

"What about him?"

"He has been waiting in your office for you to receive him for the last hour."

Dubay groaned. "Why didn't he go to his hotel?" he muttered. "Bring him a bottle of my Romanée-Conti and my apologies. And ask if perhaps he'd like to retire to his rooms. I will attend to him in the morning."

Soeur Marie shook her head slowly. "This is the Bishop of Autun—"

"I am aware of that," he said sharply. "This is a more pressing matter. Please," he said. "I must find Mademoiselle Thibault."

She folded her arms. "The Romanée-Conti?"

He nodded. "Yes, yes, thank you. You are an angel."

"I know," she replied, opening the door to the nave.

He closed the door behind him and walked toward the altar, the determined click of his shoes on the worn stone muffled by the deafening murmurs of hundreds of pilgrims and visitors. He scanned the crowd as he walked, each dark head checking his heart, the broken sunlight turning the church—his church—into a warren of dark caves and flitting ghosts. He passed the altar into the chapel, finding only pilgrims and photographers, praying to the Magdalene and snapping shots of the painted Ste Catherine column.

He hurried around to the entrance to the crypt below the altar, the ancient church's original holy place, and found it completely dark; no pilgrims had yet ventured into that cold sanctuary. He took up a candle from the altar and walked carefully down the narrow steps; no sign of Meredith, only the glittering reflection of the Magdalene's reliquary. He dropped to his knees. "Please," he whispered, eyes closed. "Please, I am trying to do your will. Lead me to her. Lead her to me."

Moments passed in the flickering light, and no footsteps could be heard on the steps, no quiet voice from the dark cold corner near the ancient altar. Dubay's shoulders sagged and his head fell forward, chin resting on his chest. An image came to him of Meredith's tear-streaked face, mouthing words at his hospital bedside, words she could not speak and words he could not hear.

He stood and climbed out of the crypt. The press of pilgrims shunted him down the south aisle, and he stood on tiptoe to see across the church. He reached the abduction of Ganymede column and stopped abruptly, two visitors stumbling into him from behind. "Pardon," he muttered, nodding them on their way. He rubbed his eyes with the tips of his fingers and shook his head slightly.

He crossed himself and walked, without a look around him, through the crowded cathedral, across the narthex, and onto the front steps. The sunset had turned the sky fiery orange, the narrow streets dark and purple beneath. He pressed forward, giving a cursory glance down the rue St Pierre, and turned down the rue de l'Argenterie.

He reached no. 23 and walked through the open front door. "Jonas?" he called. "Jonas?" Dubay ran up the stairs and found Jonas sitting on his bed, head in trembling hands. Dubay knelt next to him and put a gentle hand on his shoulder. "I have not found her, yet," he whispered. "I take it you had no luck with

Marie-Laure?"

Jonas jerked his head. "No," he mumbled through his hands. "She wasn't feeling well and I kept asking her to remember if she'd seen Meredith and she just kind of muttered, like she was talking in her sleep. Her eyes were all glassy..."

Dubay dropped his hand. "Has Guillaume returned?"

"Yeah," Jonas said, sitting up and rubbing his forehead. "He kicked me out. He said I was bothering her, and why wasn't I taking care of her while he was gone, and get the hell out. So I did," he said, shrugging.

"Damn. Damn," Dubay said, starting to pace. "Was the doctor there with them?"

"He came in as I was leaving."

"She is at least in good hands... She did not say anything about Meredith before you left?"

"No," Jonas said, patting his pocket and looking around the room. He stood and opened his suitcase, peered under the bed, threw the covers off and sat back down, flicking his lighter on and off. "She did say to remember 1 Corinthians. Whatever the hell that means."

"1 Corinthians what?" Dubay asked, sitting down next to Jonas.

"Three thirteen? I don't know. I didn't ask her what she was talking about. She didn't even seem to know."

Dubay lay back on the bed and covered his face with his hands. *What does she mean? What are you trying to tell me?*

"What do we do now?" Jonas asked, still playing with the lighter.

"What *you* do now," Dubay said, sitting up with effort, "is sleep."

Jonas shook his head. "No way. No, I have to get the glass back. I have to help her."

"I will contact the gendarmes as soon as I leave here—they will look for her. But I have faith that tomorrow Meredith will return, and it will all be clear. The Vigil of the Magdalene..." he whispered, half to himself. Jonas nodded absently and lay back, falling asleep within seconds. Dubay took the still-hot lighter from his hand and flicked it on. *Please. Let it be clear.*

Dubay returned to his office, threading through the cathedral's crowds and the cloister's whispering darkness. He turned on the desk lamp and dropped into his chair, shifting the papers and books on his desk, avoiding the folded note propped up against the lamp. With a deep breath, he grabbed the note and opened it. *Disappointed... usual for the Abbot to receive the Bishop personally...highly unusual...trust the glass will be ready for viewing tomorrow...*

He dropped the paper back on the desk and gritted his teeth, a wave of anger rising. *Pompous, arrogant bas-* He unclenched his fists and sat back, breath coming in short bursts.

With a steadying breath, he picked up the phone and called the gendarmerie. After detailing the situation and receiving assurances of cooperation, he hung up the phone and picked up the *Confessions,* turning to the page where the photo of Mercedes sat undisturbed. He stroked the tattered edges, running his thumb across her smiling face. "I will find her. I promise," he whispered.

The sky was grey and damp when Dubay awoke early the next morning at his desk, stiff and creaking. After another call to the sergeant of the gendarmerie, in which he received assurances that yes, they were looking for Meredith, and no, they had not found her, he shuffled into the bathroom and showered quickly, the icy water waking him with brutal effectiveness. He had just set down the razor and was toweling off his burning neck when there was a tentative knock on his office door.

"Abbot Dubay? May I come in?" Frère Pascal asked, his voice shaking.

"Yes, of course, come in," Dubay called from his room, pulling on a silk robe.

Frère Pascal pushed open the door and set a coffee tray on the desk, balanced precariously on top of the piles of papers and books. "Soeur Marie would like to know when you care for breakfast," he asked, looking anywhere but Dubay's bedroom.

Dubay walked into the office and poured himself a cup. "Mmm," he said, sipping the coffee. "I do not require breakfast this morning. Thank you."

"But–" Frère Pascal said, eyes wide. "She said I must not let you get away with no breakfast today."

Dubay smiled and felt the tension in his shoulders abate. "Thank you. Please tell Soeur Marie that I promise to eat today, truly. I simply do not have time to do so this morning."

"Yes, Abbot," Frère Pascal replied, looking at his feet.

"That will be all, brother," Dubay said, smiling and turning back to his small room. The office door closed behind him, and he dropped the robe on the bed and pulled on his impeccable trousers and tailored shirt, fastening the gold cufflinks smoothly. He slipped on his fringed loafers and shook his head. *What vanity.* He stood and checked himself in the mirror. All at once it came to him.

Lauda mater Ecclesia,

lauda Christi clementiam:

qui septem purgat vitia

per septiformem gratiam.

Maria soror Lazari

quae tot commisit criminal,

ab ipsa fauce tartari

redit ad vitae praemia.

The normally deep furrows of his forehead had smoothed away, his blue eyes shone bright and almost eager. Dubay made his way down through the dark cloisters, and into the cathedral. Even at that early hour, pilgrims by the dozen approached the altar and knelt, crossing themselves. They stood back reverently as Dubay passed and he smiled a "Bon matin" to each.

He lit a candle and walked the familiar path down to the ancient altar. With a twinge of guilt, he shut the iron gate behind him and locked it.

The crypt was as he had left it the night before, silent and dark. The strange carvings on the columns wavered in the candlelight and he was caught for a moment, watching them dance and move to a music he could not hear. He turned to the Magdalene's reliquary and sank to his knees.

An hour later he emerged into the grey morning of the cathedral. The massive space was stifling, the July heat returning with the influx of hundreds upon hundreds of pilgrims and tourists. Dubay rolled his head and groaned; the creaks and pops in his neck signaled a weariness he hadn't felt in years. He scanned the crowd as he rubbed his neck, searching for Meredith.

"Michel. Michel, there you are," called a voice from behind in the chapel. He turned to find Madame Chevrey leading her group of dignitaries and hangers-on to join him at the altar.

"Good morning, Geneviève. You look well," he said, kissing her on both cheeks, but looking beyond her, scanning the already growing crowds for Meredith.

"Unfortunately, I cannot say the same for you," she said.

"Oh I am quite well, thank you," he smiled.

"Hmm," she shrugged. "I assume you know everyone?" she asked Dubay, turning to her group and waving her hand absently.

"Yes, of course. Delighted," he nodded, looking past them toward the chapel.

"We need to discuss the arrangements for turning the glass

over to the Cluny after tomorrow. Where is it?" she asked, stepping in front of Dubay.

He took a deep breath and smiled. "You assume a great deal, my dear. I believe Jean has been in touch on this subject?" he asked, drawing her by the elbow toward the cloisters. "The glass will remain here," he whispered. "It is the only solution. You know that. I am surprised that you, of all people, would be advocating its removal. It must be displayed where it was found, where it was intended to be left."

"If that is true, which I am still not entirely sure of, then why display it? Why repair it?" she replied, shaking her head.

"Because, it is an offering to the Magdalene, and it must be made whole."

"Michel, it is a cultural treasure, too."

He shook his head. "It is a spiritual offering. The fact that it has great beauty and historical value is secondary. Please," he said, his scarred hands that of a supplicant. "It needs to stay here."

She folded her arms and frowned. "I do not make those decisions. I can only recommend."

"In that case, you know my mind," he said, looking past her again into the crowd.

"Michel, if you press to keep the glass here, there may be repercussions."

"Such as?" he asked, looking back at her.

"Such as reduction of funding for the cathedral."

"That would be unfortunate," he said, jaw tightening.

She nodded. "I agree."

"Well, what if the Bishop intervened–"

"It may make a difference," she admitted.

"I will discuss it with him as soon as I am able. In the meantime," he said with a forced smile, "I have other business to attend to. Will you excuse me?"

"Abbot Dubay," she said, stepping in front of him again. "The preview?"

"Ah, yes. We must cancel it."

"What?"

"There are some last-minute items to attend to, and besides," he said, pointing at the dark windows, "it is far too overcast to show it to its best effect. Tomorrow, tomorrow, my dear. Before mass, you will see it."

"Dubay," she replied, her face reddening. "I will not be put off."

"Tomorrow," he smiled, kissing her cheeks and hurrying toward the narthex. He checked on the threshold, watching the tide carry a dark-haired woman along the north aisle toward the altar. "Meredith," he breathed, turning to follow her.

"Dubay," a booming voice echoed through the narthex. "A word?"

He turned to find the Bishop of Autun, surrounded by his retinue, his elderly, jowly face emanating deep annoyance. Dubay looked back into the cathedral, and after a moment, picked out

Meredith, swaying gently in the crowd, wandering aimlessly from column to column.

"Dubay?" the Bishop intoned, now no more than a few feet away.

Turning around, he forced a smile. "I am glad to see you here," he said, leading him into the cathedral. "I trust your rooms are suitable?"

"They will do. I need to talk to you," he said, narrowing his eyes. "Now."

"Certainly, yes of course," Dubay replied somewhat absently, watching Meredith's progress toward the altar. "Let us step up to the chapel, the press of people is less –"

"I think it best if we talk privately."

"With all respect, your grace, I cannot leave at the moment. There is something I must see to immediately."

The bishop stood up to his considerable height. "How dare you?" he whispered fiercely.

Dubay looked back into the cathedral and for a moment lost sight of Meredith. He stepped away from the bishop further into the cathedral, jostling visitors as he did. Meredith reappeared, leaning against a column. He turned back to look at the Bishop whose face was now approaching purple. "I am afraid I simply cannot leave at the moment."

"I do not have the authority to *appoint* the abbot of Vézelay," the bishop growled, smoothing thinning white hair away from his forehead with a red, sweating hand. "But I do have the authority to *remove* the abbot of Vézelay."

"You must do as you see fit, as must I," Dubay said. "Please excuse me," Dubay inclined his head slightly and turned on his heel, picking his way through the crowd, the bishop blustering like an angry bull behind him.

He made his way through the press to the transept, where Meredith shrank back, pale and wide-eyed, against the column of the liberation of St. Peter. He was surprised to find Jonas, his face drawn, with deep circles under his eyes, standing with his hands out, pleading wordlessly.

With a nod at Jonas and a deep breath, Dubay stepped behind Meredith and bent his head close. "I am here to confess you," he whispered into her curls. Meredith stiffened with a sharp intake of breath. She turned slowly, arms shaking around a package wrapped in a grimy sheet. Her eyes were wide and vacant; she smelled of blood and sweat.

"How are you, child?" he smiled, holding her steady by the shoulders.

"Blessed Magdalene," she whispered, sinking to the floor. "Protect me."

Dubay knelt next to her and smoothed a curl away from her face. "From what, child?"

"That man," she whispered, jerking her head toward Jonas. "He followed me here."

Dubay looked up; his breath caught at the look of fear and sadness on Jonas' face. "He is a brother in my order. You have nothing to fear.

She nodded slowly.

"You are hurt," he said, inspecting her hands and bare feet. "We must tend to these first. And perhaps see to some food."

"No!" she whispered urgently. "I must be confessed, and hold the vigil," she insisted.

"Then may I relieve you of your burden?" he asked, laying a hand on her package.

"No," she said, clutching it to her chest. "This is for the Magdalene alone."

"Very well, very well," he said, helping her to her feet. "You will be confessed, and we will hold vigil together, and you may lay your offering. Wait here."

Dubay walked over and took Jonas by the shoulder. "We need to go down to the crypt. I am sorry; I do not think you should be there. She is frightened."

"I found her down my street," Jonas whispered, eyes wide. "I tried to talk to her, but she ran away from me. I–I couldn't get the glass. I'm sorry," he said, closing his eyes.

"Follow behind, lock the gate, and wait on the stairs. Be ready to help her, whatever she needs. Can you do that?"

Jonas nodded slightly, eyes still closed.

"Are you listening?" Dubay asked, shaking him. "You must be ready to help her, whatever happens."

Jonas opened his eyes. "Yes," he said, standing up straight. "Yes, I'm ready."

Dubay nodded and turned to Meredith. He took her arm gently and led her through the crowd to the winding stairs. He held her hand as they descended the worn steps into the semi-darkness. Halfway down, she slipped her hand from his. "I know the way," she muttered faintly.

They emerged into the low-ceilinged room and she gasped. "What is it?" he demanded, glancing back to see Jonas settling on the bottom of the staircase.

She sank to her knees before the reliquary, holding the offering like a child. "It is – it is so beautiful."

Dubay relaxed and nodded, again kneeling next to her. He crossed himself and prayed in a low, chanting tone.

"Lauda mater Ecclesia,
lauda Christi clementiam:
qui septem purgat vitia
per septiformem gratiam..."

Meredith smiled and joined him.
"Maria soror Lazari
quae tot commisit criminal,
ab ipsa fauce tartari
redit ad vitae praemia."

Dubay stopped and looked at her. "How do you know that?"

Meredith looked at him, eyebrows furrowed. "All of Burgundy knows the Cluny prayer to the Magdalene."

"Yes..." Dubay said, narrowing his eyes. "Yes, of course. Your Latin is uncommonly beautiful," he whispered. He narrowed his eyes further, blurring the edges of Meredith's face. *It is like Mercedes in the flesh.* "My God," he said, clenching his fists.

Meredith recoiled slightly. "My Lord?"

He stared at her, her face swirling and shifting in the half-light, at once Meredith and Mercedes and Jonas' Magdalene, frightened and haughty, unbearably beautiful. He squeezed his eyes shut, head reeling.

"Your grace?"

He nodded but did not open his eyes. "Let us pray," he whispered.

Pater noster qui in coelis est

Sanctificetur nomen tuum

Adveniat regnum tuum

Fiat voluntas tua et in terra sicut in coelo

Panem nostrum quotidianum da nobis hodie

Et dimitte nobis debita nostra

Sicut et dimittemus debitoribus nostris

Et ne nos inducas in tentationem,

Sed libera nos a malo. Amen.

Meredith crossed herself as she chanted the last lines.

"What sins have you to confess, child?" Dubay asked, watching the light flicker and dance along the Magdalene's reliquary. He clenched and unclenched his fists.

"I have disobeyed my father," she said, chanting tonelessly. "I have lusted. I have been made prostitute, offering my body in return for my mind."

"The holy Magdalene was saved from this sin," Dubay whispered.

"I have loved the work of my hands more than my eternal soul," she continued. "I must make my confession and offering yet the Enemy found me on the road, found me and turned me aside from the path and I was weak, and it was the image of the Magdalene that drew me on, drew me to this place and yet I sinned at every step on the way."

Dubay looked at Meredith and laid a hand on her shoulder. "We all sin, at every step on the path. But we have been given grace to wash the sins away."

Meredith started shaking her head. "No. No. You do not understand. The forests were dark, and I was alone, and–" she stuttered to a stop.

"And what?" Dubay whispered.

She pulled away and shook her head again, more violently. "I was alone, I was alone and they came from the trees and the darkness was coming and they tried to take the offering and… and I …" Meredith crawled back, away from Dubay, deeper into the shadows of the crypt.

He did not follow, but stared again at the reliquary. "And what happened?" he breathed.

"They tried to take the offering. I killed them," she whispered. "I killed him–her. I–oh my God. Michel. Oh my God," she whispered, eyes wide and horrified. "I killed her."

Dubay crossed himself.

Chapter Twenty-Five

"I – I KILLED HIM...HER..."

What did she just say? Jonas leaned forward, stretching to hear the whispered conversation. The strange numbing sensation in his hands, felt when he saw the glass for the first time, returned. He shook his hands, distracted, craning his neck to hear what they were saying. A soft shushing whisper wreathed him, the suggestion of a woman's voice.

"No!" she shouted suddenly. Jonas jumped, heart in his throat, expecting the sickening sound of shattering glass.

"Oh, there are too many here," she whispered urgently. The noise of the gathered pilgrims above was too much. *What the hell is going on in there?*

Jonas crept forward and peered around the corner. Meredith stood, arms stiff at her sides, staring at what had been the holy altar. "The Magdalene, the Magdalene," she wailed, shaking her head wildly. "Where is my offering?" she demanded, turning to Dubay.

Jonas recoiled into the shadows of the stairwell. Meredith's eyes were wide, animal-like, her face flushed and glimmering with sweat. Dubay stood and held her shoulders, nodding and murmuring, his silver hair plastered to his forehead. *Why the hell are they all sweaty? It's freezing in here.*

"I must—I must—now is the time, now…"

"You are very ill; we need to find you a doctor," Dubay said, urging her toward the stairs where Jonas huddled, knees pulled to his chest.

"No," she replied, pulling away. "I must atone… it's burning. It's burning!" she whispered, rushing to the glass and catching it up in her arms. Jonas stifled a groan and squeezed his eyes shut, shivering.

"Meredith. Meredith!" Dubay said, taking the glass gently from her hands.

"No!" she groaned, reaching for the glass.

Oh my God. Jonas half-stood, holding his breath.

"Meredith, you are sick. You have a terrible fever. We need to get you to a doctor," Dubay said.

She shook her head. "It is burning. There are too many…my God, my God, so many people."

Dubay shook his head and then stopped suddenly. "What is the year?"

"The twelfth year of the reign of Louis the Fat."

"Ah. Ah. Oui." He crossed himself. "Bien sûr, bien sûr. Je suis trop stupide. Child, you must lay your offering before the church is consumed. Quickly. Quickly," he said, handing her the glass and wiping his forehead with the back of his hand.

Oh my God, what is he doing?

"Yes," she smiled, her eyes closing in near ecstasy. "Yes." She took the glass and laid it reverently on the ground before the altar. She knelt before it and murmured a prayer, crossing herself over and over. The room suddenly grew bright, glowing from the far corner that Jonas couldn't see.

"Now. Now!" Dubay urged.

What the hell is he talking about? What are they doing to the glass? Jesus Christ. Suddenly, Jonas was transported: a vision of fire crowding in on a great mass of pilgrims, and long blond hair –his long blond hair–singing and flaming red. "Jesus Christ," Jonas whispered, shaking. The image burned away into a wisp of smoke.

Meredith nodded and smiled brightly, then swayed, eyes rolling back into her head. Dubay caught her before her head hit the floor; Jonas clenched his teeth and fists.

"Meredith," he cried. "Meredith, wake up."

"Meredith, wake up," Jonas whispered. A memory, deep and dusty, returned: Jonas, a child, pounding on his mother's chest. "Mother, wake up. Wake up!" Tears started and he bit hard on his lip to keep from sobbing. He was halfway into the crypt, heart pounding and half-blind with tears, when Meredith jerked in Dubay's arms, her eyes flying open.

"Oh my God. Oh my God," she said, crawling back away from him. "Michel. I was so stupid. It was twilight, and… God, I remember it all now–"

"Meredith, be quiet," he whispered.

"No, no, no…I …"

"Meredith, you are sick, you have a fever, you are not yourself."

"Yes, I am, I am," she said, sitting up and grabbing his scarred hands.

"I do not want to know," Dubay whispered, pulling his hands away, slowly, as if in a dream.

Jonas grasped the iron railing in the stairway until his fingers went numb, his breathing shallow.

"I took the corner too fast –"

"Meredith, be quiet."

"It was twilight and I'd had too much to drink and I was going too fast and the curve came out of nowhere–"

"Meredith, be quiet," Dubay whispered, shaking his head.

"And she wasn't wearing her belt, but God who did back then, and–" she said, gaining strength.

Dubay convulsed and was suddenly wracked with sobs.

"And neither were you, you idiot, and when we hit the tree I blacked out for a minute but then I woke up and there was your blood all over the windshield and oh shit," she cried, sobbing, "I thought you were dead and I couldn't breathe and then I looked back and where is Mercedes and and and…"

"Meredith, please stop now," Dubay shuddered. "Please. I cannot hear this."

"I have to tell you, I –"

"I do not want to know!" he roared, standing up and towering over Meredith. "Leave me that at least. Leave me that," he said, shrinking back against a rough-hewn column.

Meredith collapsed to her side, pulling her legs up to her chest, pounding the ground and her head with her fist.

"Stop that," Dubay said quietly.

Jonas took a half-step into the room.

"No. Why? Why have you been so Goddamned forgiving? Damn you! I killed my sister and I almost killed you, and you just stand there... You fucking saint," she sobbed. "You fucking martyr."

Dubay stared long at the low ceiling. After a long moment, he said quietly, "I do not pretend to understand God's plan. But it is as it was supposed to be."

"That makes no sense," she shuddered. "God forgot about us. I killed Mercedes," she whispered. "I ruined your life. Look at you. A priest. You should have been like Marie-Laure. You should have had children, and a life..."

"Why do you think I do not love the life I have?" Dubay asked sharply. He slid down the column and sat cross-legged on the ground, his dark vestments covered in ancient dust. "Look– look at that glass," he said, pointing. "Is it not a miracle? Perfection in light and color, hidden for almost 900 years–I was meant to find it."

Jonas shuddered with suppressed sobs.

"What are you saying?" Meredith asked, red-faced and exhausted.

"I do not have all the answers. I can only follow the signposts along the road."

Meredith shook her head.

"Meredith. It is the only way I can explain it all. Otherwise I will shatter," he said, covering his face with his hands.

"Do you miss her?" Meredith finally whispered, tears streaking her face.

"Yes."

"She was—"

"She was someone I did not worship as I should have," Dubay sighed, rubbing away tears.

Meredith looked at the ceiling. "I'm sorry."

Dubay nodded and leaned back, his face pale and drawn.

They sat together in silence for minutes on end, watching the glow of the glass and the sparkle of the reliquary. Jonas ached to join them, but stayed in the shadowy stairwell.

"What day is it?" she whispered hoarsely.

"July 21st."

"Huh. My head hurts."

"I am not surprised." Dubay looked down at his hands. "Do you remember anything from your blackouts?"

Meredith looked up at the ceiling. "I do."

"How much?"

"All of it. My God," she replied, squeezing her eyes closed. "Poor Jonas. God, Jonas," she mused, wringing her scarred hands. "What a broken mess he walked into. Why the hell didn't he run away when he had the chance? "

Dubay shrugged. "He was here to make things whole."

Meredith dropped her hands and looked at Dubay. "What do you mean?" she whispered.

"Jonas was meant to make all of it whole. You were meant to be touched by it. It was God's plan to bring you here, tonight, to help lay this offering to rest, help release that pilgrim's troubled soul, to finally release your guilt. For Jonas to begin to make himself whole again. I believe this," he whispered. "I have to believe this."

Meredith nodded and closed her eyes. Jonas shivered and ran his fingers along the livid scar on his temple.

After a few moments, Dubay pushed himself wearily to his feet. "I believe you should see a doctor. Your feet are quite tattered."

"I didn't even notice," she whispered, rubbing her forehead.

"I'll take you," Jonas said, stepping into the crypt, gingerly after so long crouched on the stairs. He knelt down and crouched next to her.

Meredith's face drained of color. Oh Jesus…how long have you been there?"

Jonas shrugged. "Long enough."

"Jonas, go away. Please."

"No."

"Please—I–I didn't—" she cried, turning away.

"No," he repeated. "I want to help you. I have to help you."

Dubay stood and put his hand on Jonas' shoulder. "Can you take her to Marie-Laure's? I will call Fréderic and ask him to meet us there."

Jonas nodded and offered his hand to Meredith. As he pulled her up, they were startled by the sound of movement on the stairs.

"Dubay? Dubay are you down here?" thundered the voice. The imposing form of the Bishop of Autun stepped into the low-ceilinged room and seemed to fill it immediately. "Dubay, what the devil are you doing down here? I have been waiting to see you for –"

"Your Grace, is now a convenient time? Have you eaten?" Dubay said, bowing slightly and attempting to usher the bishop back up the stairs. "I have some more of that wonderful Romanee-Conti–"

The Bishop refused to be moved. "What is going on down here?" He looked around the room and was caught by a glimmer of light at the ancient altar. "Is that the glass?" he demanded, pointing across the room. "Is that the glass, laying in the dust and dirt down here?"

"Yes, your grace—I—" Dubay began.

"Why is it here? It should be under lock and key. What are you trying to do here, Dubay?"

"I–"

"You clearly are not an appropriate caretaker for this treasure," he said, stooping over and making his way to the altar. "I'm taking it to Autun, where it will be protected and cared for properly."

"No!" Meredith yelled. "It's not yours! It's hers! Leave it!"

"Michel," Jonas pleaded, watching as the Bishop's massive hands hovered over the glass.

Meredith escaped Jonas' grasp and lunged for the Bishop.

"Meredith, no!" Jonas pleaded.

The Bishop twisted away from Meredith as Jonas grabbed her around the waist and dragged her back. "Dubay, remove this woman immediately," he said over his shoulder, leaning down again to retrieve the glass.

"I will not–" Dubay began, but was interrupted by the Bishop's gasp.

"It–it is hot," the Bishop hissed, peering at his reddening fingertips. "What have you done to it?" he demanded.

Jonas finally released his breath, closing his eyes and leaning his head against the glass of the reliquary. Meredith sagged into him and he held her.

"The glass must remain here," Dubay said, stepping between the Bishop and the offering which still rested on the floor before the altar. "It is an offering to the Magdalene and it must stay in her house."

"You are answerable to me, Dubay. Me! The glass will rest where I say it will rest. It is too valuable to be left to–"

"It must stay in her house," Dubay interrupted. "And I will do *everything* in my power to ensure that."

The Bishop stood and looked down at Dubay, and then again at his blistered fingers. "We will discuss this tomorrow. Before *I* give the mass. In the meantime, get that woman some help," he said, gesturing at Meredith as he swept out of the small crypt and back up the stairs to the main cathedral.

Jonas pulled Meredith's left arm around his shoulders and supported her around the waist. "Come on, let's get you down to Marie-Laure's," he whispered, steering her toward the stairs.

"No–I can make it on my own," she said, pulling her arm away. "Just go, Jonas."

"Let me help you. Please. Please," he whispered. He pulled her arm back around his shoulders and she again sagged into him as they made their way to the stairs. Jonas turned and looked across the small crypt to where Dubay stood at the altar. "Are you going to be OK?"

Dubay was holding the glass, looking through its jeweled stories to the reliquary beyond. "I will be fine," he smiled.

Chapter Twenty-Six

JONAS LOOKED DOWN on the milling crowds in the cathedral, swirling eddies and crashing tides of color. The arches, multicolored and massive, seemed miles and miles away from the cane chairs of the nave. But floating there in the early grey dawn, it seemed as if he had only to lean down and with a finger bring all the colors together.

He picked a bright hue out of the crowd: a swish of red, fading to orange in the dim morning light. It was the Magdalene, swinging and spinning in her wide scarlet skirts. He leaned down, hand outstretched, straining. He fell, somersaulting and tumbling, the writhing figures on the capitals shouting encouragements and jeers in words he could not understand. The crowd stepped away from the fetish; she stopped spinning and with a smile caught him in her arms.

Jonas awoke with a gasp. He sat up and looked blearily around the dim room and then fell back onto his pillow, rubbing his eyes. He sighed and pushed himself up, dropping his legs over the side of the bed. With a groan he stood and scratched his stomach under his t-shirt, then shuffled into the studio. It was still strewn with the wreckage of the chair, an avalanche of papers and tools. He stepped gingerly through the piles and found his leather-bound planner. He flipped the pages to July 22 and the words written in his careful hand across the page: *Project ends.*

Jonas carried the book to the windows and leaned against the casement, paging through the days. July 24, 10:50 a.m.: *AA49 CDG-DFW*. July 29, 1:00 p.m.: *Follow up at St. Joseph's—leave at 12:00!* August 2, 7:00 p.m.: *Steve's birthday dinner—Capitola*.

"Guess I better start packing," he muttered, closing the book and dropping it to the floor. He pushed the window wide and squeezed himself onto the windowsill, feet braced against the casement. The first pink blush of dawn appeared above the rooftops; he watched it spread across the sky, watched the gilding of the north ramparts, watched windows up and down the narrow street swing open to catch the last of the cool morning air.

An hour later he sighed and unfolded himself, creaking and sore, from the window and limped back into his cramped bedroom. He pulled on his jeans and shoved his sockless feet into his high tops and knelt next to the bed in a last fruitless attempt to will cigarettes to appear there. He stood and made his way downstairs and out into the rue de l'Argenterie, hesitating. He shrugged and turned right, climbing the street toward the cathedral.

A group of congregants, including shop owners and waiters he recognized, were milling around the plaza and loitering on the steps. Among them was a man leaning in the shadows against the wall, silver-haired and impeccably dressed in a crisp white shirt and perfectly tailored trousers, watching him intently. Jonas walked past, toward the *tabac*, and then stopped suddenly and turned around. "Michel?" he said, eyebrows knitted. "You're not giving the mass."

"No," he replied, tight lipped, looking past Jonas down into the town. "I have been encouraged to take a leave of absence."

"You're shitting me."

"I am not. The Bishop was not pleased with his reception, nor was he pleased that the glass was 'endangered', nor was he pleased that I snubbed him in public. And like all of the men that have held that position, he is not pleased that he cannot appoint the Abbot of Vézelay, so they harry us and plot against us and find ways of putting us out of the way," he said, his voice rising. "He knows he cannot remove me outright – the congregation and the brothers would not countenance it – but he can send me away for a time indeterminate and put one of his own in my place."

A group of congregants turned to look at them; Jonas took Dubay by the elbow and led him down the steps and across to the gardens. "But why do they care? It's not like Vézelay is some massive power in the church, is it?" he said, pushing open the gate and standing back to let Dubay through.

Dubay shrugged. "No, but the grudge is long-held—almost a thousand years. And men love their power."

"What are you going to do?" Jonas asked, shoving his hands into his jeans pockets.

Dubay picked dead leaves off a rose bush and smiled. "First, I shall visit my brother Paul and his family in Nuits St Georges and wander in the vineyards and drink our excellent wine. Perhaps I will go up to Paris. Perhaps I will pick up my research and finish it. There are many possibilities," he said, turning to Jonas. "And you?"

"Go home, I guess," he shrugged, wandering toward the farther gate and the park beyond the cloisters and chapel. "I have a meeting next week with the basilica in San Jose."

"So you will not be staying?"

Jonas shook his head. "No. Guillaume and Marie-Laure are taking care of her…"

Dubay pushed the gate open. "She was fragile last night. I do not think she meant–"

Jonas waved the words away. "She was totally clear. She wouldn't even talk to me when I took her down to Marie-Laure's. "

"Jonas," Dubay said, staring out across the park toward the evergreen Morvan, "stay a few days. And then decide."

Jonas shrugged noncommittally and rested against the rough trunk of a spreading chestnut. He closed his eyes and sighed. "This has been the weirdest few weeks I've ever had. And that's saying a lot."

Dubay chuckled. "I can imagine."

"Did you—did anything weird happen to you? I mean, besides Meredith?"

"Ah. Well, yes."

"Like what?"

"I—heard what I thought was Mercedes' voice. It was so welcome, a waking dream, but...it was not her. It was—well, it was not her."

Jonas nodded, picking at spears of grass and wrapping them around his finger.

"And I had the strangest sensation last night that the building was on fire around me—when Meredith was wavering," Dubay whispered, sitting down next to Jonas. "That is when I realized what was happening."

"What do you mean?" Jonas asked, turning to look at him.

"The church burned to the ground on the eve of the Magdalene's feast—that is to say, July 21, 1120—with a crowd of pilgrims inside, gathered that evening for the vigil. Over 1,000 died that night."

"No."

"It was the first of many fires that have burned this place down," Dubay said, gesturing at the solid edifice. "Meredith was reliving the events of that particular night. I believe she was making the glass whole for the pilgrim who died in the fire before her offering was laid."

Jonas' heart began to thud. "The pilgrim knew she was going to die in a fire," he said, looking up at the cathedral. "Remember the last panel of the border? She knew…and yet, she still came to lay her offering, knowing she would die."

"Perhaps she didn't know the fire would consume her before the offering was properly made. Meredith made the offering whole, you made the glass whole. We are all three of us pilgrims here, I think."

Jonas considered this for a moment. "See, but I don't get why she was reliving the accident," Jonas said, tracing the scar on his temple. "It's weird."

"I do not know, Jonas. She had many years of guilt exhausting her—she and the pilgrim were doing each other a favor—releasing each other at last. Perhaps it was the intervention of the Magdalene? I cannot tell you the workings of God."

Jonas looked back at the cathedral. After long minutes, he turned to Dubay. "Is Marie-Laure going to be OK?"

"Yes, yes. Fréderic believes it was simply exhaustion, although there is a possibility she had a mild stroke. He must have some tests run before he can confirm that."

"She was weird when I saw her. I should have stayed to help her, but Guillaume was there…She's going to be OK, right?"

"Yes, I believe so."

Jonas nodded and took a deep breath. "And what about Meredith?"

"She wore her guilt like a mantle these twenty years; throwing it off was incredibly exhausting, I am sure."

"She looked like a ghost."

Dubay shrugged, but said nothing.

They sat together, silent in the green park until the bells began to toll for Terce and the Magdalene Mass. Dubay stood and brushed off his trousers. "Are you coming to the mass?"

Jonas stood and shrugged. "I don't think so. I'm gonna go back and start packing up."

They walked together towards the garden and paused at the gate. "I will come say goodbye before I leave this evening," Dubay said, placing a hand on Jonas' shoulder.

"You're leaving so soon?"

"Yes."

"They're idiots."

"Yes."

Jonas smiled. "I thought this all happened for a reason?"

Dubay grinned. "Yes, of course. But it does not mean that they are not idiots. I will see you this evening."

Jonas nodded and turned away to skirt the garden wall, past the ruins of the old monastery. He stopped suddenly and jogged back. "Michel," he called, and Dubay appeared again at the gate. "What's happening with the glass?"

"Madame Chevrey found me late last evening and declared it magnificent."

Jonas nodded. "And? Is it staying here?"

"She and I will not rest until that is assured."

Jonas nodded and turned to make his way down to the town, followed by the ringing of the bells and approaching the rising tide of the faithful.

The evening sky was amethyst by the time he'd carefully wrapped his tools and sorted through his paperwork. He sat on the bed in the tiny bedroom, fingering the edges of Meredith's portrait he'd found buried under schedules and shards of glass. A knock at the door broke his reverie. "It's open, Michel," he hollered, placing the portrait on top of the framed photo of Sainte-Chapelle in his suitcase.

He walked into the studio and swept the last remains of the broken chair into a waste bin. At the sound of steps on the landing, he asked, "How was the mass?"

"I wasn't there," Meredith replied.

He dropped the broom and turned around. "Oh. Hey."

"Hey." She stood uncertainly in the studio door, shadowed in the faint dusk light.

Jonas took a few tentative steps toward her. "Are you OK?"

"I think so," she shrugged, stepping back.

He nodded and walked over to the open windows. "Are you going to stay in Vézelay?" he asked over his shoulder.

"I don't know. I don't know what to do now. I'm sorry," she said. "I didn't want you to have to take care of me. You shouldn't have to spend your whole life taking care of crazy women."

"You're not. Well, not really," he shrugged. "And I wanted to. I needed to." Jonas said, blowing smoke out into the night.

"It's beautiful."

"What is?"

"The glass."

He turned and smiled. "It is, isn't it?"

She nodded. "Even with my face," she said, suppressing a shudder.

"Because of your face."

"Listen, I'm sorry–"

"Don't."

Meredith folded her arms. "Were you scared?"

"Yes."

"Me too."

"How's your head?"

She shrugged. "Hurts."

"How are your feet?"

"They've felt better."

"And how's Marie-Laure?" he asked, leaning against the tall window's frame.

"Better. Resting."

"Isn't that what you should be doing?"

She shrugged. "I wanted to catch you before you ran away."

"I wasn't going to–"

"Yes you were."

"I figured you didn't want me around."

"I was scared, and tired. And–ashamed."

"Marie-Laure sent you here."

"No. I came on my own."

"I'm glad," he whispered finally.

"I had a dream last night," she said, edging into the room.

He cocked his head. "Was it your own dream?"

"Yeah."

"Was it a good dream?"

"Yeah," she smiled.

"Good."

"So, when are you leaving?" she asked, stepping in front of him.

"Day after tomorrow."

"Ah."

He seized a curl near her ear and twirled it around his finger. Her eyes fluttered shut and she shivered.

"Is this a dream?" she asked.

"What do you think?"

Acknowledgements

I AM GRATEFUL to the people of Vézelay for allowing me to take poetic license with their village and landmark.

Writing this book allowed me to spend wonderful hours reading online and researching in musty libraries. I am particularly indebted to author Sharan Newman and her fantastic bibliography for 12th century France, which was a very welcome find.

Particularly useful in my research (and wonderful reads on their own) are the outstanding: *Vézelay, the Great Romanesque Church* Veronique Rouchon Mouilleron (1999); *Hugh of Poitiers: the Vézelay Chronicle* John Scott and John O. Ward (1992); *Capetian France 987-1328* Elizabeth Hallam (1980); *Medieval Folklore: A Guide to Myths, Legends, Tales, Beliefs, and Customs* Carl Lindahl, John McNamara, John Lindow (2000); *Life in Medieval France*, E.R. Chamberlain (1967); *The Penguin Dictionary of Saints*, Donald Attwater (1985); *De Sacramentis*,

Hugo of Saint Victor (trans. Roy J. Deferrari) (1951); *Sword, Miter, and Cloister: Nobility and the Church in Burgundy, 980-1198*, Constance Brittain Bouchard (1987); *Monastic Life at Cluny*, Joan Evans (1968); www.newadvent.org; www.costumes.org; The Internet Medieval Sourcebook; and the UNESCO websites.

I am indebted to the members of the (now defunct) Originalfic writer's workshop: Andrea Winkler, Catherine Schaff-Stump, Crystal Di'Anno, Jenn Racek, Juliane Schneider, Katy Carroll, Leeann Bonaventura, Michelle Earles, and Yolanda Joosten, who were the midwives for this book when it was first written in 2002-03.

I am also indebted to my friends Scott Atkins, Renee and Michael Roderiques, Catrina Horsfield, Kenna Therrien, Ronda Grizzle, and most especially my comrade-in-arms Heather Domin. They were all incredibly supportive and their feedback, suggestions, and camaraderie have kept me going and kept me (relatively) sane in the intervening years (particularly Heather, who *understands*.)

Dad, Chris, and Felice have been loving, encouraging, and helpful throughout the process, from the first word written to the last pixel pushed.

My mom was always my biggest cheerleader, and the first fan of *The Pilgrim Glass*. I wish she could be here to hold this book in her hands.

And finally, I couldn't list those who made this book possible without including my husband Craig. He has been loving, supportive, encouraging, and patient, and I am very, very grateful.

CPSIA information can be obtained at www.ICGtesting.com
Printed in the USA
LVOW050035150812

294322LV00002B/93/P